wildflower hope

Center Point
Large Print

Also by Grace Greene and available from
Center Point Large Print:

The Memory of Butterflies
Wildflower Heart

**This Large Print Book carries the
Seal of Approval of N.A.V.H.**

wildflower hope

The Wildflower House Series

Grace Greene

CENTER POINT LARGE PRINT
THORNDIKE, MAINE

This Center Point Large Print edition
is published in the year 2020 by arrangement with
Amazon Publishing, www.apub.com.

Originally published in the United States
by Amazon Publishing, 2019

The text of this Large Print edition is unabridged.
In other aspects, this book may vary
from the original edition.
Printed in the United States of America
on permanent paper.
Set in 16-point Times New Roman type.

ISBN: 978-1-64358-739-4

The Library of Congress has cataloged this record
under Library of Congress Control Number: 2020943880

Wildflower Hope is dedicated to those who grieve and overcome loss. It is dedicated to those who struggle with emotional or physical crutches of any kind, whether self-medicating, shopping, or something else—any of the things we consume or activities in which we engage to comfort and distract ourselves, many of which are harmful to us or become harmful over time. Loss and struggle are hard but are a part of life. This book is dedicated to those who stumble and fall but keep getting up. This book is dedicated to those who focus on the strength of resilience and not on the stumble.

Prologue

My father, Henry Lange, died in June, two months after he and I moved to Wildflower House.

People speak about grief and its stages—denial, bargaining, acceptance, and so on. I don't doubt the truth of it. In fact, it seems to me that just about anything in life, whether a disliked task or recognizing you've wronged someone and should make amends—or even being wronged, yet needing to be the one to forgive—goes through similar stages. We navigate and rationalize our way through life and death, and all the in-betweens, until the actual end, and then all the effort expended and pain endured in this life become moot because done is done.

Except for the loved ones left behind to pick up the pieces.

I wandered through the high-ceilinged, nearly empty rooms of Wildflower House, and along its wide, lonely hallways. Over and over, I found myself in my father's room. His ashes—in a beautiful brushed-pewter urn engraved with his name and dates—stood on his dresser. Seeing the urn, and myself reflected in the mirror behind it, I couldn't miss his hazel eyes. I had Dad's eyes and Mom's straight dark hair. But those were surface features. There was so much more inside me that I'd gotten from my parents. Much that was good, but also much that was not so good, including a sad lack of self-confidence, and a tendency to build walls around my heart and brain to protect myself.

Dad died in June. His hopes and secrets perished with him, but he left me with a maze of unresolved questions and with Wildflower House.

It was up to me to figure out what to do with them.

Chapter One

"Kara?"

My name echoed along the hallway.

I responded, "I'm in the kitchen."

Nicole Albers strode into the room. She was an ageless sort of woman—slim, blonde, and always professional. She was about ten years older than me, somewhere in her early forties, but I suspected she'd looked much the same a decade ago and would into the next decade too. She was carrying a large business tote and a handful of postmarked envelopes and ad circulars. She set her tote in a chair and waved the mail in my direction before placing it on the kitchen table. "I grabbed these from your mailbox. Looks like they've been there for a couple of days."

"I didn't feel like walking down there yesterday."

"Then drive to it. It's not a good idea to leave the box unchecked. Someone could mess with the contents, and you'd never know anything was taken."

I answered her concern with a dismissive look as I moved the stack to the counter. "It's always junk mail, so I'm not likely to lose much worth keeping."

She asked, "How are you doing?"

"I'm fine." *Not.*

"How's the project plan coming along?"

"Project plan? I know all about project plans. Did you forget I was a project manager in my previous life?"

Nicole called my bluff. "So you've set one up?"

"Not exactly." I shrugged. "It's early days. I'm still working from a handwritten list and a box of notes and samples."

Something about Nicole looked different. It took me a second, longer look to identify what.

"You're wearing shorts," I said.

She glanced down and brushed her hand against her shorts and thighs. "Is it a problem?"

"No. You look great. It's just that you're always dressed for work—ever ready to do serious business."

"I *am* ever ready, but today I'm taking the day off. I didn't schedule a single appointment." She looked around the room. "Where's that box and list? I want to see where you're at with it."

I took a bottle of chilled fruit water from the fridge. "Thirsty?"

"Sure. Thanks."

I poured her a glass of water. As she drank, I lifted the box of samples—the idea box—from where I'd left it in the corner. I set it on the table in front of Nicole. She irritated me. Her manner was abrupt. Abrasive. And she'd been very close to my father—a relationship from which I'd been excluded by being kept in the dark about it. But not by Nicole. It was wrong for me to hold that against her. Especially when she was using her skill, her connections as a lifelong resident of Louisa County and a longtime real estate agent, and her personal time to help me turn Wildflower House into a creative retreat.

Nicole took one look inside the box and shook her head. After a feeble show of sifting through the assorted papers, she stepped back. "You and I need to sit down together to make firm plans and set dates. Kara, you need a business plan. I can set you up with a top-notch accountant. He'll help you run the numbers and all that."

"I know what I need." I was about to warn her that while I appreciated her coordinating the legal end of this project, I would drive the decision-making, when she said, "Can't do it today, though."

"Oh?"

Nicole tucked a stray hair behind her ear. "Maddie Lyn needs a little extra attention, so she and I are playing hooky."

Maddie Lyn was Nicole's niece. She was almost five. Maddie's mom had died before I'd met any of the Albers family. Legally, Nicole was Maddie Lyn's guardian, but Mel, Maddie's grandmother, shouldered most of the child-raising responsibilities, all the more since Seth, Maddie's uncle, had left a month ago.

Seth had played a major, almost parental role in her life for the last year or so—a significant impact in terms of Maddie's young age. It was hardly surprising that his move cross-country had unsettled her.

That makes two of us. Aloud, I said, "Where is she?"

"Front porch. She has her crayons and a coloring book. I told her not to color your bench."

"Really?"

"Sure. She's reliable with crayons, so no worries."

"I mean, you really left her out there alone?"

"What's wrong with you, Kara?" Her smile was slightly chiding. "Maddie Lyn is safe on the porch and can amuse herself for a short time. If she needs me, she'll call for me."

"It's hot out there."

"It's still morning, and it's shady on the porch. I'm not staying long. I dropped by to find out where we're at with the project." Her smile dimmed. "More than that, I wanted to see how you're doing."

"I should ask the same of you. Are you okay?" The dark areas under her eyes seemed to be disappearing more rapidly than mine, but I didn't make any assumptions about that. I knew Nicole had had deep feelings for my father, and I couldn't imagine—didn't want to imagine—the depth of her grief. She'd done her crying, as

12

I had. But it was her nature, as it had been my father's, to move on. *Compartmentalized,* someone had said of them both.

Seth. It was Seth who'd said it.

I put my hand to my heart as its beat responded to the thought of him. Seth had been my almost sweetheart before he'd left to take a job in Los Angeles. I missed him. I tightened my jaw and looked away.

As if reading my mind, Nicole said, "Have you heard from Seth?"

"He called a few nights ago. Have you spoken to him?"

"Mom did. She said he sounds good. Maybe a little homesick. But I suspect she heard what her heart wanted. He and Maddie Lyn did a video call."

"I'm sure Maddie was delighted. I hope the job works out for him. He's an excellent writer." I paused, then added, "When I spoke to him, he seemed a bit swamped learning the ropes of a public relations business. I tried not to complain. I don't want him to think he should be here, you know? Or make him feel guilty about letting us down by leaving. He needs to focus on what he's doing out there in the new job."

"As we'll focus on what we're doing here." Nicole spoke firmly as she pulled a folder out of her tote and plopped it on the table with gusto. "Read these when you have some time.

It's information about building codes and other permitting requirements that you need to know. Tell me when you're done, and we can discuss it in more depth."

My heart sank. A welcome rescue came as I spied a small face peeking around the doorframe. Wispy corn silk–colored curls caught the light.

"Maddie Lyn? Is that you?" I asked.

She stepped forward with a shy smile and held out a cup with a hard plastic pink straw sticking up through the lid. I took her gesture to mean she needed a refill.

"Thirsty?" I asked. "I'll get you some juice."

The little girl smiled but scanned the room. She'd been here before with her Uncle Seth, so I knew she wasn't checking out the decor. She handed me her cup, and I went to the fridge.

"Maddie Lyn," Nicole said. "I asked you to please wait out front. I'll be done super quick. Just another minute."

"Maybe she—"

Nicole raised her hand, cutting me off with a firm smile. "Maddie Lyn, I'll be right out. Thank Miss Kara for the juice, and please wait on the porch."

Maddie nodded, whispered a barely audible "Thank you," and retreated. We heard the screen door shut.

"Seriously, Kara, it's up to the adult to be firm." Nicole pressed her manicured fingertips together.

"Consistent love and discipline. Reliable routine. These things give a child a sense of security."

Maybe, I thought. I didn't have any mothering experience myself. I'd almost had that chance and had lost it. But I suspected Nicole might be aiming a tad wide of her intended mark. She was great when it came to business, and she knew everyone in the county, but maternal instincts? Not so much.

I asked, "Maddie seems much quieter than usual. How's she adjusting since Seth left?"

"That's why we're doing something special today. She misses him, no question."

"He's like a father to her. It's not easy being left—left out or left behind—by the people you love." I sighed.

Nicole said, "That's true. She's been bugging me about coming over to your house. Is she hoping she'll find him here? Despite knowing he's working a new job on the far side of the country? Maddie's too young to grasp the distance. I'm sure that's why she came into the house just now. Probably thought she'd tiptoe in and find him waiting to surprise her."

"What the brain knows and what the heart hopes for are often different things."

"Who knows what's going on in someone else's head and heart? At best, it's a guess." Nicole looked sad.

I empathized. She was finding it difficult to manage her four-year-old niece's heart and expectations. Nicole was logical in the same way that my father had been—well meaning when they remembered you were there, but not natural nurturers.

"Let's not keep her waiting. She's eager to spend the day with you." I moved toward the kitchen door, hoping Nicole would follow. "By the way, I'm hiring that contractor you recommended to renovate the kitchen. He's supposed to start next week with pulling out the cabinets."

The cabinets and appliances were old and stained and awkwardly spaced. The lack of balance, the stains, and the questionable cleanliness had bugged me from the first.

Nicole didn't move from beside the table. "Try to remember that construction projects, including renovations, always take longer than you think they will."

"I don't mind," I said. "No rush. I'm looking forward to redoing this kitchen more than anything else. New appliances, new plaster, and fresh paint. I'm going with a light yellow and lots of white with splashes of melon. I want it to look new and crisp."

I was about to add that I thought kitchen appearances were particularly important for guests but caught that downcast look on her face again. In that moment I also noticed the slight lines on her forehead and at the corners of her eyes. It almost stole my breath.

She said, "I've wanted to ask you . . . have you decided what to do with Henry's ashes?"

My response was instinctive and harsh sounding. "What do you mean?"

Nicole said, "Sorry if I hit a tender spot, but it's been a month now."

Take a mental step back, I reminded myself. It was okay, even natural, that Nicole would ask. Emotions were so treacherous. I needed to put mine aside or rise above them.

"I'm sorry, Nicole. I'm not ready to discuss it yet."

"If you need a friendly ear or a sounding board, I'm available." She turned her back and started digging through the sample box again, this time as if it mattered. She cleared her throat and asked, "Is it working out with Moore Blackwell? I didn't see any progress with removing the wallpaper."

"He and I are going to review the plan. Dad wanted to strip all the paper, but I want Mr. Blackwell's assessment on whether we can rehab some of it instead."

"Seriously? Why?"

"Some of it, especially the dining room paper, is in pretty good shape, unlike the parlor paper."

She looked doubtful. "I recommend getting it done all at once."

"Instinct," I said.

Nicole frowned, then sighed. "I don't understand."

"Dad viewed this as a renovation. He planned to live here and enjoy the project and pursue new hobbies." I laughed, but wryly. "Take on hobbies like gardening and such, even though he'd never engaged in those activities before. But that doesn't matter. It was his plan. A creative retreat is different. The surroundings, inside and out, should add to the customer experience. A certain ambience—a sense of history, but with modern conveniences and a little luxury—can be a marketable draw. If I'm wrong about the wallpaper, I can always have it removed later. What will I have lost? A little time? Some rework?"

"What about upstairs?"

"Only a couple of rooms are papered up there. I'm still deciding about those."

"It's your choice," she said, with a sigh of resignation. "As you say, you can always remove it later."

"Nicole, I don't pretend to have experience or finesse with the finer points of decor, but it feels wrong to rip the paper down just because we can. It's difficult or impossible to re-create 'old,' yet at the same time I don't want to keep 'old' for the wrong reasons. I'll rely on Mr. Blackwell's experience and my own instinct." I shuddered when I said that. Those were brave words for someone lacking in confidence and commitment. But the words had been said, and I wouldn't back off and sound foolish.

Nicole nodded. "Okay. It's good to listen to the experts." She walked toward the back door. The exterior door was open, and she stopped in front of the latched screen door. She stared out at the backyard.

I knew what she was looking at. I felt it. She was viewing a memory, as if it were a solid thing, and the knowing of it prickled along my flesh and made my eyes sting. Nicole was seeing the field of wildflowers, the break in their colorful ranks where the riding mower had cut a swath into them, and the spot where my father had died. But he wasn't there—nor were the flowers. As Nicole had reminded me, all of that had happened a month ago.

"I'm going to check on Maddie," I said, my voice cracking.

Nicole ignored me and stayed at the door.

The day was still stuck on this side of noon, I was exhausted, and it was Nicole's fault. I leaned against the front doorframe, feeling burdened with things I didn't want to think about and couldn't control. The breeze through the open door brushed my face. I pushed the screen door open a few inches and peeked out. Maddie looked up from her coloring book. We shared a smile.

"Are you doing okay out here, sweetie?"

"Yes, ma'am."

"It won't be much longer, I think."

She nodded and went back to coloring.

In the kitchen, Nicole was still standing as I'd left her, facing that thin piece of screening and the backyard. She heard me return and asked, "What about outdoors? What are you working on out there?"

"Dad already arranged with Jim Mitchell of Mitchell's Lawn and Landscaping for the grounds work. He's sending one of his best people, Will Mercer, with a small crew. I'm going to ask them to tackle the overgrowth on the sides of the house first and then free the carriage house."

"Free the carriage house? That sounds odd." She pressed down on the door handle as if about to exit. She asked, "What about the wildflower field?"

Out of patience, I nearly shouted at her, *What about it?* But I didn't. The flowers that had grown there a short time ago were a large part of my reason for being here with Dad. When I'd first seen the wildflowers, their colors and scents had drawn me into their midst like the bees and butter-flies that flitted in and among them. Dad had died here on the day he'd tried to cut them down. A fatal stroke had interrupted his plans, but Mother Nature had finished the job for him—with hail. The field and flowers had ended in a stinking, green, mushy mash. Now the mud had dried, and the whole area was a wreck with only the grass around the perimeter standing tall. Too tall.

Nicole said, "The grass needs cutting."

I snagged my lower lip between my teeth to keep my initial response in check. In the silence a small sound, a tentative plinking of piano keys as if little fingers were testing them, drifted along the hallway on the breeze. Nicole pressed her lips together and looked sternly toward the kitchen doorway.

"Let her be," I said. "She isn't hurting anything. She's been far more patient than I'd expect a four-year-old to be, especially one left alone on a porch."

I watched Nicole's face and saw her expression change when she decided to drop the subject. She shook her head and said, "Maddie Lyn and I should be on our way. Do you have a finish date you're working toward? I'll plan out a timeline for who to contact when."

Suddenly my breath felt short. I put my hand to my throat. "No," I said.

"You aren't considering backing out, are you? You forget I sell houses and I'm good at it. I know what a client looks like when they're coming down with a bad case of buyer's remorse."

There might be truth in what she was saying, but it annoyed me that she'd seen it and felt so very free to say it out loud to my face. I stood taller.

"As you yourself said, I'll take the advice of others into consideration, but I'll reserve the right to decide my own future, including the future of this project. I'll let you know when I'm ready to make those contacts."

She pressed her lips together again.

I moved toward the hallway, and this time Nicole followed. I continued walking, saying, "I appreciate your help. I *need* your help, Nicole. I wouldn't dare undertake this project *without* your help. But sometimes it would be more helpful if you'd chat more and push less."

Nicole didn't take offense. She never did. Or at least she never showed it.

She nodded. "I understand. The choice to stop or move forward is yours. Always and only yours. This whole concept of a creative retreat and event space is an amazing idea with lots of potential, but you'll enjoy this venture more if you fully commit to it. And that, too, is your choice, Kara." After a pause, she said, "Are you sure you wouldn't like me to take a look at the carriage house with you? I haven't been inside it yet, but I could offer advice."

"No, we need to clear the vegetation away first. Right now it's a jungle, hard to even get close to, and this is your day with Maddie."

"Okay. Call me if you need me, or if you want to talk about any of this."

"I will."

In the foyer, both of us paused beside the piano bench. The seat was unoccupied, but the hinged piano key cover was still raised. The screen door gave a slight shiver as if it had just closed.

We smiled at each other.

I said to her softly, "I'm committed, Nicole. Mostly."

She gave me a long look and responded, "You'll do fine, Kara."

I walked her to the door with great relief. That moment in the kitchen when I'd panicked—when Nicole asked about a completion date—had scared me. Before we began discussing this project with local artisans and authors, before we started promoting the place and got anywhere close to accepting reservations, I needed to be absolutely sure and comfortable with the progress. It was so early in the project. Doubts were normal, weren't they?

Nicole helped Maddie gather her crayons, coloring book, cup, and so on. She looked at me, saying, "You're welcome to join us."

I was touched, but I said no. "I'm going to empty the kitchen cabinets today. Doesn't that sound like fun?"

"Do you need help?"

"No. I'll do it at my own pace, but thanks."

Maddie waved from the back seat as they drove away. I turned to go into the house. As I stepped through the open doorway, a gust of wind blew a sheet of music from the piano. The paper sailed upward and then floated down gracefully to the floor. I picked it up. "Simple Gifts."

Seriously? Victoria—my used-to-be best friend—had played this music. She'd been staying here with me after Dad died—until I'd kicked her out. After she left, I put the sheet back in the bench, and it had been tucked away there, untouched, since.

Of course. Maddie. I laughed at myself. Maddie had opened the bench lid and had taken the sheet of music that was on top. She'd probably been pretending to play it while Nicole and I were in the kitchen.

The description on the page noted that it was a Shaker hymn. Yes, I'd known that. And it had been used by Copland in his *Appalachian Spring* composition. I'd known that too.

I squinted at the fine print. *Music and Lyrics by Elder Joseph Brackett. 1848.* Almost a hundred years later, it had formed part of *Appalachian Spring.* And many decades after that, I'd heard that music play in my head when I'd first arrived at this house and seen the wildflower field in the bright sunlight.

I didn't try to sing the tune but read the words aloud:

> 'Tis the gift to be simple, 'tis the gift to
>   be free,
> 'Tis the gift to come down to where we
>   ought to be,

And when we find ourselves in the place
  just right,
'Twill be in the valley of love and delight.
When true simplicity is gained,
To bow and to bend we shan't be
  ashamed,
To turn, turn will be our delight,
Till by turning, turning we come 'round
  right.

The greatest problem was that what *should* be simple, like finding a little happiness and contentment, was usually the most elusive or difficult to achieve . . . and keep.

. . . *place just right . . . love and delight . . .* I would welcome such gifts.

It all sounded good, but specific instructions would be much more useful than colonial dance steps.

What I did know—and had learned the hard way—was that you couldn't count on people staying or on happiness being regular fare. My mom had left Dad and me when I was fourteen. She'd had emotional problems for a long time before that. Two years after she left us, she was found dead of an overdose several states away, near where she'd been raised. My grandmother hadn't invited us to the funeral or memorial service. In fact, she'd asked us to stay away.

I'd grown up in a life where bad news was

experienced and then dismissed into a black hole of sorts, never to be revisited. My dad had always lived in the present. The past was the past. But Mom . . . maybe she'd never been able to escape her yesterdays or whatever it was that had haunted her.

I put the sheet music back in the bench.

In the kitchen I picked up the mail from the counter. As I thumbed through the stack, it was clear I'd been right—offers of insurance and ads for products I'd never use. But in the middle of the junk mail was a hand-addressed envelope. I recognized the careful writing with its wide-open, almost childish loops and a strong flourish at the end of the *a*. I didn't need to see the return address, much less open the unwanted note inside, to know that it was from Victoria.

She was still intruding, trying to worm her way back into where she wasn't wanted. I felt all the more justified in my opinion of her.

I poured a glass of water and sipped it slowly to calm the sudden turmoil in my stomach, the slight burning in my gut.

Until three weeks ago, I'd trusted Victoria. She and Niles and I had been friends since meeting in college. Niles and I married after graduation and moved to Northern Virginia to start our careers. Victoria had followed, finding work and an apartment nearby. We'd continued our friendship through the six years there.

I saw it laid out like a trail we'd left behind us. College, marriage, jobs . . . until the night when Niles told me he wanted out, that he'd been seeing someone. We'd argued on that rainy night, and the car accident had happened. That memory was a big, gaping hole in my trail of life events. I remembered little except darkness and pain, interlaced with blinding light and shrieks of metal tearing. And on the other side of it, there was no Niles. No husband. No marriage. Not even my pregnancy had made it through.

Dad had been there to help me. He'd seen me through more than a year and a half of recovery. When Dad died a month ago, Victoria had come to support me. Until, that was, I discovered she'd interfered between me and my husband just before our marriage had blown up. I'd seen the photos on her phone. She and Niles had been hugging and laughing and snagging selfies only days before the accident. Without me there or even aware.

Victoria had insisted her actions had been well meaning. That she hadn't done anything wrong. But whatever she had or hadn't done, there was no doubt that she'd been a more loyal friend to my cheating husband than to me.

Shame on her. Yes, the shame was hers, but I hadn't liked the ugliness of our final encounter, so I'd sent a note wishing her well but making it very clear that I didn't want to hear back from her. Ever. I should've known better than to try to end things in a civil manner.

Victoria saw things only as she wished to see them—and that view was usually slanted to her advantage.

I held her letter suspended over the trash can for a moment. Should I open it? Just in case? No.

I released it, as I'd released my former feelings of friendship for her, and let it fall into the remains of breakfast to join the rest of the garbage.

Chapter Two

The crew from Mitchell's Lawn and Landscaping was due to arrive at eight a.m. I'd set my phone alarm to sing at seven fifteen to be sure I was up and functional before that.

Mornings were a struggle for me these days. Since Dad died, I'd had difficulty falling asleep at night. This was merely an adjustment period. I saw no need to get involved with sleeping pills when the leftover meds from my auto accident were handy and did the job well enough. That accident, almost two years ago, had left me with serious injuries and scars to my arm and thigh, plus a scar near my temple at the hairline, along with an extreme sensitivity to bright light and sound that usually preceded the onset of severe headaches. The injuries were mostly healed and rarely troubled me now. In fact, I was so much better since the move to Wildflower House that at some point in the last three weeks I'd lost my cane and hadn't bothered to go looking for it.

The white pills had been prescribed for pain. The blue ones were mild sedatives to help me relax. Most nights they eased me nicely over the threshold into sleep. In the mornings, though, my brain was often foggy, and my body felt a little disconnected.

I wasn't hooked or anything like that. In fact, I was grateful to have the help and thankful I hadn't disposed of them. The days at Wildflower House were good, but the nights . . . some nights my brain was busy with worries and what-ifs. Other nights I simply lay there awake with a feeling I couldn't quite decipher. A sense of waiting, maybe?

I suspected those dark, lonely nights would've bothered me anywhere I lived, but I might have handled them better in the city, where I would've had a job and close neighbors and more distractions.

Yet I stayed here.

This past March, almost four months ago, I'd seen Wildflower House and the field of flowers for the first time. Dad had only just told me he was retiring and moving. I'd been stunned and concerned, and I'd come alone to see the house.

I'd fought through the tangled jungle in the side yard and emerged into a mass of vivid color and varied petals, all kissed by sunshine. Instead of the painful sensations I'd experienced since the accident, this field of flowers had been nearly blinding in its wonder and had seemed to reset something in my brain. That was when I decided to move here with Dad. I told myself I would stay here until the end of wildflower season. But everything changed when he died.

Dad was gone. The flowers were gone. And

this morning I was standing at the kitchen window, drinking my second cup of coffee and discovering that getting up early hadn't been early enough.

On the bench down by the creek—too distant from the kitchen window for me to make out details—someone was sitting. A man. I glanced at the wall clock over the fridge. Seven thirty a.m.

My heart skipped with the thought that it might be Seth. He might've made a surprise visit home and chosen to wait outside rather than disturb me so early . . . which made no sense whatsoever. Likely, it was one of the landscapers.

I went to the front of the house, where I could get a good view of the driveway from the parlor window. A truck was parked there, blue and dusty with a large dent on the rear wheel hub. Racks attached to the side held ladders, and assorted paraphernalia peeked over the top of the bed.

Definitely not Seth.

I hurried upstairs and pulled my hair back into a ponytail. I brushed my teeth and washed my face, donned jeans and a shirt, and then went out to the back porch. I stood there for a long moment listening to birdsong and admiring the blue skies high above. The early puffs of clouds that had hung low over the creek at dawn were clearing out, and mist was rising from the grass. It made the scene look atmospheric, much like an impressionistic painting. Today would be a hot one. It was July in Virginia, after all, but more than that, there was an edge to this morning's warmth that promised high humidity.

As I neared the bench, the man stood and turned toward me. His dark hair was longish and shaggy and pulled away from his face in a loose band low on his neck. The band wasn't adequate to the job, and his hair slipped out, but his expression was pleasant. His broad, square jaw and wide shoulders gave him a rough look, but he also appeared strong and capable. He wore an unbuttoned cotton shirt with a gray T-shirt beneath it, blue jeans, and dark work boots, and he looked ready for work.

"Morning, ma'am."

"Good morning to you too. I was surprised to see someone down here."

"Yes, ma'am." He held up a thermos in one hand and its plastic cup in the other. "Couldn't resist enjoying my coffee by the creek. Nice bench. Nice spot. Hope you don't mind."

"Not at all. By midday, under this summer sun, it won't be so pleasant. It's going to be hot today." I walked right up to him. "I'm Kara Hart."

"Yes, ma'am. We met before. I came that day with Jim Mitchell when we were discussing the work Mr. Lange wanted done. Name's Will Mercer."

32

He hardly looked at me. I caught a glimpse of blue eyes before his gaze slid away and down to his thermos.

"I remember that day," I said. "I know you and Jim already spoke with my father about the work, but I'd like to revisit that discussion. With Dad gone, I'm changing what he'd originally planned for Wildflower House."

"No problem. What sort of changes?"

"My father was focused on renovation, but I have a business in mind. A retreat for creatives and also a facility for day events. It won't change the basic work like clearing the front and side yards, but I'd also like the area around the carriage house improved. And the front acreage needs to be particularly inviting. If you have any suggestions, please do let me know."

He nodded and drank his last sip of coffee, then recapped the thermos and twisted the now-empty plastic cup back into place on top.

I hadn't seen a genuine thermos in use in . . . well, in years. He saw me staring. He gave me a longer look this time, and with a small grin he held up the battered thermos. "Old fashioned. It was my granddad's and my dad's."

"Sentimental?"

He frowned in a confused way; then it cleared. "You mean because it belonged to them?"

"Yes."

"No, not that. No point in being sentimental

about objects, but at the same time there's no reason to toss something if it still has use left in it."

"Oh."

"How about we go look at the grounds? You can tell me what you'd like done, and then we can discuss where to begin."

As we walked up the slope toward the house, I waved my hand at the open area of the backyard. "I haven't decided what to do about that yet. The yard used to be full of wildflowers. The hailstorm we had last month destroyed them."

The area of devastation was like a huge sore covering most of the yard. Grass grew in two bands as walkways, one on either side between what had been the field of flowers and the tree line. As Nicole had said, that grass needed cutting. There was no hope we'd see wildflowers again anytime soon.

Will said, "Those flowers are done for this year."

I was startled by his words, which so closely echoed my own thoughts. I insisted, "Some may come back, especially later in the season. Maybe."

"Doubt it."

I dug in my mental heels. "They might."

"So you want to wait and see?"

"What? No. I just meant . . . never mind."

"Weeds will come."

"Weeds? They aren't weeds. They are wild-flowers. Were, that is."

"No offense, Ms. Hart. I meant actual weeds. Weeds are opportunists. They'll take advantage of that empty area. It's what they do. Dandelions. Crabgrass. Spurge. Nature's ground cover. And it'll happen pretty quick in this climate, this time of year."

"Of course. Weeds."

"They'll get a head start on any flowers that might try to return and choke 'em out."

"Then what do you recommend?"

"Up to you, ma'am."

Not very helpful. If his work style was to feed me worries but withhold solutions, then this wasn't going to work. I didn't know what bothered me more—his unwillingness to exchange ideas or his strange refusal to meet my eyes for longer than one fleeting second at a time.

I crossed my arms. "I'll make the final decisions, but before I do, I'd appreciate your *expert* guidance."

There was a long silence, during which we both stared at the area in question. I could observe him, though, from the corner of my eye. Finally he nodded and said, "I'll give it some thought and let you know. For now, I recommend cutting the grass. Other decisions can wait."

I pressed a hand to my face and shook my head.

"I'm sorry. I sounded like a bully. Truly, I didn't mean it like that."

He looked at me—a longer look this time. His eyes were very blue. "No worries. I know it's a sensitive subject given what happened."

Dad's death. That's what he was talking about. Will Mercer was trying to show respect and extend sympathy. A shudder seized me as I recalled finding my father lying in the flowers and already beyond help. Without the barrier of the house or even the screen door or the kitchen window between me and the memory, it rolled over me. I called forth every iota of steel inside me to control it. I squeezed my eyes closed and focused on putting that steel into my spine. Pulling my shoulders back and standing straighter, I said, "Thank you, Will. I'll give this more thought, and we can revisit the subject later."

"Are you okay?"

I kept my face averted. "I'm fine."

"Yes, ma'am."

"Not ma'am. Please call me Kara."

"I meant no offense."

"Of course not." I managed a small smile. "I know it's southern courtesy. I'm born and raised in Virginia myself. But I prefer you to call me Kara, if you will."

He nodded.

The tension between us seemed to have passed.

We walked together more comfortably as we discussed how to handle the side yards, the front yard, and the carriage house. Will's words about my discomfort over the erstwhile wildflower field were spot on, and I gave him points for discernment. Plus extra points for consideration because he didn't refer to it again.

By the time we arrived at his truck and he stopped to put his thermos on the front seat, I had decided that we could work together well. He'd grow comfortable around me. I didn't doubt it. With a little familiarity between us, he'd grow more confident about offering ideas.

He said, "I have a couple of guys coming. Lon and Derek. They'll be here soon. We'll work in the side yards in the morning and in the front acreage in the afternoon. Should stay nice and shady under those pines out front. We'll do the same tomorrow, then assess where we're at."

"Hot work."

"Yes. Pretty much expected this time of year." He was already turning away. My pleasant smile was wasted. Again.

"Are we clear on which bushes and trees to keep? Some of them are ailing or too overgrown, I know, so I'll trust your judgment, but I don't want everything cleared out wholesale."

"Yes, ma'am." He coughed. "Kara."

"I'll need space for parking too. If you can recommend an area that will be convenient for visitors but also able to be landscaped with a professional, businesslike appearance, I'd appreciate it."

"How many vehicles?"

"I don't know. Maybe ten cars?" I laughed a tiny bit. "I'm sorry. I'm still working out the details."

"Is the parking area for that retreat thing?"

"Yes. A creative retreat." I shrugged. "It was an impulsive decision. I'm not normally that person. I'm usually better prepared before I take on a project."

Will smiled. "You'll figure it out. Meanwhile, I'll get on with the rest. Plenty of work to be done. Any questions or concerns, let me know."

With a nod, he dropped the truck's tailgate and started unloading equipment.

I walked away but stopped on the porch. Will didn't look up, so I went on into the house and watched from the window.

His voice and words had sounded respectful. But his body language, his refusal to sustain eye contact, made me curious and a little suspicious.

I thought back to when I first met him in early June—only days before my father died. I'd gone out to the yard to join Dad's conversation with Jim Mitchell about the landscaping. Will had been there, but I'd hardly noticed because my thoughts had been about Seth. Seth had almost kissed me moments before in the kitchen. Almost. I'd been floating on air, or so I'd felt, as I walked outside. Dad had made the introductions, and he and Jim had done most of the talking. As far as I could remember, Will hadn't uttered a single word.

Within days, Dad was gone. And right after the funeral, Seth left for LA. Not long ago at all, yet so much had happened.

Was Will shy? Could that be the answer?

A small smile settled on my lips.

Adults could be shy. A man who liked working outdoors, who preferred physical labor . . . that occupation could be a good fit for a man who was an introvert. Physically, he was built for that kind of work. Those shoulders . . .

So I had a reasonable explanation. Will was shy.

It didn't matter. He had his work to do, and I had mine. *Yes, mine.*

Will's question about the parking lot had been simple and obvious, and I hadn't known the answer. Not knowing had sparked something in me.

How many parking spots?

I should already have figured that out, and so much more. That said, this creative retreat idea of mine had been voiced publicly less than three weeks ago, with very little conscious thought applied before that.

Impulsive, indeed. What had possessed me?

What did they say? Those wise sages people

often quoted? *Don't make important decisions after a big life event like death or divorce?*

But the idea must have been taking root in my brain. I must've seen something, heard something, at some point in time. And at the right moment, it had just sort of bloomed in my conscious mind. I'd declared my intentions to Nicole and Mel. If I'd realized they'd take those words as a commitment, would I have thrown them out so boldly?

Yet in retrospect I was glad I had—that I had put that commitment on myself with the crazy declaration. I could still change my mind about the project, but those words . . . well, they sort of kept me on course.

I had homework to do after my shower and another cup of coffee.

What else was it those sages said? *Today is the first day of the rest of your life?* Maybe it could be true.

After my shower I was ready for a restart on the day. When I went downstairs, I saw two other vehicles, a truck and a battered SUV, parked next to Will's. His crew had arrived.

In the kitchen, I picked up Nicole's folder with the permitting and building info. I carried it with me as I decided where to set up my work space. The kitchen wouldn't do. The contractor was coming early next week to tear it apart.

The dining room table was huge—plenty of work area—but I anticipated that Moore Blackwell, the man Dad had hired to remove the wallpaper and replaster the walls, would be starting work soon, too, possibly next week.

The sitting room? There was space for a desk in the corner alcove. But even aside from the wallpaper-removal question, this was the room everyone saw first when they entered the foyer. That was why I'd put Hannah Cooper's blue vase squarely in view on the fireplace mantel. Nicole had given the vase to Dad and me as a housewarming gift. Hannah was an artisan in clay and something of a local celebrity, at least as far as her pottery went. I'd never met her, but Nicole said she had clients far outside our little community. From what I could see, her celebrity was well earned. There was something about the vase that begged to be touched, as if the glaze itself might give way and let your fingers reach right into its heart. Depending upon the angle and the light, you could pick out the form of a girl shadowed in the glaze and in the shape of the clay, and she seemed to have wings.

Dad and I had positioned Hannah's vase on the mantel below my needlework—the blue delphiniums. After my accident I'd taken up needlework almost compulsively and had found comfort and distraction in it. Dad had suggested framing and hanging the delphiniums in precisely

41

that spot. Then, after Dad died, I'd stitched a couple of sampler-type pieces about wildflowers and Wildflower House and had had them framed, but I hadn't hung them yet.

No, the sitting room wasn't the place to set up my work area.

The parlor on the other side of the foyer was also out of the question. That cabbage rose wallpaper was definitely coming down. The smell of old cigars was so strong in there at times that I could almost see mustached men in vests with dangling watch fobs sitting and puffing away.

There was a reality to my situation that was both good and bad. Dad had been successful in business. As his sole heir I'd inherited money, but not enough that I could spend it without regard. If I chose the wrong course, I would find my funds had vanished along with my big plans. On the other hand, if I'd had to seek financing, I would've had to run the numbers and apply for loans. My impulsive decision might well have ended as abruptly as it had come. I might have packed up my belongings and scurried back to the city and a nine-to-five job. I'd been successful in my old project-management job, and even though I'd been out of the workforce since my accident, I was confident my former employer would give me an excellent reference if I asked.

None of that mattered now. That was the past. I was here and moving forward, but I owed it to everyone, including to Dad's years of hard work and his legacy, to do my due diligence.

I almost walked past the room I needed. The middle room. It was on the right, between the grand staircase and the closeted hallway with the servants' stairs. It was the least interesting room in the house. No nooks or crannies. No turrets. I tended to forget that room existed.

The room had two windows, both presently covered with ivy and other green growth, and the air inside was stuffy and dusty. I fanned myself with Nicole's folder.

Dad had stored an old four-legged folding card table in the attic along with the unpacked boxes. I could use a kitchen chair or a cushioned one from the dining room. With a little sweeping and a few sprays of air freshener, this space could work.

Before fetching the broom, I set the folder on the foyer table. It was more of a chest, really, with large, deep drawers. On impulse, I opened the top drawer and lifted out the large framed photograph of the girls and young women who'd attended school here when the Kinney family had built this house. Some had boarded at the house. Girls in knee-length white dresses with big bows in their curls stood in the front row. Young women with longer gowns and hair done up in buns were behind them, and two older women in heavy black dresses, whom I thought must be teachers, flanked the ends. They were all posed on the front porch. This front porch. *My* front porch. The first time I'd seen this photo, I'd felt like each set of eyes had a story to share. I didn't know their stories, but women's opportunities had been limited at the turn of the prior century, so I could guess.

This photograph and the samplers I'd stitched about wildflowers and welcome had seemed so important to me in those days following Dad's death. Yet by that point, the real-life flowers had already been beaten down by hail and encased in mud. I hadn't been able to do anything to prevent Dad's death or the loss of the flowers. But this photo of the female students had called to me, and it continued to. It seemed to have some meaning that tied into my feelings about my father and the flowers. My life. And this house. This project of mine.

I struggled to define how those faces might've inspired this retreat idea but failed to put real words to it. Maybe it had to do with permanence—or the lack thereof? Or biological frailty? Of trials endured and hopes lost? Things we'd wanted to do but hadn't and how our missed opportunities often morphed into "never dones"?

I'd stitched:

> ❧ *Wildflowers are tough. They root in unlikely, often hostile environments, yet they manage to grow and bloom.*

- *Wildflowers are fragile. Careless or deliberate acts can easily destroy them.*

- *Wildflowers grow where the seeds find themselves. They must succeed or perish. If they don't grow, no one notices. It's as if the seed or the flower never existed.*

- *Wildflowers are beautiful for a season. Some may be beautiful for seasons to come. The wildflower will never know the difference because it either is or isn't. Only the bees and the butterflies—or a human heart—may feel the lack.*

    —Stitched by Kara Lange Hart
    at Wildflower House

I had intended to hang them, all three frames, but every time I picked up a hammer and nail, the memory of my dad would grow strong. I'd hear him striding down the hall. I'd look up, expecting to see him walk into the room. A couple of times I thought I heard his voice or the loud sigh he'd sometimes give when faced with an unwelcome or perplexing problem. I would pause, almost like a compass unable to find its true north.

I'd lost him too soon.

He'd come to my rescue after the accident. He'd sat at my bedside and handled all the details of my life, including closing up the town house

Niles and I had lived in and packing away our goods for storage. Dad helped me along the journey to regaining my health and putting my life back together.

So I hadn't hung the frames yet. I promised myself that I would get the task done when the time was right.

If Dad were here, he'd ask me why I was being wishy-washy. He wouldn't expect or want an answer from me. He'd say, "If it's worth doing, then go for it. Anything else is a waste of time and energy."

In a moment I'd get the broom, then go upstairs and bring that folding table down, but for *this* moment, I sat on the piano bench. I didn't play. Had never learned how.

The foyer chest, the piano, even the photo of those women belonged here in a way I didn't. Sue Deale, the Forsters' heir, had sent these items and more back here—to their former home— because her own home was overwhelmed with the furniture and keepsakes she'd hauled out of here before Dad bought the house.

Belonged. The piano belonged here more than I did.

I sighed. And my sigh sounded like my father's.

It seemed to me that fate had often interfered with my life. Each time things seemed to be going well, fate would step up and give things a spin. I could feel that it was about to happen again.

It hadn't been enough that my mother had left when I was young. Fate had had more in store for me, including that accident and the loss of my husband.

I pressed my fingers to my temples. Under the fingertips of my right hand, I found the raised flesh of the scar again—my keepsake from the accident now almost two years past, the accident that had made me a widow, ended my pregnancy, and reset my life without warning or permission.

And in a roundabout way had led me here, to Wildflower House.

Chapter Three

Yesterday, Will Mercer had asked how many parking spaces I'd need. Today, I heard the sound of men's voices outside, muffled by the foliage-covered windows and occasionally punctuated by the roar of a chain saw or a leaf blower—mostly presumed, since I couldn't see much through those windows. The rise and fall of the voices and the louder noise of the equipment provided evidence of activity and served as welcome background noise in an otherwise-silent house.

The morning had started slowly for me. My brain had been busy, but good busy, excited about the project moving forward. I'd slept well enough last night after taking the blue pill, and the second cup of coffee this morning worked to get me into gear.

The idea box was now in the middle room. I'd picked out the notes relevant to a project plan and business plan. The decorating samples and product pamphlets stayed in the box for now, on the floor next to the folding table on which my laptop was situated.

I sat. Boldly, I typed *Business Plan* on my laptop screen and then waited. And waited.

Type something, anything, I told myself. *Just do it.* Finally, I did, but I produced only random bullets about what I'd want for the creative retreat—things like types of usages, numbers of guests I could potentially house at any given time, and even how many of those pesky parking spaces I might need. I was breaking out in a sweat over it, but I filled most of the page. It was a jumble, but it was a start.

Next I opened the spreadsheet program. In the first column I listed what I considered the most likely expense categories.

It was remarkably exhausting. I knew the process would get better and easier, and I was proud of myself for finally doing something real to drive this project. The plan wasn't ready for prime time yet, but it would get there.

I wasn't used to working on a project that I, myself, had initiated. As a project manager, I'd functioned within the parameters set by my employer's approved practices and the specific requirements of the project itself—all laid out for me and my team by the project owners. I was comfortable working within that framework. As a child, I'd learned to function comfortably and efficiently within the parameters set by my mom and dad. That was natural enough but also essential given our family's special challenges.

Had I never moved beyond that?

A horrible thought. My eyes stung, and I pressed my fingers against my lashes to stop the sudden tears.

Mom had had problems. Officially. Most of the time she'd sit at the kitchen table and stare at the window. On good days—the days when I came home from school to find her dressed in normal daytime attire—she would order supper in. On bad days, those days when she was still in her pajamas or robe when I got off the bus, I would cook. In between school and bedtime, I sat with her, either telling her about my day or doing my homework.

Mom left us when I was fourteen. She'd run off before but had always returned. Until that last time.

It had hurt then, and it continued to, as unresolved pain usually did.

Together, Dad and I had made our post-Mom lives work. We had our lists of responsibilities. The few tasks he assigned to me, like laundry and dusting and homework, I handled, while he kept his business growing and a roof over our heads. Dad saved me when things had gone wrong in my life, like the accident. Even the one decision I'd made on my own—to marry Niles—in retrospect felt suspiciously like I'd been following the expected, most comfortable path. *Meet a nice guy . . . fall in love . . . get married . . .*

It had all gone so wrong.

I'd never initiated anything new or bold in my whole life—except for that day soon after Dad's funeral when Nicole and Mel asked what I was going to do with Wildflower House. Would I stay or sell? And I'd said, "A retreat . . . a place for small groups to come. Maybe writers. Maybe artists."

Thinking of it still made me breathless.

It had been outrageously impulsive. Totally out of character.

Creative retreat, indeed.

I'd wanted to disavow those words soon after. But Mel and Nicole had been immediately on board, supporting me in my brash plan.

I needed someone to brainstorm with, to chew over possibilities and details. Nicole had offered to be that person, but personality-wise it wouldn't work. Maybe Seth. At least he would've tried. But he was far away.

Frustrated, I closed the laptop lid. I picked up the idea box to set it on the table, and it fell. Paint swatches and pamphlets of window coverings and bathroom and lighting fixtures hit the floor and slid in every direction.

Seriously?

As I stared at the scattered papers in dismay, I realized I wasn't hearing work noise from outside.

What were the guys doing?

I peeked out front and saw another pickup. This one was tan colored, dented, and scratched up, but it was clearly a truck that meant business in life and play. I also saw a pile of branches, sticks, and lots of green stuff near the right side of the house. I went to the side windows. These would need a major cleaning after the jungle had been tamed. Despite the grimy film on the glass, I could already see a difference in terms of the amount of daylight filtering through.

A pitcher of ice water with sliced lime and strawberries was in the fridge. The kitchen cabinets were mostly empty, but I had a few glasses and plates stacked on the counter. I could offer the workers something to drink. I stepped out to the back porch and saw no one, but the heat hit me. The house, especially the lower floor, stayed so cool inside I could forgo the air-conditioning most mornings. But outside? *Ugh.* Outside was just plain hot and muggy. Iced tea weather. The workers would probably prefer iced tea to lime-and-strawberry water anyway.

Back inside, I shut the windows and doors and turned on the AC. I put water on to boil and took tea bags from the tin. Honey hibiscus lemon. Perfect. I left the tea bags on the counter while the water heated and returned to the middle room to gather up the samples, pamphlets, and paint chips from the floor. As I worked, I heard new sounds coming from the side of the house.

Even the windows in this middle room were basic, without the elegance of the tall windows at the front of the house. It was a plain room, and between the grime on the glass exterior and the leaves of the vine trying to secure its grip out there, there was no view. As I looked, the vine shook and its leaves shivered. I felt a rush of excitement. *Soon,* I thought. Soon there'd be a view and lots of sunshine.

Next to the middle room, between it and the kitchen, was the narrow hallway with the enclosed servants' stairs. That hallway had a door that opened onto a small porch on the side of the house. Its door was blocked by the same vines and vegetation that obscured these windows. We'd lived here for three months, and I'd never opened that door or stepped onto that porch. Making it usable had been on Dad's to-do list—a long list he'd enjoyed refining, tweaking, and adding to. His whole idea for moving here had been for the fun of renovating—and not just the house. He'd had such plans for the grounds. He'd even mentioned wanting an orchard. But his time here had been too short, and the list had stayed long.

I retrieved the last of the fallen pamphlets. My computer and the in-progress business plan needed my attention. I should get back to work instead of worrying over iced tea and what the work crew was doing outside. Was it procrastination? Avoidance? Or simply the fact of living, breathing people doing interesting stuff outside my house? Regardless of why, I didn't resist the lure. I could always find quiet time to tend to business. Right now there was life and activity going on at Wildflower House, and I gave myself permission to be part of it.

I fetched the key ring from the kitchen drawer and went straight to the dark, narrow hallway. I gripped the doorknob and twisted. The knob didn't turn, so I fidgeted with the assorted keys and chose one.

The first key I tried worked, but the door itself stuck. I grasped the knob with both hands and pulled. The door moved, but it wouldn't come free of the frame. I tugged again, harder, and it moved on its own, pushing in toward me with force. I flew backward, not trying to catch myself but using my arms to shield my head from hitting the floor or the close walls.

"Ma'am? You okay?"

I thrust my hands forward defensively, moving them against the threat, ready to protect myself.

"Kara?" Will caught my flailing hands, but gently. "I saw the door was stuck. I pushed . . . but only a little. Are you hurt?"

By now, I'd made it to a full sitting position and had caught my breath. Will had released my hands but now reoffered his to assist me up. Before I could accept or decline, he pulled it back abruptly, apparently shocked by the dirt. He wiped both hands down the sides of his khakis.

"Sorry. Working outside and all, well . . ."

Meanwhile, the perspiration—sweat—that soaked

his hair and T-shirt dropped from his face onto my shirt. Will saw the wet spot, and if his red face could possibly get any redder, it did. He looked utterly embarrassed.

I said, "I was pulling so hard I overbalanced when the door opened." I did a quick assessment. Nothing hurt except my butt. I laughed a little, trying to defuse his embarrassment and my awkwardness. "I'm okay. I just wasn't expecting help with the door at exactly that moment."

He stared. He pushed the sweat-drenched hair off his forehead. "Are you sure?"

Honestly, it bothered me that his state troubled him so much. He was working in the yard in July, for heaven's sake. Sweat and dirt were inevitable.

He frowned slightly and met my eyes, asking, "Is something burning?"

Was that a euphemism? Some sort of reference to his flushed face and my own discomfort? Was my face red too? I almost laughed and agreed with his joke, but then my nose noticed what his already had.

It was a hot smell. Not smoke. But directed heat—too much of it.

"The stove. Boiling water," I said.

I moved quickly, aware of Will's hands on my arms helping to propel me upward and onto my feet. I moved as if I'd never had a serious injury, had never needed a cane. Adrenaline fueled me, no doubt.

The water had boiled away. The bottom of the pan inside was discolored. Not burned too badly, but it was probably ruined. Not thinking, I reached for the handle. Will stopped me. He'd already found the dish towel and used it to grab the pot and carry it to the sink.

I turned off the burner. Despite the protection of the dish towel, after he set the pan in the sink, Will waved his hand in a quick cooling motion.

"Are your fingers burned?"

He grimaced. "No. Just hot. No damage done except to the pan."

"I'm glad. Thank you," I said. "I was making tea. I was distracted."

"I'm sorry."

"You helped. What are you sorry for?"

"Because of the door—"

I interrupted. "It was my fault. I wanted to see what you and your crew were doing. I should've walked outside the usual way."

He looked taller and broader in my kitchen and uncomfortable. His presence stymied me for a moment. I offered, "Would you like some water?"

"No, thanks. I've got a cooler outside. We bring our own. Important to stay hydrated in this weather." He looked down at his wet T-shirt, then nodded. "Excuse me while I get back to work." Without another word, he exited by way of the back door, leaving me standing there with a ruined pan in the sink and the noxious smell of hot metal in the air around me.

They'd brought their own. Of course. Why had I thought I should offer refreshments? Because it gave me an excuse to interact? I groaned. Was I that lonely?

The screen door closed behind Will, but he'd left the door itself open, and I knew the side door was surely open to the heat and insects since neither of us had stopped to close it. The breeze wafting through the kitchen felt humid, but it diminished the burning smell, that hot metallic evidence of distraction. I went to the front door and opened it wide to keep the air flowing through, then returned to the side door.

I'd walked through the side yard many times and had caught glimpses of the side porch through the green overgrowth, but standing at the open door, I was now seeing it as a whole unit, small and weathered but intact. This small porch could be attractive after it was cleaned up, painted, and decorated. I stepped out, and a man yelled.

I froze midstep. Will again. He was standing a few yards away.

He said, "Some of those boards look iffy. Be careful until we check them out. You don't want to fall through."

I satisfied my curiosity from the doorway. "It's the first time I've really seen this porch."

He nodded and gestured toward several rangy bushes crowding the railing, saying, "Those bushes don't look like much."

Wanting to be agreeable—after all, he'd practically saved my house from burning down—I said, "You can pull them out or cut them, however you think best."

"I suggest keeping them."

"Why?"

"They're lilacs and camellias. We'll prune them. With better sun and air, they'll probably come back next year. They'll smell good outside the windows and next to the porch when they bloom."

"Oh," I said, and I felt that *oh* inside, kind of warm and soft in my chest. I said it again deliberately, wanting to repeat the feeling. "Oh, that sounds lovely. We'll give them a chance to make a comeback."

Will smiled, and his face brightened.

I smiled back. After a long, awkward moment in which I felt foolish because I couldn't think of anything clever or pertinent to say—and Will didn't say anything at all—I settled for, "I'd better get back to work."

"Same here." He nodded and walked away.

I returned to the kitchen. The ruined pan went into the trash. Never mind tea. As I was putting the tea bags back into the canister, the doorbell rang, quickly followed by a solid knock and a voice calling out, "Ms. Hart?"

I'd left the front door open, so Mr. Blackwell must've knocked on the house itself.

Moore Blackwell was the wallpaper expert. It was hard to mistake his voice, which ranged from deep and smooth to gravelly and matched his tall, thin, somber appearance. His skin was olive, and he seemed to have a permanent five-o'clock shadow. I imagined his beard had defeated many a razor. But while his appearance was imposing, he was actually a very kind man. I knew because of how he'd responded with my on-and-off-again plans in the weeks following Dad's death. *Death.* I said the word silently, testing it. Yes, it still hurt.

"Come in, Mr. Blackwell," I said as I walked down the hallway to the foyer.

He stepped into the foyer. He was holding a jar with a decorative top, and he offered it to me.

Brown liquid. "Honey tea?" I asked.

He nodded. "My Sheryl sent it. Told her you sounded kind of rough on the phone. Your voice sounds better now, though."

I'd been grieving and doing a lot of crying when we'd spoken. I said, "It comes and goes."

"Well, I hope it stays gone, but regardless, I expect you'll enjoy Sheryl's tea." He brushed his now-empty hands against each other. "You said you want to make changes to the project?"

"I have some ideas I'd like to get your thoughts on. As you know, Dad planned to strip all the paper, but is it possible to save some of it? Not in the parlor, and probably not in the sitting room. But what about the dining room? It's in better shape than the other rooms. If that paper can be cleaned, I'd like to incorporate it into the overall decor. A blending of old and new, along with incorporating the house history. If you think the idea of saving the wallpaper is unworkable or impractical, please say so."

"Comes down to expectations."

"As in?"

"If you want to keep the wallpaper, then I think it's doable. When I was here before, talking to your . . . well, when I was here before, I checked the adhesion. The dining room paper seemed good. It'll never look new again, but that might be your expectation if you're wanting an antique look."

I nodded. Yes, perhaps I was.

"Most renovations I work these days pretty much gut out all the old stuff. It's quicker and better for resale."

"Actually, I'm planning to open a creative retreat here."

"Ma'am?"

"Yes, a place for classes, day events, and even for groups to stay over."

He scratched his cheek. "Like a bed-and-breakfast?"

"Close enough."

"Whatever work you have in mind, I'm happy to oblige."

"Thank you, Mr. Blackwell. I'd like to begin with cleaning the dining room paper and stripping the parlor paper. When can you start?"

"I'm free now."

"Wonderful. I also have work about to begin in the kitchen. I hope you can manage around each other."

"No worries there."

"Excellent." I held out my hand to shake. "Thank you, Mr. Blackwell. I'm sorry for the delay, and I appreciate your patience."

"Couldn't be helped." He shook my hand and then sniffed the air. "Something on the stove, ma'am?"

"Boiling water. Or was. I left it too long."

"Happens, Ms. Hart."

"You're right about that, Mr. Blackwell. Things do happen."

I couldn't wield a chain saw, and I wasn't about to try removing wallpaper, but I could do something. It might be a mindless task, but I could do it with my own hands. I wanted to be part of the physical progress.

Before he'd left for the day, Will had confirmed that the porch floor was sound enough, but he'd warned me to be mindful of splinters. After the last of their vehicles had departed, I threw clean rags over my shoulder; filled a bucket with warm, soapy water; and toted it out to the side porch.

I filled a second bucket with clean water for rinsing and carried it out too. The long summer day was still plenty bright, and heat hung over everything, but the side porch was in the shade. I didn't mind working up a sweat as long as I didn't have an audience.

Kind of like Will Mercer that morning? I laughed a little as perspiration prickled at my scalp and beaded along my spine. My T-shirt was soon spotted with wet. I laughed more and wrung the cleaning rag out over the bucket, feeling better than I had in a long while. As I scrubbed the window glass, sweat bloomed through the fabric of my shirt and my shorts. I scrubbed all the harder. I felt the stirring of ownership.

As I soaped and twisted the rag and then wet it again, I was doing more than cleaning and putting my mark on the house. I was hoping to sweat out some of my negativity, my doubt, while I was at it. Now that I didn't have anyone near—not Dad, not Niles, and not even Victoria—to distract me, I saw it clearly.

Out with resentment. Away with tiptoeing through life, not wanting to give offense or to disappoint people. No more holding it all in until I blew up over nothing.

I scrubbed at the side windows with a will. I drank a ton of fruit water to stay hydrated, and I was covered from head to toe in grimy, gritty sweat. It felt disgusting but also really good.

I would sleep well tonight without extra help, except perhaps treating myself to a long soak in the tub with a lavender bath bomb.

I took that sweetly scented bath and spoiled myself, complete with candles, and when I fell into bed, every muscle knew my rest was well earned. And I slept. Until three a.m.

Suddenly I was awake, and for no reason that I could discern, unless it was because I hadn't taken a pill. I lay there for a while listening and heard nothing special, so I stayed in bed to see if I might drift back off. No luck. Finally I went to get a drink of water, then took a stroll through the house.

I liked how Wildflower House looked in the dark with the moonlight filtering in through the windows. It gave me a feeling of peace, spoke of permanence and infinity. Cave dwellers had seen that moonlight. Those yet to come would see the same. I kept wanting to turn to someone, to touch their arm and tell them, *Look at that moon . . . see those stars . . . the hallway and stairs bathed in starlight look so magical . . .* But there was no one to tell.

I returned to my bed, smoothed the covers, climbed in, and lay there awake.

Empty never felt as empty as it did at three a.m. It was the loneliest feeling on earth.

At four a.m. I gave in and took a blue pill. When he'd prescribed it, the doctor had said it was a mild sedative, nothing heavy duty. But it had the power to help me over that threshold into sleep, and that was enough for tonight.

Because I'd taken the pill so late—or early, depending on one's perspective—I wasn't surprised that I slept later than usual. It hardly mattered since I was the only one here to notice. I woke at my own pace, feeling the sunshine streaming in through the window and tempting my eyes to open. I pushed aside my personal morning fog and envisioned my day and my plans. Finally I stretched my arms and legs, easing the stiffness from my old injuries, before sitting up and standing gingerly.

Was I ninety years old? Some mornings . . .

Coffee next, I thought, as I moved slowly across the bedroom.

On my way to the stairs, I saw a twig—a single brown twig—lying in the hallway. I picked it up and examined it. How had it gotten here? I'd walked downstairs during the night, but I hadn't gone outside.

I must've tracked it in earlier in the day and reencountered it during my nighttime travels, and it had hitchhiked up with me.

There was no other explanation.

Holding the twig, twirling it between my fingers, I told myself not to make more of it than there was. I had work to do and a business to craft.

Chapter Four

I started my day in the middle room. The project room. One day it might serve as my permanent office or maybe a guest room for people who had trouble managing stairs. I added a bullet to my draft business plan about offering the middle room as a first floor guest room.

The plan was messy, but it was growing, and that was good because you couldn't fix what didn't exist.

Late morning, I stopped for a break. Will and his helpers were on the grounds somewhere, but I hadn't heard or seen anyone. I stepped out to the back porch.

The backyard sloped down to Cub Creek. Except for in the open expanse of yard where the wildflowers had grown, there were trees and more trees, many and varied, all around, including on the far side of the creek.

Mother Nature had not only dropped hail on my beautiful wildflowers, but she'd also assaulted the roof and my car. The insurance company had covered the roof damage, which had been surprisingly minimal. With Nicole's help, I'd hired skilled roofers, and the damage had been repaired promptly. My car had been totaled and replaced. But the flowers? No one could fix those.

I leaned against the porch railing and brushed at my stinging eyes, my vision suddenly blurry.

Was I crying again? Really? Over dead flowers now? Or was I still crying for my father? Maybe these tears were about my husband and my mother. Or myself. I'd created a mountain of soggy tissues over the past month.

"Sorry to interrupt."

I jumped, surprised, and hastily wiped the evidence of my pity party from my eyes and cheeks. I managed to smile before I faced him.

"Will. Hi."

He asked, "Want to take a look at the carriage house?"

From the porch and from this angle, the red-tiled roof of the carriage house was just visible. The building was actually set back in the woods, and the old footpath between here and there was wildly overgrown. In the past, carriages or other vehicles had reached it by way of a rutted track that led off the current driveway, nearer the main road.

The whole aspect of it with its peaked, tiled roof seemed even more uninviting and inaccessible from this vantage point than it had when I'd braved the jungle of thorns and mystery plants to get a close-up look. I'd come away from that adventure without poison ivy or poison oak blisters or snakebites, so I counted that a win. I hadn't been tempted to go back.

But here was Will, and he was waiting.

"Yes, thanks." My feet were bare. "I'll slip on my shoes."

He nodded.

When I returned, we walked toward the carriage house. There were still sticker bushes and such to avoid along the way, but Will's crews had cleared a lot of the scrubby growth and created more of a path.

He said, "Fair warning. You'll be able to go inside the building now, but there's lots yet to do, so watch where you put your feet."

I stopped. "What?"

"Snakes. Spiders, maybe. Haven't seen any troublesome ones, but it's good to keep an eye out."

"Of course." Troublesome ones? He didn't say that he hadn't seen *any* . . .

The first set of doors was open, but the interior was very dim.

"Wow. I thought the doors were locked."

"Just choked by weeds."

A lanky man came out of the shadowed interior in the main area of the carriage house. His jeans and T-shirt were soiled and baggy. He appeared to be raking cobwebs out of his hair with his fingers. I shuddered, but not at the dirt.

"Ma'am," he said, nodding.

Will said, "This is Lon. He was checking for snakes and other cautions."

Cautions. The phrasing was odd, but I knew what he meant.

Lon exited the carriage house, moving with a loose, almost disjointed gait, and joined us. "Yes, ma'am. All clear as far as I can see."

Now that the stone walls of the carriage house weren't half-covered by vegetation, I saw they had a decidedly gray-blue cast. I wanted to touch the stone. I walked past Will and Lon and did exactly that, pressing my hands against the hard, rough face of the rock.

Despite the July air that had heated up the day, these stones were cool. The surfaces were lumpy, chiseled looking, but smoothed with age.

Before, all I'd really seen were the weeds and vines and sticker bushes. I'd seen the wrong things. A few hours of manual labor had changed the picture and my perception entirely—like an optical illusion in which the negative image unexpectedly flipped back to the reverse, positive image.

I blinked. I couldn't help myself.

"Are you okay?" Will asked. His voice was low, wary, as if I might be one of those cautions.

"I'm fine. I hadn't seen the stone properly before. It's beautiful."

He waved toward the walls and ceiling. "Inside is dry and tight. You're planning to use this place as part of your retreat?"

I nodded. "I thought it might work for an art studio, like for painting or pottery."

"With a little work, it'll be great for that." He added, "You'll need better lighting and upgraded power."

"Thanks. That's exactly the kind of information I need."

"Lon can clean it up some inside. Sweeping and such, if you want."

Will gave me a half grin. Despite the dirt on his cheek and the grimy, sweat-soaked T-shirt, I noticed that his eyes weren't just blue. In this light they were a perilous blue, a blue somewhere between the deeper shade of Hannah Cooper's blue vase and the lighter delphiniums in that needlework piece displayed over the mantel.

I caught my breath.

Perilous blue? Nonsense. That wasn't even a color. It was merely the contrast of his unusual eyes with his black hair and his rough appearance that made me look twice.

"Would you like to look inside? Lon made sure there's no—"

"Cautions?"

He grinned a little and shrugged.

"I'd love to look inside." I walked into the carriage house ahead of him, then stopped abruptly. It was dark.

A flashlight beam suddenly played around the room as Will said, "There was electric out here in the past, but it doesn't work. Anything could've happened. Mice. Roots. Moisture. Whatever." He moved the light around the ceiling until it lit on a dangling bulb. "See? That line will have to be rerun."

The building smelled very musty. I put my hand to my nose, but discreetly, and coughed a tiny cough.

"It'll air out."

"I'm sure." My eyes were adjusting. "What's that?"

"Stairs to above."

"Have you been up there?"

"Lon checked it out. Didn't want anyone to be surprised by raccoons or possums or rotten boards. Seems sound enough."

What did that mean? "Are you saying it's safe?" I pointed at a door in the wall below where the stairs climbed to "above." "What's that?"

"A small office in the old days, I'd guess."

The door opened easily, but it only added to the mustiness. It smelled to me like another age, like maybe when people shod and harnessed horses and hitched them to wagons for trips into town. The accumulated dust of decades was overwhelming. I coughed again, harder this time. I gestured toward the door and walked back outside.

Will followed. "That dust will clear once the building's aired out and it's in use again."

"I'm sure you're right. And it's quite roomy. Will it be difficult to upgrade the electric?"

"No, but you'll want an electrician. And the roof is bad."

I looked up. I saw a few cracked tiles and mossy areas. "Does it need to be retiled or totally replaced?"

"It's been failing for a while, so replaced. Luckily, no major damage inside that I can see, and the rafters are sound. You'll need a roofer—someone skilled in roof tiles."

"I'll talk to Nicole. Do you know her? I'm sure she'll recommend someone. In fact, she can probably make recommendations for the other work, too, like the electrician. I'll check with her."

As we approached the house, Will said, "Was that you who cleaned those side windows? They look great. Nice work."

"Thanks. It felt good to be doing something—a real, actual something toward making this house happy again."

He gave me an odd look.

"I guess that sounds a little strange. Making the house . . . well, happy. Slightly crazy."

"Not at all," he said. "It sounds about right to me." He grinned and wiped a handkerchief across his face. "Maybe that just means we're both crazy."

It was a friendly, cozy moment as Will and I laughed together. We walked on but hadn't gone far when I noticed a person—no, two people, but one was much smaller than the other—coming up the slope toward the house.

Without thought and reacting only to the call of my eager heart, I waved at the oncoming people, calling out, "Seth! Here!"

I gave Will a quick look of apology and said, "Please excuse me. It's Seth." I took off, but not full-out running because I didn't trust my thigh not to seize up and dump me on the ground in a face-plant.

Seth wasn't moving all that fast himself because Maddie was clinging to him. As I neared, he freed his hand and threw his arms around me, lifting me off my feet. However brief, it was still a great hug. My parents had been distant emotionally, and hugs had been rare in my life. I wanted to stay securely in his arms, but instead I disengaged because Maddie was there. I knelt in front of her. She was grabbing for her uncle's hand, trying to reclaim his attention. I didn't want to be the person she associated with coming between her and Seth.

"Uncle Seth is home, Maddie Lyn. What do you think about that?"

She moved closer to his leg and held his hand all the tighter.

"Your shirt is so cute." It was white with appliquéd bumblebees flying across it. She didn't smile, but she gave me a longer look and fingered the edges of the appliqués with her free hand. Some of the anxious look left her face. "Thank you for coming over with your uncle to visit me."

I stood again, touching Seth's shirt. It was blue and felt soft like silky cotton beneath my hand. I wanted nothing more than to find my way back into his arms.

"Seth. It's so good to see you and such a surprise."

He glanced down at the top of Maddie's head and then winked at me. With playful formality, he announced, "Maddie Lyn and I have come to invite you to a birthday party."

"A birthday?" I asked, adding in a little extra delight for Maddie's benefit.

She smiled and hid her face behind their tightly clasped hands.

"Whose birthday? When is the party?" I asked, including them both in my question.

"Now," Seth said.

I was shocked for real. "Now? As in right now?"

"Sorry, Kara. There was no time to plan ahead. Never thought I'd be able to get home for her birthday, but it worked out at the last minute."

"Maddie's birthday? I didn't know." How could I, since no one had mentioned it to me before this moment? That bothered me. "You flew in last minute? Wasn't that expensive?"

"My employer is covering the cost as long as I return right away." He squeezed Maddie's hand.

"I wasn't about to miss my Maddie's birthday."

I was wordless, stunned by the reminder that I didn't belong . . . not really. Just some kind of add-on.

Seth added, "I apologize for no notice. I wanted to surprise everyone. Didn't want Mom going to a lot of extra effort for such a short visit, but"— he shrugged—"she did anyway. As for the party, no worries about a present for the birthday girl. Right, Maddie?" She nodded. Seth said, "Mom is icing the cake as we speak. I found out what she was planning as I was driving here from the airport. I called you right away, but you didn't answer. So when I got to the house, Maddie Lyn and I put on our superfast sneakers and dashed over to find you."

Still feeling odd about the last-minute timing, I forced a smile. "Perhaps Maddie will accept a belated gift?"

"No doubt about it." He touched my arm. "Are you free to join us?"

"Sure. I'll go grab my phone." I paused. "Do I need to dress up?"

"Nope. It's a family thing. No one's fancy . . . except maybe Nicole." He nodded toward the house. "You go ahead. We'll wait here."

"It's a family thing," he'd said. And I was invited, last minute or not. As for Seth specifically, I told myself not to feel hurt that he hadn't told me he was coming—I wasn't the almost five-year-old here. Seth had wanted to surprise me. He'd said so. That was pretty special.

"Be right back," I said and dashed inside.

I brushed the carriage house dust from my hair and face and put on a fresh blouse. Seth and Maddie were still standing there, hand in hand, when I came out the back door.

Now that we were headed back toward the path to the Albers home, Maddie's mood changed for the better. She released Seth's hand. She was practically dancing as she skipped ahead of us.

"She's excited," I said.

In a soft voice, low enough that Maddie couldn't hear, Seth said, "I intended to surprise you, but not quite this way. Mom told me what she wanted to do after I'd landed. That's the only reason for the last-minute invitation." He grinned. "But I still surprised you, right?"

His hand brushed mine, and I caught it. I held it only for a moment, not wanting to worry Maddie Lyn. But the feeling of his hand in mine, our flesh warm together, lingered deliciously.

I said, "She's so thrilled to have you here, and a birthday party too."

"Technically, her birthday is in two days, but I have to be back in LA before that for an important meeting."

"A short visit." It was hard to hide my disappointment.

"Crazy short. I'm flying back tomorrow. But

77

I'm glad I could work it out. As for us, I haven't forgotten we never went on that date we'd planned."

"Not your fault. Not anyone's. Between losing Dad and you getting the job offer . . . well, we had to put our personal plans on hold."

"We'll have our date when I come back next time—if you're still interested and haven't given up on me."

I gave his arm a gentle shove.

"Thanks for understanding," he said. "I was surprised at how clingy Maddie Lyn was when she saw me. I guess I shouldn't have been."

"It's hard for her. You're her father figure."

We stopped on the small wooden bridge over Cub Creek.

Seth took my hand again and said, "It's been just over a month since we stood here and you told me goodbye—to go to LA so that I could come back all the sooner."

"Words to that effect, anyway." I smiled.

"And a kiss I'll never forget."

I caressed his cheek. He leaned toward me. I leaned in too. My lips were already tingling, remembering the feel of that last kiss, when a small voice called out, "Come on! Hurry!"

"Cake awaits," Seth said, drawing back. "Rain check?"

I slipped my arm in his. "Always."

Maddie ran back to claim us. She positioned

herself between us and put a hand in each of ours to better tug us down the path and toward the party.

Inside, I chafed at the interruption, but I knew—I remembered well—how disruptive it could be to lose a parent. Seth was Maddie's father figure, and though his absence was temporary, it must feel scary and sad for a child who was about to turn five.

The Albers house was a long brick rancher that had been added on to over the years. It was roomy, but the three-car garage in the side yard was much newer and nearly dwarfed it. The path opened onto the backyard, and we walked around to the front door. As we entered the house, I looked around. This was my first visit. Seemed like at least one of the Albers family showed up at my place regularly—and I was usually glad to see them—but I hadn't crossed the bridge to this side of Cub Creek until today.

Mel's kitchen wasn't fancy, but it was tidy and warm. The wallpaper may have been popular when the house had been built. It pictured tea-kettles with flowers and had faded over the years into a sepia-toned aspect that was, in itself, part of the coziness.

That coziness, however, contrasted oddly with the mood around the table.

The cake was delicious, but it was only me,

Mel, Nicole, Seth, and of course Maddie gathered around the kitchen table, and the adults were a little too determined to make it fun. Everyone focused so intently on Maddie, the birthday girl and only child present, that the interactions felt strained.

There was laughter, but sometimes too sharp or forced. Or maybe that was my imagination. I knew Seth would walk me home, and I was looking forward to having a little time alone with him, but as we were leaving, Maddie insisted on joining us. I sensed we might be treated to a tantrum or a meltdown if she wasn't allowed along. Her uncle, the only daddy she'd ever known, was here for this one night. I empathized with her.

Pushing my own disappointment aside, I took her hand in mine and smiled an invitation. She squeezed my fingers, and we headed with Seth out the door.

Maddie kept a tight grip on our hands and sang a medley of tunes as we walked along. I recognized a few as Disney-princess songs. Some snippets of song I didn't recognize at all. But the uninhibited serenade effectively restrained conversation between Seth and me.

We had time, right? If we meant something special to each other, then we'd make the opportunity to mean more. I could be patient. I remembered his patience with me that first day we'd met and even after. It was Seth who'd welcomed me to Cub Creek, Seth who'd introduced me to the nooks on the grounds, and Seth who'd told me the story about Rob and Mary Forster, the house's original owners, and how the wildflower field had come to be.

In a rare quiet moment during our walk back, I said, "I was thinking about the wildflowers and the story you told me about how Mary could no longer keep up the yard and how angry she was when Rob cut the grass down to the roots, threw out the seed, and let it go . . . until spring came and the flowers grew en masse."

"Why are you thinking about that?"

"Because I'm thinking about *you*." I smiled with a teasing grin.

Maddie Lyn burst into the alphabet song. Seth shot me an amused look before adding his voice to Maddie's.

When we three reached Wildflower House, Seth gave me a quick hug and a kiss. While his lips were near my cheek, he whispered he'd call me later. I waved goodbye as Seth and Maddie walked hand in hand back down to the creek. As they neared the woods, Seth swung Maddie up into the air, and she landed on his back with her arms over his shoulders and wrapped around his neck. His arms provided a perch for her legs. Her legs dangled—evidence that she was growing up fast. But for a while yet she was still young enough, and with her laughter filling the air, they vanished into the forest's edge and the approaching twilight.

It was an emptier space without Seth's presence and Maddie's laughter. I tried to hold the feeling of their presence close to me a few minutes longer by thinking of Seth and the nooks.

Seth had introduced me to the gazing ball grotto, the largest of the nooks, on the second day of our acquaintance. I thought of that nook as Seth's grotto. I'd been the recipient of his kindness, his intelligence, and his humor. His mind and manner were flexible and open. One moment he'd be teasing me about being afraid of the basement while making sure I knew where the furnace and fuse box were located; the next we'd be sailing toy boats in Cub Creek with Maddie; and other times we discussed our favorite literature and poetry while the breeze rustled the boughs overhead.

Did Seth and I have a relationship? Something more than almost sweethearts? Would we? I thought we could, but until he returned to Cub Creek to stay, how would we know? His new employer had said he could work from here after he was well versed in the business. I hoped he'd be able to make the move home soon.

At Wildflower House, the day lingered longer in the backyard because it faced west and the open slope let in more sunlight and resisted the darkness longer. I stood on the back porch and watched the sunset colors bloom over the creek and forest as the sun descended.

With full dark, the insects, notably the mosquitoes and lightning bugs, came out to hunt and play. I enjoyed the lightning bugs but not the mosquitoes, so I went inside to fix a snack. I took the plate into the sitting room and set it on the table between my chair and Dad's. I switched on the television, then settled into Dad's roomier chair, where I could tuck my legs up under me. It was quiet despite the TV.

Maddie's birthday party was the most social thing I'd done in forever.

I'd lost touch with my friends from school. I'd been friendly with my coworkers, but not actual friends. Only Victoria . . . well, that was past too. Over.

When Niles and I had been building our lives together, in those early hectic days of marriage and new jobs, and even before that, during the college days when Victoria and I first became friends—*everything* felt like it mattered. Every day had been lived in anticipation and drama.

But people got older, right? Life and fate took their toll.

I turned the sound up louder to shut out my thoughts.

The replay of my favorite version of *Pride and Prejudice* was on. Hard to beat Colin Firth as Mr.

Darcy and Jennifer Ehle as Elizabeth Bennet. This was the miniseries version that went on for hours and felt almost like an old friend. Niles had laughed whenever he'd seen me watching it. He'd said I'd been born in the wrong century— sometimes I agreed. Niles had been a person of energy and ambition. I had appreciated that ambition sometimes; sometimes not. I'd thought that "sometimes; sometimes not" was part of marriage. Compromise and give-and-take. I hadn't discovered until the night of the accident that our understanding of marriage had been our biggest disagreement of all. Niles had blamed me for being me. For being content in our life. For being . . . boring and bossy. He'd blamed me so that he could justify finding amusement with other women.

If the accident hadn't happened, if Niles hadn't died, where would I be now?

Life was filled with cautions, as Will might say, so there were no guarantees. I would've had a child, though. A toddler by now. Boy or girl? I'd never know.

The loss nagged at me, maybe because it didn't feel quite real. Niles and I had gone out to dinner for our sixth anniversary, and I'd been trying to find the right time to tell him we were expecting a baby when it had all blown up—both between us and with those headlights suddenly coming at us. Next thing I knew, I was in the hospital, drugged and in pain, and Dad was at my bedside. By that point, it had all been over except the recovery. But some of the things that had been real before the accident had still felt real in the aftermath and were hard to let go of.

The phone rang. Seth's name was on the screen. I grabbed for it.

"Seth?"

"Sorry about today, Kara. It was good to see you, though my big surprise—showing up on your doorstep to charm you—didn't quite work out. Thanks for understanding. Maddie's finally in bed. She's worn out. You were great with her."

"I know she's glad to have seen you."

"I wonder if it was a mistake. A short trip like this—all that time and energy flying cross-country for a twenty-four-hour visit, and poor Maddie is going to feel even more disappointed when I leave tomorrow."

"I disagree. She'll miss you, yes, and a longer visit would've been better for all concerned . . . including me." I added the last bit with a lighter tone. "But you were here and made a birthday memory with her."

Women's voices suddenly filled the background.

"Sorry, Kara. Mom and Nicole want to talk. I need to discuss things with them."

"Things?"

"Family stuff. The usual. I'll call you tomorrow?"

"Sure. That's fine."

"Good night."

"Night, Seth."

He was gone. I sat there, feeling directionless.

I turned off the TV and carried my plate and glass to the kitchen.

It was just past nine p.m., I was thirty, and I was heading to bed. What was wrong with this picture?

"Things will look different in the morning," I told myself out loud. "They always do."

I sat on the side of the bed and snagged the drawer pull on the nightstand. As the drawer slid open, the brown plastic prescription bottles rolled and rattled, and I grabbed one.

Chapter Five

No dreams troubled my night, at least none that I remembered. I slept solidly. But when daylight began to fill the room and I woke, I didn't feel rested. I sat up, and my head went woozy, as if I might be coming down with something. I hoped not. Who would take care of me?

Sitting on the side of the bed, I performed my usual morning arm and leg stretches before standing—the ones I'd been doing routinely since the accident. My old injuries no longer required therapy, but the act of stretching my feet, my ankles, and my legs was a gentle way of easing into morning. Plus, the delay gave my foggy head a chance to catch up with my waking state.

. The sun streamed in through the bedroom windows and brightened the room around me, poking holes in my mental fog. It warmed my flesh, and the breeze coming through the open window teased me into staying upright.

I had a mouthful of cotton. That happened when I took the blue pills. It would pass as soon as I had a drink of water with a caffeine chaser.

Deliberately pressing my feet to the floor, I stood. Something pricked my foot. A leaf was stuck to the tender flesh of my arch. A few dark grains of earth were scattered on the floor nearby.

A leaf. Dirt. I sat down again and picked up the leaf. I twisted it in my fingers, examining it. Green, so it had recently been torn from whatever plant it belonged to.

But on the floor?

I must've tracked it up here last night when I went to bed.

What had I done before coming up to bed? I'd taken that walk with Seth and Maddie, and I'd stayed out in the backyard until dark. Then I'd watched TV and eaten a snack.

There'd been a twig in the upstairs hallway yesterday.

The obvious explanation was that I lived in the country and was outside often.

No reason to make something out of nothing.

I dropped the leaf in the trash on my way to the bathroom.

As promised, Seth called, and he called at noon, which surprised me since he couldn't have reached LA already.

"My connecting flight is delayed. I was going to call you later, but if you're free now, can you keep me company?"

"With pleasure. In fact, I'll take you outdoors with me." I laughed.

"Almost like taking a walk with you, but not as good as the real thing. Where are we going? Down to the bench by the creek?"

I stepped outside. "Maybe. It's a gorgeous day."

The landscapers were working off to my right as I walked down the hill. They looked busy, and I kept moving.

Seth said, "Tell me about the day."

"It's going okay."

"I mean *The Day*. Tell me what you see."

A rough wave of emotion rushed over and past me. The Day, as Seth called it here at Wildflower House, surrounded me. As much as I had come to love the house, it was the outside that resonated most strongly with me, even with the flowers gone.

"The work crew is clearing the side yards and cleaning up the front. There's a lot to be done."

"One thing at a time."

"One thing at a time. Everything in its season," I said as I walked down the grass path bordering the dried remains of the flower field. "Earth laughs in flowers."

"Ralph Waldo Emerson wrote that."

"It was what I thought of the first day I saw the wildflowers. Did you know that I planned to leave at the end of wildflower season? That's what I promised myself when I decided to move here with Dad."

After a longish pause, Seth asked, "Are you considering leaving now? Because there's a flaw in your reasoning, you know."

Hesitating on the top stone step leading down

to Seth's grotto, I asked, "A flaw? I have many of those and have made many mistakes. But what's the flaw in this instance?"

"There is no end to wildflower season . . . except maybe the dead of winter, and even that is a resting season for the seeds and roots. There are spring wildflowers, summer flowers, and even those that bloom in the fall. If you were going to leave at the end of wildflower season, then you've locked yourself in until winter. And frankly, winter is a beautiful season. If you haven't seen the snow like a blanket on the slope, heavy on low-hanging branches, clinging to the rocks in the creek, then you've missed a beautiful scene. So you should reconsider that line of reasoning."

"Sounds icy," I said, trying to be clever, but my tone came across as harsh. I added, "Dragonflies are suddenly everywhere outside. Must be dragon-fly season now. And that will have to satisfy me because there's no real hope for more wild-flowers this year, not after the damage from the hailstorm."

"I know all about that hailstorm damage. I was there right after, remember? I found you in the mud. I rescued you."

"A gentleman wouldn't mention that."

"You kissed me, mud and all."

"I recall that as a joint effort, sir."

He sighed. "We're overdue, Kara."

"You are so right."

In a lower voice, he said, "Someone just walked by. I think they were listening."

"Lucky them," I said.

"As for luck, you were lucky about the minimal hail damage to the house. Any problems with that?"

"No, the storm damage is all fixed."

"How's your new car working out?"

"Well enough. I'm not picky about cars. If it's reliable and has a few extras, I'm happy." I laughed. "I'd like it to stay away from hail, of course." I descended the stone steps to Seth's grotto. "Guess where I am."

"The grotto nook."

Surprised, I asked, "How did you know?"

"I can hear the breeze, or rather the swish of the wind in the leaves."

"You speak words like poetry, Seth. Maybe you should give up writing human interest stories and marketing copy. You are a poet at heart."

"No poetry. Takes too much discipline and has too many rules. The challenge to bend or break them is too much for me."

"I understand. I can't write poetry, but I enjoy reading it. Or used to." I'd stopped reading for pleasure at some point during my six years of marriage.

Seth asked, "Which poems?"

"That I love? Offhand I'd say 'Tintern Abbey' and 'Hamatreya.' "

"As in Wordsworth and Emerson, respectively?"

"You're familiar with them?" A tiny, pleasant spark warmed me. I turned my face up to the sun filtering through the boughs overhead.

"Of course. I write, don't I?" He paused and added, "Give me a moment while I calculate." He made deliberately funny clicking noises in the receiver, then stopped and said, "Well, I'd say you are a combination of romantic and philosopher."

I responded in a flirtatious tone, "I didn't know my preferences were so revealing."

"We reveal ourselves in all that we do."

Too true, I thought, suddenly uncomfortable. Revealed by what we do and don't do . . . my flirty mood evaporated. I said, "That's true, assuming there's someone around to notice."

"Ouch."

"Not directed at you," I said too quickly. I amended my words. "Well, maybe it is directed at you, but I don't blame you. I know you're working hard, but I don't know what you're *doing*. The few hours you were here seem almost like a dream. Yesterday aside, you've been gone forever, Seth."

"Not quite that long," he said softly. "I'm still the newbie on the job, Kara. They seem pleased, though. It's only been a month. A hectic, crazy month. I thought I was pretty darn good at wrangling words before, but the most consistent lesson I've learned in all my years of word craft is that I'm smarter than I used to be and often embarrassed by how little I knew before."

"I feel the same, at least about life and this project."

"The retreat?"

I sighed.

"Wow. That was loud. I just heard that halfway across the country."

"Ha ha. Funny."

"Did you ever run a creative retreat, Kara? Or an event site for weddings and such?"

What could I say? The truth? "No. Never."

"But you've dreamed of doing something like that?"

"Not in a million years."

The long silence that filled the phone connection came from Seth. I was waiting, prepared to be told I was foolish. That I'd stepped way beyond my capabilities and was doomed to fail. To become a laughingstock. And then Seth laughed.

We weren't on a video call. I was deep-down glad. He couldn't witness my humiliation as he laughed at me. I stood abruptly, ice spreading in my chest, fire starting to burn in my head. My stomach roiled.

Seth said, "I am impressed. I don't understand it . . . why you decided to do what you did, but Kara, you have way more guts . . . no, courage and—what's the word?—audacity. That's it. I never suspected. You have audacity." He lowered his voice. "Meanwhile, this area of the airport is pretty empty, but the family sitting a few rows over are looking at me suspiciously. I guess I got a little loud. But Kara, you have made my day."

He had laughed. Maybe not *at* me, but in admiration?

Suddenly my defenses were down again. "Do you think I'm crazy, Seth?"

"Crazy? No, why would I think that?"

"It's a big risk. Dad left money, but I could sink it all into this . . . enterprise . . . only to see it fail. Perhaps I should've taken the safer road."

"The road back to the city and a regular job? That's what I expected you to do. I stand amazed by you, Kara."

"The retreat idea wasn't some cherished, long-held dream, but it feels like a real thing to me. As if this can really work. I'm excited, but I'm also very scared."

"Go for it, Kara. Don't let anyone, including yourself, tell you what you can or can't do."

"Don't tell Nicole, okay?"

"What?"

"Don't be obtuse, Seth. Don't tell her it was a decision without forethought. Without substance."

"Nicole is thrilled. Don't worry about her. She'll help you in any way she can."

I watched a leaf flutter to the ground and land in

the soggy mass of old dead leaves accumulating in the small, neglected pool. Had they kept fish in it? It was more like a shallow, long-forgotten wishing well.

"Kara?"

"I'm here."

In a calm, even tone, devoid of his earlier teasing, he said, "Ultimately, you can go for it or not. It is risky. But there's no guarantee in traditional employment either. Businesses go bankrupt or downsize. The only thing you don't have a choice over is whether to be in charge."

I was trying to figure out how to respond when he added, "It's your life. You must always be in charge of your life, Kara. You can't default on that responsibility to anyone. Ever."

I closed my eyes and leaned forward. I was grateful. Not for his words but because he wasn't here to see me. The ice and fire I'd felt when he'd laughed had melted into slush inside me. Seth wouldn't have laughed if he'd known how ill equipped I was to be in charge of anything other than project process steps or laundry.

"Kara?"

Deep breath. "Yes?"

His tone was clear and kind. "I'm going to share my best advice. Remember it when you are in doubt. Only make decisions in the morning. In the bright new light of morning. Too many doubts linger in the afternoon and turn to swamp water by night. Those hours that follow the morning are for work, not for supposing or decision-making. Late in the afternoon or even at night, when doubts arise—put them aside until morning. You are in charge. Tell them they have to wait. You'll see the truth most clearly in the morning light."

"Okay."

"Repeat it back to me?"

"What?"

"Tell me. I need reassurance sometimes too."

I smiled and wished Seth were here to share smiles with me in person. Hold my hand, even. Maybe put his arm around me. We might finish our interrupted kisses . . . instead, I recited, "Morning light is for making decisions. Work the rest of the day. At night, when the doubts get loud, tell them to shut up until morning. They belong to the morning."

"Close enough."

"Thank you, Seth."

"My pleasure. I need to walk over to the new departure gate. Are you okay?"

"I'm fine. And I'll be finer."

"I wish I could be there. I'd like to wrap my arms around you and reassure you. I'd like you to realize that you are the most capable person I've ever met."

"Not me."

"You. When you smile, and even when you're pretending you don't care what other people

96

think—you are like a bright light. I know that doesn't make sense, but it's true."

I sniffled and pressed my fingers to my wet lashes.

"See you soon, Kara."

I told him goodbye and knew he could hear the rough emotion in my voice. It was a little embarrassing, but maybe it was also a good thing since I couldn't quite come up with the words my heart wanted to say. Maybe the unmistakable emotion helped convey the message.

We hung up, and I sat there, my hands and my phone unmoving on my thighs. Dad's gazing ball was on its pedestal. It reflected the leafy branches above and the abstract pattern of sky between the boughs. That space between moved and shifted as the breeze swayed the branches. I missed Seth. I rubbed at the fingerprints on my phone screen. My phone missed him too.

As I sat there feeling gloomy, a gnome grinned at me. He was half-hidden behind a pile of leaves at the base of a pine tree. Mary Forster, the former owner of this property, had created these forest nooks, and many were populated with garden gnomes and elves and assorted other yard decor. You never really saw them until you did, and then you couldn't miss them. While I might be lonely, I wasn't so far gone that I was ready to commune with small plastic statuary, colorful or not. Feeling a slight stiffening in my spine, I rose and brushed leaves from my pants. I had work to do.

And what had Seth told me?

He'd said I was audacious. That I was a bright light. The words tingled all the way down to my toes.

He'd also agreed that the project had risks.

And he'd advised only making decisions in the light of morning. After that, the day must be devoted to work. And play. I added that last bit myself. When I next spoke to Seth, I'd tell him he'd left that critical part out. Play was important, and he still owed me a date. The birthday party didn't count.

I returned to the house. I had a new idea, one that I hoped would help me grow my project and business plan. I would take some of the leftover paper from the roll Seth had used to protect the floors on the day Dad and I had moved in. I would spread it out on the middle-room floor, where it could stay without being on display to everyone who walked in, and I would draw a layout of the property. Not specific—not a technical survey—but a summary of the main nooks, including Seth's grotto, as well as the carriage house, the woodland paths . . . an idea paper. A page of dreams that could engender more ideas, and I could translate those ideas into specifics to augment my plan.

Seth had brought the paper rolls into the house

just before Dad and I had moved in. When I'd met Seth, he'd already been laid off from his newspaper job and was doing odd jobs for his sister, Nicole, related to her real estate business while also helping to care for Maddie.

Walking home yesterday evening with Seth and Maddie had brought back memories from my first visits to Wildflower House, of standing in that field in the middle of flowers and hearing music in my head, *Appalachian Spring*, and then of being in the house, where the floors, though dirty, had seemed to stretch for miles through the open area of the sitting room, hallway, and foyer. That day, I'd pulled up the music on my phone. I'd wanted to hear its melody fill the rooms, soaring and swirling into the high ceilings and the alcoves. Alone that day, I'd lifted my cane above the floor, and putting most of my weight on my good leg, I'd twirled. I'd twirled because I could perform that limited movement on one good leg, and I'd done it because the music hadn't just been in the room around me—it had been *in* me. It had lifted me above my woes and out of my flesh-and-blood self.

I'd twirled. I'd danced because I could.

I hadn't seen Seth walk through the house delivering the rolls of heavy brown paper intended to protect the floors from the movers, but he could not have missed seeing me twirling. When I'd seen the first paper roll he'd left and realized a man, a stranger, was in the house with me, I'd been embarrassed—more embarrassed than afraid.

I'd known Nicole was Dad's real estate agent but hadn't met the other Alberses yet. Seth had introduced himself. He pretended he hadn't noticed me or the music. He let me keep my dignity. I was grateful for that.

What I'd never told anyone, including Seth, was that the day he'd seen me twirling across the floors, that night I'd dreamed of a dark-haired man—not Niles—and I'd felt awkward about it, as if I should be mourning my husband still. The man had walked into my dream and held out his hand, inviting me to dance with him. He'd been wearing immaculate blue jeans and a shirt so white it had hurt my eyes. Seth, of course.

I'd kept that dream to myself.

Now in my project room, I tried another spin, but constrained so as not to trip over the idea box or knock my computer off the table. It wasn't quite the same.

I wanted to be that Kara—the woman who twirled. The dancing child I'd never been. I wanted to free her, to see her more clearly and more often. I wanted to be a bright, audacious light in my own life.

That night as I climbed the stairs to bed, the leaf came to mind. I paused at the top. I'd never felt unsafe here at night. I'd had no sense of any intruders. If I had, even once, how on earth would I ever get any sleep?

But.

The dirt on the floor could be easily dismissed, but not the leaf. And what of the twig I'd found before? Did it mean something or not?

I looked back down. My view was broken by the turn of the stairs, but it was mostly a well of darkness, especially on cloudy or moonless nights, when there was no light to pierce the large stained glass window on the landing. I had locked up the house as per my habit and had turned on the outside lights, front and back. Not that that was terribly meaningful. It was private out there. People could be dancing ring-around-the-rosy naked beneath the stars, and unless they made sufficient noise or I happened to look outside, who would know? Or unless they littered . . . but even then I'd notice bits of trash strewed about come morning.

Apparently I was still capable of being amused. That reassured me.

I stood there, tapping my fingers on the handrail. Outside was one thing. Inside was a different situation altogether. And the leaf and twig had been inside.

Tracked in by me, I reminded myself. But I still felt uneasy.

I remembered something I'd read or maybe

seen in an old movie. I went to the bathroom and took the container of body powder back to the stairs. The stair tread was dark wood, but it would be in shadow at night, and a light coating wouldn't be noticeable unless you were expecting it.

Done. I returned the powder to the bathroom. Back at the stairs I stared down and sighed. My peace had been sullied, and likely over nothing. Maybe I needed an alarm system. Probably security lights outside, too, with motion sensors. It would be a pity, though, to disturb the deer.

For the first time since I'd been at Wildflower House, I locked my bedroom door. I placed the key on the dresser near the door, within easy reach in case I needed to get out quickly. I hated to lock it. It was like admitting that not all was truly well here—not safe in the night. Once you admitted that and acted upon it, could you take it back? Ever?

So be it. I'd figure out the rest in the morning. But I bargained with myself—no sleep aids. Tonight I didn't want to sleep quite so soundly. Just in case.

Chapter Six

I came awake slowly. As consciousness eased out sleep, I remembered.

I was alive and in one piece, and I'd slept well without any pills—a small victory, and I felt encouraged. Even my morning brain felt more awake and upbeat than it had recently. From my vantage point in the bed, I could see that the key was on the dresser and the door was still closed. I looked at the floor beside the bed. It was clear.

Excellent.

What about the powder on the step?

I took the key, turned the lock, and opened the bedroom door.

Morning light flooded the upstairs hallway. I stood at the open door, listening and looking. All seemed as it should. The only sounds were the creaking of this old but sturdy house and my own slightly rushed breathing.

The floor looked clear between my bedroom door and the stairs.

Carefully, cautiously, I stepped out of my room—still listening hard—and walked to the head of the stairs. I looked down at the powdered step.

The powder was there, undisturbed.

Even if I'd been an idiot and now had a mess

of powder to mop up, it was good to have the reassurance.

When I was dressed and ready for the day, I grasped the railing and took a big step over the powdery tread, and then it was easy walking the rest of the way down to the kitchen and the coffeepot.

Mug in hand, I paused in the sitting room for a quick look out front and recognized Will's truck. Next to it was parked a truck that belonged to one of the guys on his crew, and another vehicle, a small car, was parked near them.

Strangers were coming and going around here. Could they or anyone else be entering my house without me being aware?

No, I rejected that. I was certain I'd sense it if someone else were intruding in my living space.

As I stood at the window sipping my coffee, I considered fear versus reality. Reality was something to be worked with—or worked around. Fears—I had plenty of them, and that was how I knew it was pointless to treat them as real.

My dad had tried to rewrite his personal history, his memories, by focusing on the happy parts of his childhood, those he'd experienced here at Wildflower House, and forgetting the rest—the unpleasant times with his drunken father and ailing mother. I hadn't known about any of it, not the pleasant or unpleasant or that it had even occurred in Louisa County, until Dad had bought

Wildflower House and had finally shared some of his history with me. My dad had been a single-minded, focused man. I wasn't as confident or ambitious as he, but I was a survivor, for sure. I was confident of that. Reality was less scary if one simply considered obstacles as the rules of the game. Once you understood reality, it became less intimidating, and you could put the rules to work for you.

I might have had an intruder. More likely not. I would look into a security system. I also needed to clean up my act when it came to taking those meds. If I was to depend on myself, then I needed to be clearheaded, even while asleep.

Reality was that mornings were becoming problematic. I suspected that the pills I took most nights encouraged a much deeper sleep, because even though I'd never been an early riser, I'd never experienced sleep hangovers until recently. But a lot of things were different now.

I wouldn't take any tonight either. I'd skip the pills. But even as I considered it, I knew I was lying to myself, especially if I was wide awake in the middle of the night as the rest of the world snored peacefully on.

Maybe Dad had had reason to be worried? Mom had taken medicine for her depression and for other emotional problems. He'd blamed those meds for making things worse. I couldn't judge that. But I knew it was why he'd discouraged me from taking medications, over the counter or prescribed, unless the need was dire and specific.

So I took them now to help me sleep, but I wouldn't be taking them much longer, because the bottles were emptying fast. With that thought, a rush of anxiety hit me.

This had only been going on since Dad died. He'd always been my fail-safe. My rescuer. I could stop anytime.

Anytime I wanted to.

Tonight, even.

Feeling good about my resolution, I wandered into the parlor, wondering if I might catch a glimpse of Will or his crew. That was when I saw her. She was sitting just outside the window on the porch bench.

It was as if a truck had slammed into me all over again. I focused on breathing and getting my thoughts straight.

I stared at Victoria's back. At her long curly black hair. She'd added a violet streak down the side. Some sort of package rested on her lap.

Every ounce of anger I'd felt the day I'd thrown her out of the house returned in a rush. If she felt my eyes boring into her back, she'd surely turn around and see me here. I stood unmoving. The pictures on her phone of her laughing with Niles flashed through my mind, with his voice from the night of the accident echoing as if superimposed, saying, *I've been seeing someone.* I'd seen those photos by accident right after Dad's funeral. And I'd confronted her. She'd denied any wrongdoing. She'd said ugly things. So had I.

Whether or not she'd cheated with my husband, she'd cheated on me, as her friend. She'd given her loyalty to Niles and kept me in the dark.

I wanted to run out to the porch and chase her away. I held back because I didn't want to relive that ugliness. Caught between those two needs, I felt like I was vibrating, almost being torn apart.

And still she sat. My heart rate increased and pounded at a low warning level in my ears. I touched the wavy glass delicately with one fingertip.

Victoria.

We'd met on that first day of college, hardly knowing anyone and both open to believing in good intentions. So long ago—twelve years that felt like a lifetime. I'd met Victoria first and then Niles. For a while we'd all been friends. When Niles and I had fallen in love, Victoria had often been excluded. It was only natural. But we'd done a lot of stuff together too.

Niles and I had married right after graduation. Victoria had always seemed to be there somewhere around us, finding a job near ours and a nearby apartment too.

I'd thrown her out of Wildflower House only days after my father died, the same day I'd seen the photos. She'd said she hadn't cheated with

Niles, that she'd been trying to convince him to be honest with me. After my anger and hurt had lessened, I tended to believe her. But she'd been tempted—I also believed that. Regardless of her intentions, she'd gone behind my back when she'd met with him, had excluded me and kept information from me that I should've been told. She'd chosen her side. As far as I was concerned, disloyalty was only a euphemism for lies and treachery.

Later, I'd sent her a note with a tiny apology for how I'd handled ending our friendship, but I'd been very clear that she wasn't invited back here or into my life. I'd known I might regret sending it, but I'd done it for her and also for me—perhaps to ease my conscience at the way I'd behaved, justified or not. I'd known she might take it to mean more than it did. Victoria was Victoria, and she would read it as meaning whatever she most wanted it to say.

The truth was it was extremely difficult to be around Victoria and not be reminded of Niles, the accident, and my losses. Not all of it was her fault, but she was wrapped up in it.

There were cars and trucks parked out front. I knew Will's truck. Lon's vehicle. My car. The unidentified car was surely hers, though I didn't recognize it.

How dare she sit on my porch, my bench, as if she has a right?

Not a right, no. But she had a reason. Victoria always had a reason.

Angry words were swirling in my head. I felt them perched on the end of my tongue and pushing against my lips.

Victoria might have a reason, but I had a choice.

She was here, and I would have to confront her, but I needed to breathe first. I backed away, then walked to the kitchen and out to the back porch.

I gripped the railing. I closed my eyes and focused on the feel of my breath coming in and out. I began to feel my fingers unclench and my heart rate slow. Within that moment of clearheaded sanity came the realization that it didn't matter.

None of it mattered. Not Victoria. Not confronting her again. I needed to be about my business. I'd already accepted my losses as best I could, and I was moving forward in the middle of a challenging but also invigorating project. I wouldn't allow Victoria to upset that balance. It was my choice and within my control. It was time to do some adulting. Adulting with dignity. I envisioned myself walking out to the front porch. Victoria would look up. I'd say, *You are not welcome here*. No more than that. I had no intention of stirring things up again between us. With one last long, cleansing breath, I let it all go.

"You okay?"

It was Will. He was standing on the terrace and looking up at me.

I forced a small smile. "I'm fine."

"You looked . . ." He shook his head. "I don't know. A little scary, maybe? Not like yourself. Sorry for interrupting."

Scary? I smiled at that. "Not at all. Just deep in thought. Did you need me?"

After a fraction of a pause, he said, "I thought you might like a progress report."

"Oh." Actually, that sounded good. In fact, it was a relief to put off dealing with Victoria a little longer. "How's it going?" I asked as I walked down to join him on the terrace.

Will looked fresher today—not that dripping mess from a few days ago when we'd collided. His complexion was much less red, his expression was bright, and I noted those vivid blue eyes again. His hair had been trimmed.

He smiled. This time he didn't look away. "Lon's been working in the carriage house, and Derek finished clearing the growth around the building."

The carriage house was a short distance into the woods, so a few trees still blocked most of the view, but a lot of the scrubby growth had been removed, and I could see more of the building now.

"I'd love to take a look." *Yeah,* that little voice

in my head said, *anything to delay confronting Victoria again.*

"Is something wrong? You keep looking back over your shoulder. Is there a problem?"

"Nothing worth allowing it to interfere with our business."

The blue tarps on the roof of the carriage house were either an eyesore or a sign of progress. Will moved up to walk alongside me as we followed what was now a wide path meandering through the trees until we reached the wide doors of the carriage house. Both sets of doors were now open. The interior was still rustic but fresher. That fine, dusty silt was gone. The earthen floor of the main room and in the old partitioned areas that had presumably housed horses was freshly swept and hard packed. The door to the small office area was also wide open, and I put my head inside, surprised to note that it had a wood-planked floor and space enough for a desk and maybe bookcases or file cabinets. The small window at the end had been washed and cracked open, allowing fresh air in and stale air out.

Will said, "The carriage would have been parked in the large open area. The stall doors were removed years ago, probably when it was updated for cars. We found some old bicycle parts rusting behind the building. I don't think anyone ever parked cars in here, because we'd see old oil stains and such."

I was staring up and around and all over. "It looks so different now." I looked at Will. "It actually looks usable."

"Yes, ma'am. Once that roof is good, the electricity can be run out here. There's an old pump outside, but I recommend running water in here too. Install a large sink over there, especially for artistic activities. You can also have wood flooring laid in here if you're interested in that."

He got it. My vision. Somehow he'd understood the plans knocking around in my head. I felt giddy and almost speechless.

Will asked, "Want to check out the upstairs?"

"Yes." I put one foot on the first step and tested it, then moved up the dim stairs. As I reached the top and my head was about to rise above the level of that second floor, I gripped the railing. The roof was high enough that there was room for a short adult to walk comfortably. I imagined items not used daily had been stored here. It was empty now except for a row of built-in chests along one wall. They were simple wooden boxes with hinged tops. I lifted one of the lids. It held a jumble of old objects. Old horse-type gear. Even a pair of dusty driving goggles. The gear was dirty but so old it wasn't smelly. I released the lid.

Will had climbed up and was standing near the stairs.

"You're right. It's looking good," I said. "The roofer should have the estimate to me in a few days. Will the tarps be sufficient in the meanwhile?"

He nodded. "Yes, they're secure. I'm glad you're happy with the work."

I laughed. "Happy doesn't cover it. I'm thrilled."

I returned back down the stairs, and Will followed. He said, "If there's anything else, let me know."

"Of course. So much to think about."

"I'm sure. All good things, though."

"Good things," I agreed. "Thank you, Will."

He left, and I was ready. Being in the carriage house, discussing business with Will, had given me time to decompress. I felt calm now. I could do this. Victoria.

I walked past the hollies and the side porch. As I neared the front porch, my feet felt heavier, dragging a little, but I kept my shoulders back and my head up. I rounded the corner and found the bench vacant.

The car that had been parked away from the others was also gone. I went to the front door and tested the knob. Locked.

She'd left. Had she grown tired of waiting?

I heard a noise and spun around. Lon had kicked some gravel while walking over to the back of Will's truck. I was so jumpy.

He pulled a cold bottle of water from a cooler in the truck bed. He caught sight of me, stumbled a little, and gave me a wave.

"Lon?"

He stopped. "Yes?"

"Did you notice a woman here earlier? Sitting on the porch?"

He looked blank.

"Her car was here." I added feebly, "I just wondered if you'd noticed when she left."

"No, sorry. I've been working."

I forced a shrug. "Okay, thanks."

"Maybe she left a note. Like in the door or the mailbox?"

"Maybe so. Thanks, Lon."

He nodded and went to the backyard.

I walked to the mailbox. It was a long trek down the dirt-and-gravel drive that bisected my front yard—the immense front yard with its towering pines and gnarled oaks. One day, after the more opportunistic growth had been cleared, this ground would be thickly carpeted with pine tags and autumn leaves year round. And one day I'd get this drive paved.

A fox scooted by on the periphery of my vision, and a bird called at me, either singing a welcome or cursing me as an invader. The tangy-sweet scent of the pines toyed with my nose.

There was no note from Victoria in the mailbox. I wasn't surprised. The important point was that she'd been here and was now gone. *Gone* was the word that mattered.

I thought of the leaf and dirt on my bedroom floor and the twig littering my hallway.

Whatever the explanation for those, Victoria wasn't the culprit. Regardless of whatever else she might choose to do, she'd never invite herself into the house without making herself known. Not even Victoria at her most egotistical would do something that rude and stupid.

Clearly, she'd come with a purpose and had lost her nerve. If she had any sense, she'd leave well enough alone.

As for the debris on the floor? I was sure it was nothing. But there was no reward for stupidity or willful blindness. I would follow up with a call to a security company.

As I walked back to the house, the trees waved in a breeze high overhead, and squirrels raced each other around the trunks, and I felt at home. Was it perfect? No. Flaws? Yes, I had them. So did Wildflower House. And maybe that was part of our beauty.

Audacious, indeed.

Chapter Seven

That afternoon I retreated to the middle room. It felt like a haven after the crazy morning. I was ready for a peaceful afternoon. I focused on my work and pushed myself to add details and thoughts to both the project plan in the spreadsheet and the business plan in the Word document. They were still wholly inadequate, but there was progress.

After a while, the breeze coming through the open front door and flowing up the hallway teased me.

Time for a treat. I was playing now, much like Maddie with a box of crayons, except I was using markers and colored pencils.

I'd sketched in the rough heart of the property, including the house, the driveway out front winding up toward the main road, and the grounds in the back to include the creek, with a pencil. The top border was the creek. The woods on either side were fuzzy borders because I was estimating where the nooks were located. The house was in the middle, and then the public road was the bottom boundary. Proportions were relative and largely optional. This was more of an interpretation than a true—

Mel called out, "You in here, Kara?"

Like mother, like daughter? Or was it a regional thing wherein a friendly callout was more neighborly than banging on an already open door?

"I'm here," I called out, standing. As I exited the middle room, I pulled the door closed behind me. "Is Maddie with you?"

"She has a playdate today."

I shook my head at the bags in Mel's arms. "Not more food? I can't keep up."

Mel laughed. "Not for you. This is different. My fridge gave out. I could fit most of it in the backup fridge in the garage, but not all. You mind?" She nodded toward my refrigerator.

"Whatever fits. In fact, there's a lot we can pull out if we need to make more room for yours."

"I'm sure that's true." Mel gave me a wry look. "Is something wrong with your AC?"

"No. I like the fresh air. It stays pretty cool in this house. Sometimes the heat builds up in the late afternoon, and I kick the AC on." I reached to take a bag from her.

"Not that one. Take the small one that's about to break my pinkie finger right off my hand."

I did as instructed.

"That one's for you," she said.

"For me?" Inside the bag I now held was a weighty block of something that smelled like heaven wrapped in waxed paper. I breathed in the aroma as Mel set her bags on the table.

"It's fudge. I make crazy-mad-good fudge."

"Yum. I'm sorry, Mel, for what I said. I appreciate all the food you've given me over the past month and a half. You're an excellent cook." I stuck my nose inside the bag again and breathed. "But this? This is different. This is fudge."

She opened the fridge door and then the freezer and gave it a cursory inspection. "You ain't eating much of anything as far as I can see. Not even when it's gifted to you on a silver platter. Well, in foil and plastic, anyway."

I looked at her, staring at her thin arms and her scrawny build.

Mel made a rude noise and said, "I see you looking at me cross-eyed, but it's my metabolism. It keeps me skinny. I'm fit because I'm always moving."

"And that's not me?"

Mel laughed again, this time with a little more mirth.

I said, "I'm pretty busy around here, you know."

"No, you are not." Mel paused to fold the paper bag and reach for the next. "Though I give you credit. You are trying. I can see stuff is happening. But as for the food—you're skinny because you aren't eating. It's natural enough. I've seen it before with grief. You'll get past it, Kara, but in the meanwhile you've got to watch your health. If you get any skinnier, you'll

119

be able to disappear by turning sideways."

She glanced at my face and then stopped. "If I'm nagging, I apologize. Guess I forgot I wasn't your mama."

My hand went to my throat. "No, you're not my mother, and I'm glad. You didn't know her, or you'd understand my meaning. You're my friend, and I'm grateful. You need to stop worrying over me. I'm a grown woman, and I'm reasonably smart. I'll be fine."

She faced me squarely. "I'm pushy by nature, and I'm worried about you. And Maddie Lyn too." She quickly added, "But only a little. Miss Maddie will be fine."

"Nicole said something similar."

"This is a big time in a child's life, you know. Getting ready to start kindergarten. Seth gone. I know time heals, but it passes differently for a child." She looked at the stack of containers she'd removed from the refrigerator and shook her head at me. "I won't say another word about food after this, but you need to eat more and get out and about. As for me and Maddie Lyn, Seth will be back soon, and then we'll all be better."

"Love goes a long way, Mel. Just love Maddie and be there for her. My advice, inexperienced though I may be as a parent, is to encourage her to talk about her feelings. I didn't have anyone to talk to about it, and it's still with me." I pressed my hand to my heart.

"About your daddy dying? You know I'm always a willing listener, Kara. No need to keep that stuff inside."

"I mean about my mom leaving. Encourage Maddie to talk about her mom and her uncle. Better for her to annoy people by going over the same things over and over than to have her draw her own conclusions . . . conclusions drawn by a five-year-old's brain and experience." I turned my back to reach into a cabinet to get a glass. "Thirsty? Can I offer you water or tea?"

Mel kept silent. She was waiting, I knew. Waiting for me to face her again. I had to, so I did.

"I have grieved, too, Kara."

Of course she had. I opened my mouth to respond. Mel raised her hand, motioning me to stop.

"I have grieved. For my husband. For my daughter, Patricia, Maddie Lyn's mom. Not so very many years ago, I buried my parents. Mom went quickly. Daddy didn't. He died slowly. The grief was the same but with a longer introduction."

Mel pulled a chair away from the table and half sat, half fell into it in a slow, controlled motion. I was holding on to the counter. I hurt inside, though the pain was hard to define. It was an old pain overlaid with fresher grief.

She said, "I'll take a sip of water, after all."

I poured her fresh water from the pitcher in the

fridge and set the glass in front of her. She ran her thin fingers down the side, relishing the chill, and then she nodded.

"As I was saying, grief is the same either way. Sharper when losing the younger ones. Sharpest when losing a child. But love is love, and grief rips that bond, and it always hurts."

"I understand."

Mel ignored me. She was taking this conversation where she wanted it to go. I was just along for the ride. I wanted to face her, to listen showing her my full attention and respect, but I had to turn away. I couldn't stop myself. I stood at the sink and stared out the kitchen window at the sunlight; at the trees, now full of summer leaves; and at the blue sky above them.

I had my own wounds to protect.

Mel continued, "Some say you get past it. I don't say so. I say grief eases. No one can live at a pitch—a fever pitch of lust or grief. You burn out. Grief eases over time. Meanwhile, you go on because what else can you do?" She hugged herself. "When it comes to grief and loss, I don't know the difference between being five, thirty, or seventy, but I think I'm more worried about the thirty-year-old standing in front of me than the bookends."

I snuck a quick look at her. She caught me. I gave up and turned back to face her. "I presume by *bookends,* you mean Maddie and yourself?"

Mel gave me a long look.

"Okay, fine," I said. "I am grieving. I don't deny it. I know it will pass with time. Ease, as you say." I crossed my arms. "I felt like Dad and I were finally finding the relationship we should always have had. We were crossing a threshold I never dreamed we'd ever get to. And then . . ."

She nodded. "Glad you had that, at least." She smiled, but it was a sad smile. "With my Patricia, I'd been on her back about not sticking with jobs and getting laid off and all. Then she was gone. Just about that fast. Regret, right? It walks hand in hand with grief."

I took the fudge block from the bag, set it on the table, and unwrapped the waxed paper. I sliced several pieces from the end and slid the paper toward Mel.

She sighed and selected a piece. A few crumbs fell onto the table, and she picked them up by pressing the fleshy pads of her fingertips against them. I gave her a napkin.

"I hope you're right," I said.

"About grief or about its easing?"

"I know it will ease. I don't want to forget, though. I want to remember Mom. I want to remember Dad. I have to keep the memories fresh in my mind."

"Well, you'll always have those."

"But they fade. The memories pass and lose their sharpness. I want to remember my dad—both his good points and his flaws. He was pretty remarkable—even more than I understood as a child—and I want to remember him as he truly was. As my dad."

"You want to hold time still. People think if they don't let time move on, they can step right back into their comfort memories whenever they need to for reassurance or security."

"No, I know that can't happen. But maybe I'm not ready to move on yet, even aside from wanting to keep the memories fresh. Once I let time fade into the past, it's gone. I need to finish processing everything first."

"I had a friend who held on to her grief so tight and took so long processing it that it used up the rest of her life. She never had another shiny moment or heartfelt joy that she didn't reject and squash right away. I thought maybe it was guilt because she was still alive. Or maybe it was fear of living on her own. Or a selfish duty, like proof of grief. Regardless of why, don't be that person, Kara."

I shook my head, refusing to acknowledge the chill that seized me. "I'm not that person. I'm moving on with my life, but it's not easy." I looked away.

"How are you doing at night? Here alone?" She waved her hands around as if to emphasize the entirety of the house and its size.

My quick indrawn breath probably gave me

away because Mel was not only sharp eyed but also sharp of hearing. I pretended my gasp meant nothing. She couldn't know that I needed a little help to deal with the night and that I no longer felt as safe as I had before finding that leaf on the floor. I couldn't tell her any of that because Mel was a doer. This was a problem she couldn't fix. Only I could.

I said, "I'm resting well enough. The house does feel very empty."

"Empty. I know about that." Mel sipped her water again. "When Maddie Lyn learned to tie her shoes herself, I thought, *I need to tell Patricia*. But no. Couldn't do that, could I? And when Maddie Lyn says something cute—even though I know I can't, I still think I need to tell her. Maybe Patricia's around somehow and does know. When my husband died, our kids were grown and living elsewhere. I was alone. How many times did something happen when I said, 'I need to tell Carl' . . . or that I turned to tell him something like 'We need to get that hot-water heater checked, Carl.' Or 'Carl, what kind of warranty did we get on the mower?' Or 'I think the well pump is making odd noises' . . ." Mel rubbed her hands together as if they were cold. "It ain't the same as just talking out loud. Sounds foolish to even think it would be. But you take what you can get, and sometimes that means talking to the walls."

Walls. Yes, I understood that. And sometimes the echo of your own voice was the closest you came to a conversation . . .

Mel sighed. "When Patricia got pregnant and wanted to come home, I was glad. Secretly glad. But glad. I was happy to have a pair of ears to speak to and to hear her voice, even if I didn't always like what she said."

I wanted to offer comfort, but I didn't know the right words.

"Oh, I said things, of course, about how she should've made better choices and all that. I'd take 'em back in a heartbeat now if I could. How was I to know we'd lose her so soon?"

"You couldn't know, but you were there for her and helped her when it counted. She knew you loved her."

Mel showed no sign of hearing me. She was stuck in her own past now.

"She had a headache that day after work. Came on sudden, right before I told her to take care of Maddie Lyn. Patricia was standing in the kitchen doorway—I can still see her clear as day. She said, 'Mom, I'm going to lie down.' Maddie was only two. How was I supposed to cook supper with a toddler underfoot? But Patricia had already left the kitchen. I raised my voice after her: 'Take care of your daughter, Patricia Lyn!' I was in the kitchen wrestling a wooden spoon away from Maddie, and I saw that terrible-two tantrum about to erupt. When Patricia didn't answer me back, I was angry. So angry. I went after her, thinking she was already in her bed, but she wasn't."

Mel shook her head and put one hand over her face. After a long moment, she dropped her hand away. The grief, the stark regret, was visible on her face. "She was on the floor. My daughter was already gone. Gone, Kara."

She breathed for a minute, then said, "So young. She hadn't had time to live yet. An aneurysm, that's what the coroner said. In her brain. She was there one minute, annoying me, and then she wasn't."

Such devastation. Such regret. It ached in my chest. My eyes burned. My shoulders wanted to curve inward, to protect myself and withdraw from this dreadful conversation. But Mel deserved acknowledgment for what she'd shared.

"I'm so sorry, Mel. What I said still stands—she knew you loved her. And Maddie is lucky to have you and Nicole and Seth, all people who love her and loved and remember her mother. You can give her so much through your memories. Maddie Lyn is so fortunate to have you."

"Yes, well, I'm not sure I'm enough. I'm old and getting older every day. She's hardly more than a baby. Needs a lot of watching. She's a busy girl with a big imagination. It's not right to park her in front of the TV to keep her occupied."

"Nicole?" I asked.

"Oh, sure. Nicole does right by Maddie, but Nicole isn't . . . motherly."

Despite myself, I laughed. "Sorry. I could say the same about my mom. Not motherly. I didn't know it back when I was a child. I thought that was just how it was. When Dad told me about his parents, he said something similar about them not being . . . parental."

"Your father was a fine man. I didn't always agree with him, and he could be closemouthed and aggravating, but he had integrity, and he knew what hard work was."

"True enough. I didn't know he'd grown up in this area until recently." I watched her face closely, suddenly realizing she might have information I wanted. "In fact, he showed me where he lived as a child."

Mel eyed me carefully. "That so?"

I waited for her to offer more. She didn't, so I said, "It was a sad, tragic place. Did you know my dad? Growing up?"

"No, I didn't. Any idea why he didn't tell you before?"

"To avoid discussing his childhood. It was . . . unhappy. His father drank a lot. Dad called him heavy handed. That's all Dad would say about him."

"Henry was a few years younger than me, so we didn't go to school together, plus I grew up in

128

the Bumpass area. When I married Carl Albers, I ended up over here with him." She cleared her throat and took a sip of her water. "Carl might've known Henry, but he never spoke of him."

"I was angry at Dad for not telling me about his childhood sooner. I would've understood him better, I think. When I asked him why, he said no one wants to relive the bad stuff. He preferred to focus on the good."

Mel said, "I see that determined look on your face, and I'm not unsympathetic. I heard a few gossipy tales about old Mr. Lange long ago, but not about your dad. I never thought of him at all until Nicole sold him a house in the city years ago."

I said, "Yes, that was after I left for college. Dad moved to the smaller house just outside of Richmond. He was still living there when he brought me home to recover from my accident. I didn't know about Nicole, had never even heard her name until Dad told me he was moving to Wildflower House."

Mel took a long drink of water before saying, "Henry and Nicole were sweet on each other on and off, but she didn't bring him around us much. While I'm not above an occasional exchange of juicy information, I wouldn't insult you or your father's memory by dredging up gossip. Consider the source, they say. Old Mr. Lange was a mean man. A miserable person. If he found peace in the hereafter, then let him rest in it, Kara."

I stared at her, wanting to push for more. Finally, I said, "Did you know that Dad had a younger brother and sister? Twins. They were about ten years younger than him. Their mother died when they were very young. They were toddlers when they disappeared. Dad came home from school and found them gone. His father refused to explain."

"You think Mr. Lange gave the babies away?"

"I hope that's it. Dad was never quite sure." I saw Mel's expression changing, and I let the unspeakable alternative possibilities remain unspoken.

Mel put her hand over her face again. When she slid it away, her wrinkles were deeper, and her eyes were glittery. "As if there ain't enough misery already in this world."

The despair that had eased from Mel's face as we'd chatted about Dad had been brought back by this talk of old Mr. Lange and the twins. I touched her hand and said, "Never mind, Mel. It's okay. I'm sorry I brought it up."

She shook her head. "Okay or not, it's a long time gone. If I had to guess, I'd say Mr. Lange gave them to the state. People did that, you know, if they couldn't care for them, especially if there was no other family to step in and help. I can't imagine him raising babies on his own."

"Dad looked for adoption records and other

legal records when he got older but found nothing. He even hired a private detective but had no luck."

"And now nearly a half century has passed. Many of the people who might have known anything are likely in their graves. I believe the courts seal adoption records. Lots of records pertaining to minors get sealed too. I think. What I know I learned from TV shows, so take it for what it's worth."

She looked away from me. "Henry never spoke to me about anything personal. Kept his personal business to himself. Remember, we were both old, and we were friendly, but we weren't old friends." She reached across and took my hand in hers. "I promise you this: if I ever do think of something worth saying, whether good or bad, I'll tell you."

That had to be sufficient. Mel had shared her heart and her grief with me. I was overwhelmed with the trust she'd shown. I sighed and rubbed my hands across my face, massaging my temples.

Mel said, "You okay?"

I stopped my hands midmotion and clasped them together, entwining my fingers. "I'm fine, really. I hope you are."

She stood. "I'd best be going. The new fridge is being delivered tomorrow. I'll come back for the groceries then."

"Fine. It's fine."

When I heard her light, quick footsteps retreating, I noticed how her slight figure was cast into shadow, backlit by the strong light coming through the hallway from the front door.

Mel was older than my dad, who'd been sixty. She had to be in her late sixties. Maybe already seventy. She had a wiry strength but none of my father's robustness.

That thought brought me to my senses.

"Mel?"

She'd reached the front door.

"Mel!"

She paused and looked back. "What?"

"You are welcome to drop by anytime. You are always welcome. And if the refrigerator doesn't arrive tomorrow, don't worry about leaving the groceries here longer."

Mel laughed. It was a sharp sound but mirthful.

It was my turn to ask, "What?"

"Twenty-six words, girl. Twenty-six words for what we both already know."

"How do you do that, Mel?"

"Count words?"

"Yes, ma'am."

"Oh, I have a knack with numbers. Counting is always going on in the back of my mind whether I want it to or not." She grinned. "Everybody's got some kind of superpower. Guess that's mine."

"Oh yeah? What about me?" I joked.

I wasn't expecting an actual answer, but Mel

went silent and gave me a long look. I was about to say something, anything, to break the increasingly awkward moment.

"Hold on, girl. You asked; I'll answer." She waggled a finger at me. "I was going to say determination. But that ain't quite right. Resilience, I'd say. No matter what, you endure. You get back up."

My heart sighed, if that was possible. I crossed my arms. "Honestly, Mel, it may be true, but it's exhausting."

"Yet you do it anyway." She blew me a kiss. "Don't stop getting up, Kara. You'll never be sorry."

I smiled. "See you later, Mel."

"Later, Kara, honey."

Shortly before Dad died, I'd been pushing him to tell me about his childhood, his family. Finally he'd driven me to the site of his parents' home. It wasn't far from Wildflower House as the crow might fly, but by road it was longer. We'd walked into the woods on a barely there trail. He told me the creek path also led there, but nature, especially watercourses, could change the landscape, and he didn't know if that path still went all the way through.

That day Dad and I sat on a fallen log with the broken-down house before us while he told me the tragic story of his childhood, of how he'd spent as much time away from the house as possible because of his father. Dad had earned money doing small jobs for people in the area, including yardwork for the family who lived at Wildflower House before it became known as that, and even before the Forsters lived there. He told me about the Bowen family, the dad, Rick; his wife; and a little boy named Stevie. As he worked in their yard, he pretended he lived there with them, that the other place he went to each night to sleep didn't exist in the same world. But the Bowens moved away, his mother died, and when the twins disappeared, he had no reason to stay.

He'd still been a child himself, no more than fifteen or so, when he ran off to Richmond. He'd passed for older, picking up jobs here and there. As soon as he could, he'd started his own business. He'd built it from the ground up and had eventually become the unofficial tire and automotive magnate of a large portion of the mid-Atlantic. That was the business he'd sold when he decided to buy Wildflower House and retire here. He'd been trying to come to terms with things he'd never dealt with, and he'd wanted to do it here at this house, where his best memories had been made.

If Mel did remember anything, I felt sure she'd tell me. The idea of a possible aunt and uncle, still alive and maybe with children and grandchildren of their own . . . I could have lots of family out there. The concept intrigued me.

If Dad could've found out what happened to his siblings, he would've. The fact that he never did was a pretty convincing argument that the information was not there for me to find either.

The powder stayed on the step for a second night because I was too lazy to clean it up. I avoided that step going up to bed as I'd avoided it going down that morning.

I closed my door and locked it. I hated to, but honestly, once I'd accepted the possibility of someone entering the house during the night, it was hard to go back to relative innocence. As before, I left the key on the dresser and went to bed.

No pills tonight, I vowed. Instead, I plumped my pillow, pulled up my covers, and, with patience, settled into sleep mode.

I lay there and stared at the dark ceiling.

Tonight wasn't about jumbled thoughts or worries. Tonight I had that waiting feeling. Waiting for what? For sleep? Just a stupid feeling of waiting.

Number by number, I watched the time change on the clockface. I got up and walked around. I ate a late-night snack. By three a.m. I was done with gutting it out.

Seth had called me audacious. Mel had said I

was resilient. That was all well and fine, but I had work to do tomorrow. I needed rest. Feeling frayed and exhausted wouldn't be helpful.

I pulled the drawer open and found the bottle with the blue sedatives, and I faltered.

Would it be so awful to just stay up? Get online and surf the internet? Play with the business plan or the map?

By the time I'd considered those options, the top was already off the bottle, and I was on my way to the bathroom for water.

A good thing about being alone was that there was no one to see me in my weakness and my failure.

One night, one day at a time, I told myself. That was all anybody could ask.

And, I wondered, how many addicts had told themselves exactly that?

Chapter Eight

Work continued inside and outside of Wildflower House. A few days had passed. Mel had retrieved her food from my freezer. I still hadn't cleaned the powder from the top step, which was rather embarrassing, but on the upside, Victoria had not returned.

The kitchen was a disaster area. The man who was performing the renovation never spoke but seemed to know what he was doing. Since he came with the Nicole Albers Stamp of Approval, I didn't worry over it. The plumbers he'd brought in had finished up their work yesterday. Now we were waiting for the new cabinets to arrive. Meanwhile, Mr. Blackwell was constantly hauling in or carrying out paraphernalia and taping heavy paper and plastic to various sections of the floors, and the ladders and buckets seemed to be reproducing behind my back.

Today I sat in the denuded kitchen sorting bills at the table while I ate lunch. The microwave still worked, and I'd heated up one of Mel's casseroles. As soon as I obtained a file cabinet and a larger, sturdier worktable for the middle room, I'd move bill-sorting tasks there too.

The carriage house roof estimate, bills for groundwork and wallpaper work, and an endless assortment of estimates and invoices were sorted into piles. Dad had viewed writing checks as part of doing business. For me, it was torture. It was depressing to see that bank balance—the money that my father had earned from the ground up by building his own business—go down. I told myself that expenditures were a part of growing a business and to stay focused.

In fact, as of this point I was only making improvements and repairs—what Dad would've done just for the renovation project.

I could eventually make a go of this—most of the time I believed that. I could feel the idea, this enterprise, growing in my mind. I could survive without making a profit for quite a while so long as I made enough to cover most of the expenses. Oddly enough, I was becoming more comfortable with the risk as I eased into this . . . this new life path. With each stroke of the pen, each new draft of the business plan, my life was becoming a truer fit. For me. And then the doubts would creep in. Self-doubt, mostly.

Economics-wise, this area was growing, positioned as it was at the rural nexus of three major cities, nearby high-dollar communities, horse farms and stables, the towns of Mineral and Louisa with their amenities and quaint shops, and Lake Anna a few miles beyond that—it all screamed potential.

The one check I didn't mind writing was to

Mitchell's Lawn and Landscaping. Will more than earned his pay, plus I enjoyed having him around. There was a synchronicity between us. I felt it, and I was sure he did too. He was always good for a friendly laugh, and I relied on him to do what was needed to get this property into shape—a shape that would work toward the end goal.

As I heard footsteps coming up the hallway, I set the enormous roofing estimate on top of the nearest pile.

Nicole walked in as she always did. I could've made a remark about it, but despite our little skirmishes, telling her she wasn't welcome to just walk in when she obviously thought she was would hurt her deeply.

If I cared all that much about walk-ins, then I could shut and lock the door, right? That simple.

Same with this project. It was up to me. I could walk away. Other options were still open. But not to see it through? My brain told me there were no guarantees. My gut said to stick with it.

At any rate, I was glad I was in the kitchen, away from the true heart of the work in progress. I wasn't ready to show Nicole my efforts in the middle room.

As she entered, she announced that the attorney—a Mr. Browne, whom she'd known forever and who'd done business with and for practically everyone in this area forever and who was thus 100 percent trustworthy and the font of all useful legal knowledge—wanted to meet with me.

"He does?"

"Of course. We discussed this." She gave me a long look. "He wants to talk about licenses, permits, insurance, and such in a big-picture kind of way and dip into details as needed."

"Sounds sensible." But inside I wavered. I'd come so far, hadn't I? But not far enough. One reasonable suggestion from Nicole was enough to send me into an immediate backslide. "Are you sure about this, Nicole?"

"Not again." She shook her head. With a sigh, she sat in the chair next to mine and put her hands on the table. "Honestly, Kara, you seem all good to go one moment, and the next you're shrouded in doubt. What's bothering you? Is it being alone?"

"I'm fine alone. I'm an adult. Heaven knows I should be used to being alone by now."

Nicole rolled her eyes. I could hardly believe it.

I leaned forward. "I am. Truly. Maybe my uncertainty is about whether I want to be alone *here*." I looked away. "But I love this house. Maybe I'm crazy. Or maybe doubts are normal. Have you considered that?"

Nicole's eyes lit on the estimate that Will had given me that morning. She picked it up to examine it.

She asked, "Is this the problem?"

"No. Yes. It's a lot of money. I think those roof tiles must be gold plated."

Nicole ignored my weak humor.

"It's a lot," she confirmed. In a calm, even voice, she said, "Let's consider it this way, Kara. You are trying to make reason and emotion mesh neatly. You want to add them together like a basic math problem—two plus two equals four—believing you can then move forward with certainty. But that's impossible. Reason and emotion are distant cousins. Sometimes total strangers. They are supposed to argue. That's what keeps life and sanity in balance."

"Dad didn't torture himself with doubts. He knew exactly what he was doing in his business every step of the way. I'm not the businessperson he was."

Nicole raised her hand. "You never saw your dad go through doubt when he was building and managing his business, but that didn't mean he wasn't. He was schooled to hide it. It was there nonetheless—I promise you."

She was speaking as if she knew my dad better than I. It annoyed me, but what she said made sense.

"So this"—she held up the estimate—"is a lot of money. But that's not the question. The question is whether it's reasonable. You can get other estimates, but we know this contractor. You were happy with the repairs he made to the hail damage on the roof, right?"

"Yes."

"He's local and available in case you need follow-up work?"

"Yes."

"So let's consider your options." She spoke dispassionately. "Let's say you don't continue with repairs and you decide to sell the Wildflower Property—"

I interrupted. "The wildflower property?"

She smiled. "I know you and Henry named it Wildflower House, but everyone"—she waved her hand in a general sweep encompassing the world—"is now calling it the Wildflower Property. Capital *W*. Capital *P*. Used to be called the Forster property, but you've made a mark. A big enough mark to rewrite how this place is known locally."

"Wow," I said. Pleasure warmed me. Pride, maybe.

"You betcha. Wow, indeed. There's value inherent in reputation. Now back to your choices. If you stop the repairs and improvements, you'll have to sell it for less because people will regard the house as having problems, feeling skittish about why you are abandoning a worthwhile restoration midwork. Or"—she held up a finger for emphasis—"or you finish the work and then sell it. The improvements you've made to the house and land will be persuasive, and the carriage house, being such a unique feature of a uniquely vintage, recently restored estate, will increase the value in the eyes of buyers for this type of property."

The power of words, I thought, impressed, *especially when spoken with confidence.* With Nicole as his real estate agent, Dad had never had a chance.

She continued, "Or you decide to stay here. You pursue your plans. If at any time you decide operating a creative retreat is not for you, then you tell me. I'll represent the property for you. It will sell, without doubt. The executives at the tech firms on the west side of Richmond are moving out this far. In fact, I sold a large property in Charlottesville to a CEO last month. Honestly, nothing is without risk, but I don't see how you can lose with this as long as you stay focused."

"You're good," I said with admiration. "I can see why Dad was so eager to buy this place." I meant it as a semi-joke, but the words fell flat.

Nicole frowned. "I assure you he wanted this property. It was his choice."

Crap. "I'm sorry, Nicole. I just meant that you are very persuasive." That sounded even worse.

Nicole pulled her shoulders back and lifted her chin. "You may be surprised to learn that I argued against it."

Surprised was an understatement. I almost

didn't believe her, but this was Nicole. She wasn't given to careless words or claims. "What?"

"I considered not telling Henry when Sue Deale said she was ready to sell."

"Why?"

"In fact, had I not helped Henry get his offer in quickly, I could've sold it for a larger commission. I warned Sue that she could make more if she let me work the market a bit. It was my responsibility to be candid with her."

I was shaking my head as I spoke. "But you told him anyway?"

"Of course. That's what he wanted. It's what he'd asked of me."

"And Sue was willing to take a loss?"

Nicole shrugged. "That was her choice. I read people pretty well, but I don't second-guess anyone, including myself." She touched my arm. "As for Sue, I understood what motivated her. She retained some control by selling to the person of her choice rather than to some wealthy executive from New York or California who was relocating for a year or two to Virginia, who wouldn't care about the house's history and its place in the local landscape."

"Dad cared."

"He did, indeed. He had good memories of this place. It was his escape from a sad childhood."

I looked away. "I miss him. He and I didn't always communicate well, but we worked things through together. We became a team after Mom left. We balanced and supported each other."

Nicole's voice grew softer, gentler. "Is that really true?"

"What?"

"Henry was a clear-sighted, objective business-person. His decisions were usually sound. He was confident in them. He rarely invited opinions . . . other than from experts. How much did you really discuss with him?" She rushed to add, as if our conversation might be cut short, "How often did you just go along? Only trying to influence him when you felt strongly enough about something to risk a disagreement?"

I couldn't speak. I was stunned into silence.

Nicole added, "Disagreement tends to divide. Isolate. But it can be truer and healthier than pretending—"

Shock brought me to my feet. My chair rocked behind me. "I disagreed plenty. Did I want dissension? No. You think he and you were so close, so in sync, but I was his daughter. He and I were a team. You have no idea how it worked between us. We exchanged ideas, and we discussed . . . we . . . he was always willing to . . ." I shook my head. "We made it work. Over time we learned how to make a good team."

Nicole nodded. She sighed, and her voice took on an unaccustomed gentleness. "Get mad at me. It's okay. All I ask is that you think about it,

Kara. You aren't accustomed to making decisions like this on your own. Few people are, really. It's tough to step out and trust your choices. Be kinder to yourself, Kara. Give yourself credit." She stood, too, and we faced each other. "You are doing an amazing thing here. Few would have the guts to try it. Sometimes I wonder, I really do, why you want this. But as long as you do, I'll help you in any way I can. Even if you get angry. I loved your father, Kara. I'll do this for him and for you." She added, "Just think about what I said."

She left. I wanted to fight. To yell. I'd never been able to do that with my dad. Certainly not with my mother. I'd yelled at Niles, and we'd had the accident. He'd died. I'd yelled at Victoria, but I'd found no satisfaction in it and had lost my closest friend.

The shaking began in my gut and spread up into my chest. I crossed my arms, trying to hold myself together.

I left via the back door and walked to Seth's grotto. I descended the stone steps that led down into the hideaway where trees dropped their leaves forever, where the small pool was covered in them, where the concrete stand stood showing off its brand-new gazing ball. Dad had purchased this one to replace the missing ball. I'd found the new one still in its box near his chair soon after he'd died. He'd bought it because I'd mentioned, in jest, that the grotto used to be called the gazing ball grotto, but the stand had lost its shiny bling.

I missed Dad. I missed my mother, too, and she'd been gone for more than half my life. There were things I would have liked to have said to her, to him. Maybe even to have yelled a time or two. But they'd been doing the best they could. Now I was left with gazing balls and garden gnomes. And Nicole.

She was annoying, but she was honest. She saw the wall I kept in place against most of the world. I disliked that she saw it and kept pecking at it anyway. I appreciated that she kept pecking at it. I was insane. Like my . . .

No, not like my mom.

I'd had to be careful with my mom. Most days she'd been remote. Removed. Some days she'd been better. But I'd always been careful not to tip her over into . . . what? Going poof? Leaving?

She'd left more than once. Sometimes teachers had asked me why my parents never came to the parent-teacher conferences, and I'd had a list of excuses ready for them. My life, my family, had existed within a delicate balance. But it was my family. It was what I knew. They were all I had when I was a child. I'd done what I'd needed to do to protect us.

Now I wondered, though . . . what if instead of making it possible for Mom to stay cocooned in her own world . . . what if I'd shaken her and yelled at her and forced her to be a mom? I shivered. She might've left for good even sooner.

The day Mom left, she'd seemed her usual quiet self. I'd packed my lunch and checked to make sure my homework was in my school backpack. I'd kissed her on the cheek, then hurried to catch the bus. By the time I returned home that afternoon, she was gone, leaving only a short, polite note wishing Dad and me well.

Looking back, I imagined she had awakened that day—had really awakened—and hadn't liked what she'd seen of her life. I'd never know. Some questions had no answers.

Dad had stepped up. He'd helped me adjust to the new situation. He'd done his part. I'd done mine. And we'd managed.

All my life, I'd gone along to get along and had made the best of things. That's what Nicole was saying.

And maybe she was saying not to judge myself and my capabilities on the past. That was then. I was working on a new future right here and now, and I wouldn't wake up one day and find myself where, and who, I didn't want to be.

Chapter Nine

It took some stretching and yawning to get myself going the next morning. I had taken a pill last night. Only one. I'd been unsettled by my conversation with Nicole. That less-than-cozy chat had stirred up a lot of old unsatisfactory memories. I'd needed a little help to sleep and had given myself permission to seek it. No harm done.

The key was on the dresser where I'd left it, but when I gripped the doorknob, it turned. Without the key. The door was unlocked. I froze, body and brain. I forced myself to breathe.

I glanced back at the floor beside my bed. No sticks or leaves. I opened the door as quietly as possible, listening as I peeked around it. Daylight flooded the hallway. All seemed as it should. The only sounds were the natural creaking of a huge old house and my own rushed breathing. The floor from the stairs to my bedroom door was clear of any debris.

So I'd forgotten to lock the door. I was sure I'd locked it, but I hadn't. It was that simple.

After a quick stop in the bathroom, I headed to the stairway. I needed caffeine to clear my head. At the top of the stairs, I stopped, my foot hanging in the air, my hand clutching the banister, dumbfounded by what I saw.

Not only had the powder been disturbed, but

there was a clear print, as if a bare foot had stepped in it and twisted slightly. The toe prints . . . the toe end of the print was near the edge as if in the act of descending the stairs. The powder on the other end of that same step was also disturbed, though fainter and harder to interpret, but it was clear that it had pushed into, had disturbed, the edge of the going-down print.

So the going-down print had happened first.

I glanced back toward my bedroom door. With the light from this angle, I saw a slight powdery residue on the hallway floor, very faint and disappearing altogether as it got closer to my room.

Certain that I must be misreading this, I stared down the flight of stairs.

The going-down prints had left smears and bits of powder on the next few steps below the top one. The coming-up print on the top step had been made last, and there wasn't even a trace of powder leading up to it.

Clearly I'd descended those steps.

I. Me.

And my feet had been clear of powder by the time I'd come back up, so I must've walked it off before returning to bed.

My knees went weak; my legs folded as my stomach lurched. I clutched the railing as I lowered myself to the floor, my eyes going back and forth between the prints on the step and my bedroom door.

I examined the soles of my feet. Were there traces of powder there? Maybe.

One thing was certain: if I'd cleaned up that powder in a timely way instead of putting it off, I would never have known.

When had I started sleepwalking? If that twig and leaf were part of this, I might have even walked outside.

A mild wave of nausea swept me.

I'd heard that some sleeping pills could cause sleepwalking. I didn't take any of those. But maybe the pills I did take could contribute to such . . . nighttime activity.

I rubbed my face and dragged my fingers through my hair.

Why would I suddenly be doing something so crazy? And how incredibly dangerous might it be to me? These stairs . . . not to mention the hazards on the main floor with all the work going on. It was a challenge getting around all the work paraphernalia without injury as it was. And with woods and a creek outside, I could wander. How far? Where might I wake up?

I'd survived a terrible accident; gone through more than a year of surgery, rehab, and recovery; and never—to my knowledge—ever had more than a restless, wakeful night.

I knew the answer. My cache of pills—white for pain, blue to take the edge off my anxiety—was playing havoc with my brain and my body chemistry. The kindest thought I could offer myself was that I'd been irresponsible. Suppose something awful had happened while I'd been under the influence? Who would have known?

The risk was huge. Anything from breaking my neck to reinjuring my thigh or . . . the list was almost endless.

I'd taken these pills before, and nothing untoward had happened, but that had been early in my recovery, and as soon as I'd been feeling better, I'd stopped taking them regularly. The doctor had kept prescribing them. I'd continued filling the prescriptions because . . . well, just because. Just in case. I went back to taking them again after Dad had died. Not every night, but most.

Irresponsible. I'd traded the crutches after the accident for the crutch of the meds cluttering my nightstand drawer—because . . . because I couldn't quite part with them.

Now what was I supposed to do?

What had Seth said? *Only consider questions requiring decisions in the bright light of morning.* I was going to amend that to *Only consider decisions in the bright light of morning* after *coffee.*

I cleaned up the powder that morning. I hadn't accounted for the problem the wood grain of the stair tread would present. It was now filled in with white. I found a bottle of lemon oil furniture polish and used that, working the rag into the tread and thinking I was getting rid of the powder but creating one extremely shiny, very slippery stair tread.

Life was full of risk. I seemed to be exchanging one problem for another, I thought, as I used a little detergent to remove the worst of the polish.

The first floor of my home was a no-man's-land of plastic sheeting, tarps, and general chaos as Moore Blackwell and his helper, Chip—or sometimes more than one helper—proceeded with the wallpaper-removal/repair component of the project. Everywhere I went, I seemed to be tripping over something. The contractor remodeling the kitchen worked according to his own idea of pacing, but as long as the microwave and fridge were operational, I could manage. My day, unless I was tucked away in the middle room working on my business-related plans, was a constant iteration of apologizing or being apologized to. For lunch, I usually took a sandwich out to the porch to eat. Today, though, there was little peace and quiet out there. The roar of saws seemed incessant, and the thuds of severed trunks slamming the ground were a little unnerving and sad.

Unnerved and sad . . . kind of how I'd felt at the start of this day, seeing the powder disturbed and realizing I might be in more trouble than I'd imagined.

I sat on the front-porch bench during a break in the tree cutting. The tree cutters were settled in a shady spot eating their lunch and rehydrating. Will and Lon were clearing away a pile of debris. Will saw me on the porch, waved, and headed over. I stood.

Did I want to talk to Will? I'd come out here where he was bound to see me, so maybe I did.

He walked past the dump truck and a mulching machine and brushed at the bits of dirt, bark, and greenery clinging to his jeans and his bare arms. His expression spoke of satisfaction.

He said, "They should finish removing the trees today. Tomorrow we'll clear the stumps and grade the lot."

"I was sorry to see those trees go."

"Too late for regrets now." He stopped and gave me a second look. "I meant that as a joke. Have you changed your mind?"

"No, I'm sorry. I'm a little off today. We need that parking lot."

"Did you decide whether to pave it? I don't recommend it. Asphalt isn't permanent, and it's a bear to tear up. There's still lots of trees out there, and they'll keep growing roots. Gravel is a better choice."

"I like the idea of asphalt. I understand why you're recommending gravel, but I don't like how it feels underfoot or rolling wheeled luggage through it. If I go with gravel for now, let's make it fine . . . like pea gravel. Also, I'd like to define the parking area with some planting beds. Nothing too fancy, but to make it look . . . I don't know the right word. Stable? Secure? I want people to park here, and as they bring their stuff in, I want them to feel as if their needs have been anticipated and provided for. Does that make sense?"

"Definitely. And your timing is perfect. We'll get the beds in ahead of fall and winter so they'll be all set to bloom in spring."

He'd moved closer as we were talking. Without thinking I picked a dried bit of leaf off his shirt. Will stepped back with a surprised look. Instead of mumbling a weak apology, I kept my eyes on his face.

I wanted to tell him I was worried—to say I'd just discovered I'd been sleepwalking and confess that I was a little afraid. I bit my lip. I couldn't possibly say this to him. Or to anyone. Because anyone I told would think I was asking for help, and maybe I was, but none of them could help me. Not Will or Mel. This was on me to solve. The ultimate *on me*.

"Thanks, Will."

He looked confused. "Are you okay?"

I opened my mouth. For a split second I thought the wrong words might fall out—maybe even a full-blown confession of my fears and flaws and mistakes—and embarrass me and Will both beyond recovery. He was a good guy and a hard worker. I valued his presence, and I didn't want to spoil that.

"I'm fine, Will. Thanks for asking."

That night I didn't take any pills. I held the plastic cylinders with their childproof (but not Kara-proof) tops and knew I could do this. I could do it this once. That was all I asked of myself. Once. Tonight.

I wanted to take a book to bed with me for a little light reading. There were only a few books in this house, and I'd already finished them. Other than the newspaper, Dad hadn't been a big reader, certainly not of fiction. My books had been put into storage along with the other things Niles and I had had in our town house in Northern Virginia. For two years those boxes had been stored there, and one of these days I'd have to go through them, but that didn't help me tonight. I sorted through the small stack of books I had with me, thinking one of them might be worth rereading, and saw the small plastic photo album.

The album was one of the few things my dad had saved for me after Mom had left. The photos were of Mom and me from the time I'd been born and shortly thereafter. When I'd found the album while unpacking the boxes, I'd been overwhelmed and even angry with Dad for not telling me he'd kept it. I hadn't stayed angry, though. How could I? It was as if a bit of my mom had been returned to me.

I hugged that photo album. I didn't take it to look at the photos—I knew those by heart because I'd viewed them over and over—but I cradled the album in my arms and eventually fell asleep.

When I awoke in the morning, I felt a tiny thrill of triumph because the book was still snug in my arms. There was no sign that I'd gotten out of bed or raided the bedside drawer, much less taken a nighttime trip in or out of Wildflower House.

One night wasn't a victory. It was, after all, only one night. But it was a sign of progress. Maybe even a sign of healing. I had hope.

Chapter Ten

The trees had been felled yesterday. Today, I took my lunch out to the front porch again, this time to watch the earthmover clear the stumps and large rocks away from the area of the parking lot.

Will was keeping an eye on that work and also on his crew, who were finishing up their work along the drive from the main road to the house. Wildflower House needed an impressive and orderly approach—one that would inspire confidence in the guests who would come here and pay money for the privilege. That prospect sent a shiver down my spine, a shiver of anticipation, not apprehension.

The emerging parking area seemed like an invitation in and of itself. It made the idea of a retreat and special event venue feel like a real thing. I would need signs up by the road and in front of the house. Something that said *Welcome to Wildflower House*. I had my samplers, of course, but those would be hanging in the foyer.

This was truly happening. This whole thing. I had lots of work yet to do, including nailing down manpower needs and where the extra bathrooms would go and all that stuff, but it was just a matter of getting it done. Occasionally it felt overwhelming, but it no longer seemed impossible. One day and one step at a time.

Will saw me on the porch and came over. He walked with a light step, despite the heat and humidity and the fact he was wearing the evidence of his hard work.

He said, "Looking good, right?"

"It is." I was excited and gestured toward the pile of rocks. "We could use those in the beds bordering the parking area."

Will grinned. "Great minds. I was going to suggest the same thing."

I smiled in acknowledgment.

He said, "Those rocks—small boulders, really—will look good. I'm thinking that given the trees and the preponderance of pines, we'll stick with an understory of shade-friendly, acid-loving plants like azaleas and rhododendrons. They're also easy care. We'll keep them mulched with the pine tags the trees contribute. Hard to get it done any easier than that, and it's easily sustainable too."

I nodded. I heard his words and agreed, but I was still stuck on *the preponderance of pines*. I loved the phrase. I was a lover of words—Mel had called that out. Will's hair had been trimmed, but he still had that rough look, yet he'd said *the preponderance of pines,* and it had rolled off his lips as if he spoke in poetry all the time.

Will was a puzzle. A nice one.

I said, "I called the roofer and told him to go

with the dimensional shingles instead of the tiles."

"Makes sense. As good as those tiles would look, with all the trees around the carriage house, it's just a matter of time before they get damaged again."

Trees . . . yes, lots of trees on this property. In fact, we had a *preponderance of pines*. I didn't speak it aloud, but I felt the words on my lips. I smiled, and Will smiled back.

I hadn't seen or heard from Nicole in a few days—not since our chat in the kitchen. I didn't know what to call that chat. Not *cozy* by any means.

When I tried to pin down specific words to hang my anger on, I couldn't. Maybe she was right about Dad and me not being a team. Maybe I was mistaken in the notion that we had been. But that didn't mean she had the right to say it out loud to my face.

When she arrived later in the afternoon, I met her on the front porch. Neither of us mentioned our last meeting, and I invited her to walk out with me to the carriage house. As we left the porch, I explained my decision about the tiled roof.

"I told the roofer to go with dimensional shingle instead of the red tiles. Shingles are less costly and more practical."

"But that style of roof, the red tile, is so striking out here. You don't see it much in this area of the country. It's quaint and unusual."

"Come see."

We walked along the path that Will's crew had created around the side of the house and into the woods. When we reached the carriage house, I waved at the building and the forest that all but surrounded it.

"Face it," I said to Nicole. "With all these trees around, it's a matter of time before the roof is damaged again. I'm keeping the trees, so I'll keep the roofing more practical too."

Nicole nodded. "I can't disagree with your logic, but I think the tiles give the building a charming appearance."

"We'll go in a different direction to achieve charming. I'll have the exterior woodwork painted in an upbeat color. Maybe a light teal. It should contrast and complement well with the stone walls."

"That would be inviting."

"I give credit to Will. We discussed the issues of the trees and the cost, and he suggested this course instead. Said he'd seen something like it in a landscaping magazine."

Nicole gave me a surprised look. "Nice. I may consider bringing Will into other projects. Sounds like he's an idea guy in addition to being a doer."

With a mock frown, I said, "Not until I'm done with him. For now, he's mine."

I was startled by how those words sounded. Nicole lifted one of her perfect eyebrows but didn't remark on it.

"I just meant that he's good to have around. Very useful." That felt like a dodge. My cheeks grew warm, and I turned away from Nicole to snag the dangling light cord.

Nicole inhaled a quick, audible breath.

Will had run a temporary electrical line to the building until the roofing was done. A big bare bulb dangled from the ceiling beam. It lit the rough old wood and the generous proportions of the building.

I was pleased at her reaction. The air was still a tad musty but much better. Nicole was reacting to the light streaming in through the small windows, which highlighted parts of the open interior—the well-aged raw wood and the old iron nailheads—while the backlight coming through the open doors was like an invitation to visit an older time. A time long gone.

I broke the spell deliberately by saying, "Imagine a couple of potter's wheels in here. Plenty of room for easels and paint tables. Tables for clay work too. Opening these massive doors allows in a lot of light and air." I pointed above us. In this central section, the ceiling was the roof itself. "I wish we could put skylights up there, but the tree problem remains. I think, instead, I'm going to have some large spotlights—industrial type—hung up there. And large fans in a couple of the corners, since it won't be practical to install AC."

"There are options for that. We can discuss them. I do think we should ask Hannah Cooper to take a look and weigh in on the pottery aspect. She's our clay expert, and she's very interested in this project. We're lucky about that. She's gifted and a businesswoman in her own right."

"Regarding business, Nicole . . ." I cleared my throat. "There's something I'd like to show you."

"Yes?"

"Not here. In the house. Do you have a few minutes?" Suddenly I was nervous. Silly me, making something big out of a small thing. Maybe that wall inside me was finally cracking. At some point I had to share the project work I was doing—the business plan and all that—with Nicole. She was an important part of this project, sort of a friend, and also one of the potentially scariest people I knew. Why scary? Maybe because I couldn't bluff her the way I could most people. She saw through my bluster every time. And maybe, because of that, I could trust her judgment on whether my efforts were worth my . . . effort.

"Sure. Lead the way."

I did. I led her to the middle room. My project

room and my room of dreams. I opened the door and stepped aside.

Nicole cast me a questioning look. I nodded, indicating she should go in. "It's early days still—remember that."

She frowned but moved inside. "What's this, Kara? You have a workroom—an office—in here?"

My laptop, the brown paper map, stacks of paint chips, markers, and a myriad of stray papers were spread across the table. Nicole picked up the legal pad where I'd scribbled notes, along with heavy doodling, and gave the first page a quick read.

She looked up at me. "Is this your business plan?"

I joggled my computer mouse and hit the enter key on my laptop. The screen came alive with the Word document displayed. Nicole sat down and scrolled silently through the pages.

I held my breath. I didn't want this to matter so much, but it did. That fact was undeniable.

She scrolled more quickly through the next pages, where I'd laid out, sweating and stressing over each of those words, my view of the present state, my long-term goals, and the interim steps.

"Not bad, Kara. We can work with this."

I bit my lip.

"Not bad at all." She saw the spreadsheet icon. "May I?"

"Yes."

She clicked, and it came alive on the screen.

I said, "It's rudimentary. I have a tab listing actual expenses. I tried listing other anticipated expenses, but there's too much I don't know. You said you could recommend an accountant? I presume someone who's familiar with small business and the hospitality industry?"

"Yes. I can do that."

"And I'm ready to meet with the experts. The local people we're hoping will want to participate. I need to pick their brains for details too."

Nicole sat back and looked at me. "The plan is rudimentary, but it's a very strong starting place, Kara. We all start at the beginning. Remember that. And we can work with this."

Her expression was pleased. She looked . . . optimistic? Excited? Her eyes were even glittering a little. She stood and noticed the paper spread across the floor.

"What is this? A map or a picture or . . . ?"

"Both. It seems silly seeing it as it is now, and even when I was working on it, I knew it wasn't what I was supposed to be focused on. But somehow, putting it all down on paper—not in words but drawing it out with pencil and markers—was . . . I don't know. Satisfying? It seemed to help unlock some of my resistance."

Nicole laughed. It was a small laugh. A

light laugh. A goodwill laugh with a touch of amazement. "It explains so much."

I braced myself for criticism. Barbs, maybe. Disappointment, certainly. I had hoped she would understand.

She knelt for a closer look. "Kara, this is good. It's the wrong kind of paper. You can do much better with a good grade of paper, and white, not this brown stuff. I didn't know you could draw. Your dad never mentioned you were artistic."

I had to replay her words in my head before I understood they were positive. Encouraging. Something reached into my chest. It felt like a fist, and it squeezed so hard that it stole my breath and forced moisture up into my eyes, onto my lashes. I reached up to brush it away before it could roll down my cheeks, dabbing at my eyes with the back of my hand to hastily hide the evidence.

I said, "An artist? I'm not. The map helped me think more clearly."

Nicole watched my face closely. Her expression had gone blank as she stared at me. She rose to her feet and walked over to where I stood. She put her hands on my arms. I was startled. Nicole wasn't generally a toucher or a hugger.

"That's artistic expression, Kara. I'm not an artist myself, but I understand that people speak in more than words. Art. Music."

"Nicole, I . . ."

"Don't examine it, Kara. Don't judge it. Let it marinate. Keep working on this project, both the documents and the map. Don't second-guess it. Promise?"

"Okay." I was stunned by the energy in her body and in her voice. It felt electric, and I felt it in her touch as she continued holding my arms. "Sure, okay."

"I'm sincere, Kara. Don't make your choices now based on what your life used to be."

I nodded, and she released me.

"Nicole?"

"What?"

"Thank you."

Nicole paused in the doorway. "For what, specifically?"

"For being a friend. My friend."

She smiled. "My pleasure, Kara."

Nicole drove away. I congratulated myself, if only for having the guts to expose my work to someone, especially her. I'd trusted my gut. My instinct. I poured a tall glass of strawberry water and drank it down, amazed that I still felt a little shaky, but in a good way now.

She'd never said it, not outright, but I knew Nicole had doubted whether I'd ever find my way forward with this project. Not whether I could . . . but whether I *would*. And frankly, she'd had reason to doubt me.

Now she knew better, and so did I.

How silly to be called an artist. I was working on a retreat. A creative retreat. This was a business.

I stood at the foyer table and opened the top drawer. There they were. The women. The girls. As if patiently waiting. *Waiting.*

I'd felt that myself, especially at night—alone and waiting.

For what? For life? For more?

For my mom to come back to me? I shivered. Why? I wasn't still caught in that fourteen-year-old's brain, was I? When Mom had died two years after she'd left, I'd cried. It had been hard. But it had also been almost anticlimactic. I had already mourned her. Only the sadness had remained, and there had really been nothing I could do but accept it.

So what was I waiting for? Self-expression? Growing my life? In more ways than via spreadsheets and needlework?

Seth called that evening. I hadn't heard from him in several days.

"I miss you," I said, "but I'm making progress, and it feels good."

"On the house?"

"Yes. Well, technically, the professionals are doing that work. I've been creating the business plan and such."

"And it's getting easier each time you work on it, right?"

I laughed. "It is. Is that how your job is?"

"My job seems to be more of a client-pleaser gig, and then I have to come up with campaigns that live up to the brilliant work I've promised."

"You are definitely a pleasing person. Handsome and charming too. But ugh, that job wouldn't work for me. I'd rather be doing this."

This time he laughed. "Exactly."

"Exactly what?"

"I have a theory, Kara. When a person gets out of their own way, they will naturally gravitate to where they belong."

We said goodbye soon after. But I was uneasy. There was subtext in his words that troubled me.

I sent him a silent wish: *Come home soon, Seth.*

I went shopping. I'd shaken off the unease from the night before after my phone call with Seth. Everything always looked better in the morning light. Today was no different.

Per Nicole's advice, I purchased a better grade of paper. I also bought a second table, a file cabinet, and a small lightweight bookcase to hold my supplies. The store loaded the file cabinet and other items into the back seat of my car. Hopefully Will or one of his workers would be willing to help me get the furniture into the house.

I was a businessperson. I was a project manager. Was I an artist? How would I know? I'd never tried. Weren't artists compelled to create? Could it come later in life? Maybe when the environment was more conducive?

After the new items were home and set up in the middle room, I removed the framed photo of the young women from the foyer table drawer and set it atop the bookcase across from my table and computer. I leaned the picture against the wall for support. It was fairly weighty. When it seemed steady, I released it and gave the ladies a thumbs-up.

Will grew plants using soil, water, and fertilizer. His tools. Perhaps this room and these items were my tools. I wasn't growing plants . . . not even wildflowers. I was growing me.

That afternoon I looked out the kitchen window and caught a glint of light—a quick spark that caused me to pause and take a second look—and saw Maddie Lyn climbing onto the bench down beside the creek. The top of her head was barely visible above the back of the bench. I looked a moment longer, expecting to see someone else following close behind. My heart gave a short leap: perhaps Seth on a surprise visit? But no one else arrived. No adult. Not even another child. Just Maddie. A barely five-year-old girl out on her own?

I stepped out to the back porch and looked again, thinking that surely Mel or Nicole would emerge from the woods, having allowed Maddie to run ahead. By now, I was already descending the steps and crossing the terrace.

Was Mel okay? I walked quickly down the grass toward the creek, picking up my pace, thinking only of reaching Maddie Lyn before she ran back into the woods and I lost track of her. How on earth would I explain to Mel that I'd found and then lost her granddaughter?

I hurried, and my thigh tightened. I was afraid I'd fall. If she dashed off, I'd never catch her, not with this thigh acting up. I slowed down and pressed my hand to the cramping muscles. I kept moving, limping, and called out, "Maddie? Maddie, honey?"

Her fingers gripped the top of the bench as she came to her knees. She saw me heading her way and lifted one hand in a hesitant half wave. I forced a smile and dropped my hand from my thigh. I was close enough now. I'd make it in time.

I crossed the last few feet to the bench, and with a welcoming smile on my face, I asked gently, "What's up, Maddie? Did you come to visit me?" Her hair was in pigtails, and she was wearing pink leggings and a flowery top. She looked fine.

She didn't nod but looked past me up the slope toward Wildflower House. I followed her gaze, then turned back and saw disappointment on her face.

I eased onto the bench beside her. I placed one hand on hers. "What's going on, sweetie?"

She fisted her other hand and rubbed at her eye. I heard one telltale sniffle, and then she seemed to recover herself. Her hand dropped from her face, and she smiled—a bare smile, hardly a smile, and a tiny one—at me.

"Are you thirsty, Maddie? Would you like to come up to the house for a drink and a snack?"

She shook her head no, but it was so slight I would've missed it if I hadn't been watching for a response.

"Would you like me to walk you back home? To your grandmother's house?"

Maddie looked down at her entwined fingers and nodded.

I'd heard this child chatter on and on when Seth had been here with her, so I wasn't concerned about the present lack of words. She'd speak when she felt like it. Meanwhile, the question was, Should I go back to the house for my phone? I'd been so focused on reaching Maddie . . .

No. While I had Maddie, silent or not, I wouldn't leave her to fetch my phone and risk her disappearing.

Taking her hand in mine, I stood. Maddie left the bench, and we walked together back toward the woods and followed the path to the bridge.

She was quiet until we reached it. There she stopped, and I stopped beside her. I looked down at the top of her fair head, still feeling the small hand in mine, and wondered if I should ask what had prompted her trip over to my house.

I opened my mouth and breathed in, forming a question, but before I could ask it, Maddie raised her hand and put a finger to her lips. I closed my mouth and listened.

Then I heard them—animal noises that had formed part of the background. I heard the bird-song first but then a deeper, rumbly grunt-grunt sound. Animals did thrive along Cub Creek, especially deer. But these sounds weren't from deer.

I put my face close to Maddie's.

"Turkey," she whispered.

That grunt-grunt changed to gobble-gobble in my head now that I knew its source. Gradually their voices diminished.

"They're gone now," I said.

"Yup." Maddie nodded and tightened her grip on my hand, and together we crossed the bridge.

I was thinking of Seth—the bridge reminded me of holding his hand and of our kiss before he'd left for LA that first time—and I stumbled. Maddie tried to catch me. I appreciated her gesture but was glad I hadn't taken us both for a tumble.

"I'm fine. I wasn't paying attention."

"Finking about turkeys?"

I laughed. "How did you know those were turkeys?"

"Daddy tole me."

She said it so easily. So casually.

"Daddy?"

"Daddy Seth." Except the *th* came out with a slight *f* sound. Like *Daddy Seff.* I'd never heard her call him that before.

I asked, "Your uncle?"

"Yup." Midstride, she gave a little hop. "Uncle Daddy Seth."

I was curious, but I let it go for now. "You miss him, I know."

She nodded and swiped at her nose with a small fist.

"I do too," I said. "And Grammy and Nicole."

"Uh-huh." She sniffled.

"It's okay to miss the people we love," I said.

"Uh-huh." She stopped. "Here."

"What?"

We were standing beside a tree trunk. Not freshly cut, so this tree had been downed many years ago. The trunk stood about waist high for me. Maddie raised her arms.

My brain tried to catch up. She wanted me to lift her onto the tree trunk? Could I? She was petite, but my old injuries . . . suppose my arm cramped? I could drop her. But Maddie believed I could. So I put one arm around her back and the other under her legs and scooped her up and lifted her to stand on that trunk. Maddie Lyn weighed about as much as a sack of feathers. Her height was more of a problem than her weight.

She patted the tree nearest the trunk. "See?" She pointed up and could just barely touch the figures carved in the bark.

Keeping my hands on her legs, afraid she'd fall since she wasn't paying any attention to how small that space was under her feet, I leaned forward. There were letters carved. Not recent, and hard for me to read, but once I got a good look, it became apparent. Someone had carved these letters—someone taller than Maddie Lyn, and the carver must've stood on this same trunk, because they were above my head too.

I read the letters aloud. "PA & MM."

"That's my mommy."

"Mommy," I repeated. Patricia. Mel's middle child. The daughter who'd died. "Your mommy."

"Yup."

I turned her to face me. "You miss her."

She nodded fiercely. "I was a baby. But I remember."

She'd probably overheard adults talking about her being too young when her mother had died to remember her.

"Of course you do." I kept my voice even. "I lost my mom when I was young, too, so I under-stand."

Maddie nodded again.

"And you miss your Uncle Seth."

"Yup."

I asked, "Did you think he might be at my house?"

After a long pause, she moved her thin shoulders in a mighty shrug.

"He isn't, you know. Seth is away now. He's learning a new job. He'll be back, but we don't know exactly when. I know it's hard to understand why he'd leave, but it doesn't change how much he loves you."

"I could go with him."

Her voice was so soft I could hardly hear her.

Shades of the past, of memories I'd put behind me of my mom leaving, of Dad saying it was good she hadn't taken me with her, flooded me. But I hadn't really put the memories behind me. I'd only locked the emotional damage away as if that would be good enough. I shuddered, then put my arms around Maddie.

"Try not to worry too much. Do you talk to Uncle Seth on the telephone?"

"Yup. On the computer. I see him. He can see me."

"That's good. Meanwhile, we'll have to tend to our business just like Uncle Seth is tending to his, until everyone can be together again."

" 'Kay." The syllable was accompanied by a huge sigh.

I lifted Maddie down. She didn't resist.

"Your grandmother must be worried about you." I guesstimated Maddie must've been gone at least twenty or thirty minutes, assuming she'd come directly to my house. Hard to know for sure. But thirty minutes would be an eternity for Mel if she'd realized Maddie was off on her own. "We'd better hurry along."

She gave me another of those inscrutable looks, then said, " 'Kay."

Something nibbled at the back of my mind. "Did your Grammy know you left the house?"

She shook her head no.

"Is Grammy there? Was she there when you left?"

"No."

"Well, Miss Maddie Lyn, I'm pretty sure she didn't leave you home by yourself."

"Annie came over."

"Who's Annie?"

"She lives on my street. Babysitter, but I'm not a baby, and she was on the phone, and I went for a walk."

"Without telling her."

Maddie squeezed her lips together.

"Then we'd better get you back quickly. I imagine right about now Annie is frantic. Maybe calling Grammy to tell her you're gone. Lost."

"Not lost."

"Lost to her."

She gave me an extra look at that, as if thinking it through.

" 'Kay."

We picked up our pace. The trees thinned as we neared the end of the path, and the house and backyard came into view.

We walked through the side yard, and I began to hear voices. Sure enough, Mel and a teenage girl were standing in front. Mel had a phone pressed to her ear and was talking, her manner agitated. Her other hand was in her short hair, a gesture of anguish. The teenager had a finger stuck in her mouth and appeared to be chewing her fingernail as she shifted from foot to foot.

Mel saw us. Maddie Lyn cast away my hand and ran to her grandmother. Mel leaned over to hug her, and Maddie wrapped her arms around Mel's legs. I stood there and tried to smile courteously, wanting to ask how this child had been allowed to go traipsing through the forest on her own but refraining because this was Mel's business and her place to ask.

"Hi, Mel."

"What happened? Annie says she blinked her eyes and Maddie was gone."

Annie didn't seem inclined to add additional commentary to Mel's account.

I kept my voice even. There was no value in fueling the upset. "Maddie Lyn came to visit, so we walked back."

Annie's phone was half-in, half-out of her back pocket.

"If I'd called, I could've saved you some worry, Mel, but I didn't have my phone with me." *Defuse Mel,* I thought. *Help her bring it down a notch.* I put that message in my voice and in the gaze I fixed on her. The important thing was that this shouldn't happen again. "Glad it all worked out okay."

Mel drew in a deep breath. She stood taller but kept her hand firmly on Maddie's shoulder. She looked at Annie.

"You can go home now, Annie. We'll settle the bill later."

Annie pulled the finger from her mouth and wiped it on her T-shirt. "Yes, ma'am, Ms. Albers." She cast a quick glance at Maddie Lyn. "I'm glad she's okay. Sorry I lost her." She took off with long strides, as if something might be chasing after her, pausing only when she reached the asphalt road, where she retrieved her phone from her backside.

Mel knelt and spoke gently directly to Maddie. "What happened? Please tell me. You won't get into trouble. No one will."

Maddie said, "I went for a walk."

Mel smoothed stray white-gold hairs away from Maddie's face. "You didn't like me leaving you with Annie. Was Annie mean to you?"

"No. She's okay."

"Okay," Mel echoed. "Go on inside and get a snack. I'll be right along in. I want to speak with Miss Kara."

Maddie spared me a quick smile and then dashed up the concrete steps, and the storm door slammed behind her.

Mel said, "She likes her snacks."

"She's a growing child."

"With a serious sweet tooth."

I replied, "And a serious case of missing her uncle. She mentioned missing her mom too."

Mel shook her head. "I don't let much get me down. I learned a long time ago that wishing and regret were a big waste of time. But wanting to be enough . . . that's even harder. I'm Grammy. Not Mommy. Not Daddy."

"I know. I understand." I moved close to her and touched her arm. "I saw Maddie down by the creek and went straight out after her. I wish I'd thought to grab my phone, but I was afraid she'd move on and I'd lose her. I guess Annie called you?"

"She did. She's a neighbor girl. Young, but I thought she could handle keeping an eye on Maddie Lyn for an hour or two. She—Maddie, I mean—is pretty independent and self-sufficient, but Annie doesn't have any younger siblings. No practice with little ones."

"Maddie indicated to me that she thought she didn't need a babysitter—'not a baby,' she said." I smiled.

181

"Babies. They grow up so fast—way before they are actually grown."

Mel's eyes were wet—it alarmed me to see her so discouraged.

"Mel. All you can do is your best, and your best is pretty darn good. Maddie is fortunate to have you. Don't blame yourself because you had to run an errand. Kids get left with sitters all the time."

"Mostly I take her with me, but not to this appointment. That doctor can keep you waiting forever. Seemed better to leave her here with a sitter since Nicole couldn't stay."

I could help. Even the offer might help. Everyone needed a backup. Or someone to have their back.

"Listen, Mel, if you ever need to leave her with me, you are welcome to. Just call. The sad truth is that Annie probably has a better understanding of children than I, but I'll do my best." *And I won't be distracted by my phone.*

"Well, that's sweet . . . but you have your own life, your own obligations. Still, I might take you up on it if it ever comes to that." She dabbed her eyes with the back of her hand. "I don't know what's wrong with me."

"You love her."

"Well, again, I know that's true, but I'm also old."

"Not that old. I've seen you work." I was trying

to cajole her past this distress. I wanted her to be the woman I'd met the day she'd come to restore the dining room furniture after Sue Deale had sent it back to Wildflower House, to where it had started.

"Come on in, Kara. Join Maddie and me for that snack. I could use a bit of sugar and caffeine myself."

"Oh, I don't want to bother you."

"Stop that. Just cooperate and come on in."

Without Seth, I thought. Just me. I was invited.

"Yes, ma'am. Sounds lovely."

Mel gave me a doubtful look. *"Lovely,"* she muttered. "Maybe I better break out the good dishes . . ." She made a noise that may have been a snorted laugh and walked away.

I followed Mel up the steps and into the house. The concrete steps. The black iron railing. The storm door. It looked like many of the houses I remembered from the neighborhood where I'd grown up. I had plenty of unhappy memories, but what I was most struck by was the belief I'd had as a child that the families who lived in those houses had been happy, with smiles and laughter and affectionate hugs—where even the scolding parents wore gently chiding but so very wise expressions. It probably hadn't been true, but I'd believed it. Now, as an adult, I understood that nothing was all good or all bad. I'd had my tragedies, but I'd also had security. That was more than many had. I hadn't wasted a lot of time with self-pity, but still . . . there were troubles . . . hurt . . . that I'd never dealt with in a real way. I wondered if Maddie would also carry the seeds of that with her as she grew—into later relationships and even adult decisions about her life.

I joined Maddie in the small dining room at the old maple dinette set, where she was already seated.

"Hi, Maddie Lyn. It's splendid to see you again."

She giggled and offered me a cookie.

Mel said, "Want some coffee?"

"Sure."

"I've got one of those machines, so choose the flavor you want."

"Umm, how about Brazilian roast?"

She nodded at the selection. "Go for it. Here's the mugs."

I did. It was a sort of tea party. I'd never had one of those. But this one had coffee and cookies and good company and seemed just about perfect to me.

I sat next to Maddie and accepted a napkin and cookie from her. "Thank you, Maddie Lyn."

"Welcome, Miss Kara."

She spoke so sincerely, without the least hint of her adventure and how I'd come to be here. I almost laughed in delight.

Mel smiled but said, "Don't be thinking, Miss

184

Maddie Lyn, that a little politeness is going to get you out of trouble for running off. You know better."

"But . . ."

"Don't 'but' me, Maddie Lyn. Your old grandmother can't take such drama."

Between bites of cookie and sips of coffee, I said, "You come visit me anytime, Maddie. You are always welcome. But"—I waved my hands with my own dash of drama—"only if Grammy gives permission first. Otherwise you'll get us both into trouble, and we might not get any cookies."

Maddie's eyes widened, playing along with my overstated drama, but then she broke out in giggles. Mel and I weren't far behind with our own laughter.

The tea party was wonderful. Maddie's solo walk had caused us alarm, but no harm was done except to Mel's frayed nerves. I dropped a quick kiss on Maddie's forehead and left. Mel walked me out. I stood with her on the sidewalk and asked about the Daddy Seth reference.

Mel sighed. "It's new, all right. One of the kids she plays with had a group of girls over. Maddie Lyn came home saying that Uncle Daddy Seth nonsense." Mel rubbed her face, then looked at me. "I asked her about it. One of the girls was pestering Maddie Lyn about whether she had a daddy or not. Apparently, this was our Miss Maddie's solution."

"I see." I tried to keep my response and my expression judgment-free. Seth had upset a lot of lives when he'd left . . . and I'd played a part in encouraging that. It was no one's fault, truly. We were all, including Mel, doing the best we could.

"It'll pass. We talked about it, and I figure I'll just let it go for now. Put it down to some kind of phase."

I touched Mel's shoulder. "I'm sure it's best not to draw too much attention to it. As you say, with love and support Maddie will work things out. Meanwhile, remember what I said. You can always call on me."

Mel gave me a hug. After a surprised pause, I hugged her back. She seemed tiny. Her shoulders were thin, and I felt the sharp edges of her shoulder blades.

As I walked alone on the path back toward the bridge and Wildflower House, I paused at that tree trunk. I thought of losses, but mostly of my own, especially of my lost pregnancy—the child I'd never had. Maybe one day I'd have another chance. After all, I was barely in my thirties. But Seth was the closest thing I had to a boyfriend, and he was far away. And we were far from being a couple.

The child. Would the baby have been a boy or girl?

I had reached the bridge. I leaned against the railing, watching the creek flow past below my feet.

My lost child wouldn't be as old as Maddie. Only a toddler by now. And the child's hair would probably have been dark since both Niles and I had brown hair. But he or she might've inherited my Dad's hazel eyes, like me.

I rubbed my face and felt the scar on my temple. Did the memory still hurt? Perhaps it was a shade less sharp, and that was why I was thinking about it in a way I hadn't before— almost envisioning the child who hadn't been. It was a relief to imagine that child and not feel acute anguish. Was this a step forward in my own strengthening? Was I growing in wellness and confidence?

This bridge, wooden and gray and rough, was the port from which Seth and Maddie had launched their toy boats to sail down Cub Creek. They'd floated past me that day at a serendipitous moment—a moment when I'd been desperately in need of a delightful distraction. That had been the day I'd fallen in the creek and the other two had joined me there with splashing and laughter.

It was a lovely memory.

Seth, when are you coming home? Maddie needs you. I do too.

I believed we could build our relationship into

something truly special, but the sense of time passing was strong.

The wooden planks were plenty sturdy underfoot, but as I leaned against the railing, gazing downstream and musing about things past, I felt a *give* to it. I stepped back and pushed against the handrail. It wobbled a little. Seemed loose where it was attached to the actual bridge. I didn't push too hard because I didn't want to break it. Whose bridge was this, and whose responsibility was it to fix? I'd ask Seth when next we spoke.

Brushing the tiny bits of wood and grit from my hands, I crossed over to my property—back to my side of Cub Creek. I had things to do.

As I walked up toward the house, I saw Will coming from the direction of the carriage house. He saw me and headed toward me. I must've had a smile on my face, because he beamed right back at me. I felt that glow. I almost screeched to a halt. How foolish was I? It was an exchange of smiles, nothing more. I pulled my elusive dignity back around myself.

"Will, hi."

"Kara. What's up?"

"Not much. I was just over at the Albers house and walked back by way of the path. Her granddaughter, Maddie, was here visiting."

"Nice. Not that I know them all that well, but she's a cute kid."

I touched my hair despite myself and ended up

smoothing it back over my shoulder. "As a matter of fact, I crossed the wooden bridge. You know the one I mean?"

"Sure."

"The railing was loose. Maybe you'd be willing to take a look? See if it's an easy fix?"

"I can do that."

"Thanks so much. I don't know who's responsible for the upkeep. If Seth was here, I'd ask him, but he's not. Thanks for helping."

"No problem."

His words sounded good, but his smile had dimmed. I gave him an extra look as he walked away. With his eyes, strong facial features, and imposing figure, Will was naturally handsome. With his black hair tamed and his face shaved . . . well, it paid off.

Had I offended him in some way? He'd seemed fine until I'd mentioned Seth.

I reined in my overactive brain. I was putting way too much thought into this.

I just didn't want to toy with his feelings if he . . .

Whoa, girl. Exactly who do you think you are? Some sort of hot babe? One real boyfriend in your whole life—Niles—a relationship that ended disastrously, and a potential sweetheart in Seth, who moved about as far away as he could while staying in the country . . . and suddenly you're worried you might be irresistible to any guy who happens to cross your orbit? Ha. I laughed.

I felt light again. Even the messed-up yard didn't give me pause this time. It would all be handled in time.

Seth's voice echoed in my head . . . *Remember this, Kara. When you get discouraged, remember, you've got this.*

I spent the afternoon online checking into potter's wheels and easels and such, looking at details of quality and pricing. I knew the internet wasn't a definitive source, but I needed a basic understanding if I was going to be talking to those who did know. Art and the stuff used to craft and create it had never been part of my life. Not really surprising, considering my childhood. I'd had the standard coloring book and set of crayons, but I'd been taught to color between the lines, and that was where I'd stayed.

Until now.

Chapter Eleven

No more hiding my work in the middle room—it was time to examine the details that must be considered for this business I was creating in a real-world setting. As I drove to meet with the accountant Nicole had recommended, I expected to be blown away or plowed under by those details.

I felt ill prepared as I walked into the accountant's office with my paperwork in hand.

Ben Hanson put me at ease right away. He reminded me that this was my enterprise and my timeline. That people might help, but that ultimately I was in charge. Seth had said I must be in charge of my life. I couldn't default on that to anyone else. He was right, and so was Ben.

He provided me with lists of usual expenses in this type of industry. They were long. I didn't look at them too closely, as my brain felt like it was filling up quickly. I listened, though. I would digest it all later in the quiet of my project room.

I thanked Ben and shook his hand. He walked me to the door. I made it into my car before allowing myself to fully react to the meeting. I was pleasantly surprised to find that I'd survived and could still smile. I could do this.

At some point during the meeting, I'd realized

that it wouldn't be long before I hit the point at which my choices of improvements would pass beyond those I might choose to do for me alone or for resale, and they would move into expenses that would directly serve the business.

It felt like a critical milestone.

I started the car and headed home.

Decisions, many seemingly obvious but hard nevertheless, would need to be made. Yet something was working in my favor, because I hadn't taken any pills in several days despite some sleeplessness. Instead, I used that time in the night to envision good things, like the beauty of the dining room wallpaper under the masterful hands of Moore Blackwell, the otherworldly peace inside the carriage house, and even my activities in the middle room. I was proud of my progress on the business plan and on my map. Maybe all that was part of being an artist. Perhaps I did have some creativity within me.

Of course, overcoming or becoming wasn't that simple. The brain noise, the doubts—they wanted to roll back in. I would continue to find ways to see beyond and through them.

How had my father done it? He'd built his own very successful business, and he hadn't had a lot of charm or social skills to rely on. It had been determination and good decisions. Probably some luck had been thrown in there too.

The other day Nicole had asked, "How much

did you really discuss with your dad? How often did you just go along to avoid disagreement?"

I hadn't liked the question, but it was true enough. Dad hadn't intended to shut me out. It simply had never occurred to him to ask my opinion. But after we'd moved here, he'd made an effort. He had tried. He'd even opened up to me about his history. His father. His broken family and dreadful childhood. Even about my mother's history of depression and how she'd enjoyed dancing when they'd met. That he'd loved her laughter and her mercurial moods when they'd dated and married, but that those shiny times hadn't survived the dark times, the depressions. Until finally that was all there was.

The stories had seemed shattering when he'd taken me to that broken house where he'd been raised and finally opened up to me. But now the facts felt incomplete. Surface versions. The obvious sad stories with hints of darker stuff dwelling in the shadows, like the nooks in the forest edges. Dad was gone, and I couldn't cajole or guilt him into telling me more. Would he have told me more? Maybe not. I'd never know. Maybe there really wasn't more worth telling. Tragic was tragic.

When I thought about Nicole's question, I didn't hear it as a criticism now. I heard it as acknowledgment of a protective device. We protected ourselves. We held back. Either a piece of our hearts or parts of our stories. Our histories. We brushed the surface and called it done and packed those darker parts away for safekeeping. By means of civility and courtesy, we allowed them to stay buried. No one wanted to upset the applecart.

Disagreement upset the balance. But it was hard for me to blame anyone, including my dad, for wanting to avoid reliving unpleasantness.

In my childhood I had learned loyalty— absolute loyalty to our family and our family problems—and I had learned the stoic perseverance necessary to manage despite them. I hadn't learned how to draw or paint, or even how to dance, and I'd never learned how to confront someone in a positive way, and I'd never learned forgiveness. Not even how to forgive myself.

Here at Wildflower House, when Dad had finally opened up to me and revealed what he'd hidden for decades, our world hadn't ended. We'd gone on just fine. Better, in fact. I'd learned that dark secrets weren't always damaging when exposed to the light of day.

Other than the one trip to the Lange property with Dad, I hadn't gone back. I owned the property now as part of what I'd inherited from my father. I had no idea what to do with it. The smell of failure and forlorn hopes was too sharp and overbearing there.

Closing my eyes, I pictured a better scene—the

one in front of me. The slope, the creek, the woods, and that great dried-up mud pie in the middle. I could throw down more seed and wait to see what would return . . . or construct something more deliberate. Imaginings flitted through my brain half-formed. Some took shape and form and seemed almost real.

I opened my eyes slowly, half expecting to see a fountain. A sculpture, maybe. Nothing huge, but striking and surrounded by flowers. Wildflowers. Colorful and bright, though a much smaller plot than the original wildflower field. The center-piece—the sculpture or fountain—could echo the sundial already in place down by the creek.

There would be more lawn space. Lush and green, it would enhance the earthen terrace effect. It would be a lovely area for small group meetings outside, maybe yoga. Maybe *en plein air* painting.

Will's crew had mowed around the edges to keep the grass down at the perimeter of the wildflower field. The field itself was now sprouting all sorts of green stuff, mostly unsightly.

The churned earth that used to be the field of flowers needed help and resolution.

I called out, "Will?"

He'd been in the carriage house, and he now stood at the open doors with the shadows behind him and the sun on his face. He walked toward the house and me. "Yes?"

"Do you know how to drive a riding mower?" I waved my hands. "Silly question. Of course you do." By now he was nearing my perch on the porch. "What I mean to ask is, Can you show me how to drive one?"

He frowned. "If you need anything cut or mowed, just let me know."

I gestured toward where the wildflowers had grown. "I'd like to do this job myself."

He nodded and waited.

"The mower is in the shed. It was my father's."

"Yes, ma'am," he answered softly.

"I want to finish what he started." I was struck by those words. *Finish what he started.* Was that what I was doing with this whole house thing? But this time I was talking about the dead flowers and finishing what my father had started the day he'd died. I couldn't restore the flowers to how they'd looked before, but I could erase that churned-up area and turn it into something more fitting to my father's memory.

Will opened the double doors of the small shed. There was a low ramp up to the opening, and right smack in the middle of the small building was the mower.

"Key's in it. Want to do it now?"

I looked up at the blue sky. Not a cloud in sight. "Yes."

He looked around. Lifted his cap and raked back his hair before repositioning it. "You could wait for a cooler day, or I can have Derek or Lon take care of it."

"I want to do it myself."

He frowned, then nodded again. As he drove the mower out of the shed and into the yard, I descended the steps and joined him.

"It's simple enough," he said, climbing off the mower. He stood beside it. "Have a seat."

He touched my elbow as if I might need steadying. His touch was gentle but so brief that his fingers had already moved on to the key before I had a chance to process the sudden warmth on my face or even my slight instinctive lean toward him.

"You'll turn this key when you're ready to start, but not yet. The gas pedal is down there. When you want to go, press on it with your foot. When you want to slow, ease up on it. When you want to stop, take your foot off all the way. You can't get into too much trouble. Any problem—take your foot off the pedal. If you run out of gas, let me know. I'll show you how to gas it up."

He stood there with his hand on the hood, his blue eyes earnest. It reminded me of that day when I'd first declared my intentions to Mel and Nicole. It had been right after Dad's funeral, and everyone had been curious about whether I'd stay or go. When I'd said I planned to stay and turn the house into a retreat, Nicole and Mel had immediately offered their help with my project. They'd been so excited, but for me the doubts had rolled in right away.

"You okay, Kara?"

"Sorry. I was remembering something."

"Your father?"

"No, something else. Just a memory."

"Well, don't go woolgathering while you're running this machine. That's about the only way you'll get into trouble doing this. Or by attempting a sharp slope. Don't drive it along the creek bank. You could end up in the water with the mower on top of you."

"Woolgathering."

"Pardon?"

"I haven't heard that term in a long time. I don't even remember where or from whom I heard it."

He laughed a little. "My granny says it. Means daydreaming. I have no idea what it has to do with gathering wool." He pointed back downslope toward Cub Creek. "Remember, stay away from the creek bank. I'll make sure that gets cut." He scratched his head. "I know it's your decision, and I understand why you think you want to do this yourself, but it's a hot, sweaty job."

"It's symbolic."

He nodded. He understood, and that pleased me. But then he added, "I should mention that a mower won't actually do much good here."

"Why? The mud is dry."

"Yes, but these blades are only going to cut what's sitting up more than a couple of inches. Most of the weeds . . . the flowery weeds, I mean . . . got pummeled, and they're encased in that dried mud. I'd advise a tiller."

Blankly, I stared at the field. A tiller? "Do I have a tiller mode on this machine?"

"It would be an attachment."

In a small but determined voice, I asked, "Do you know if I have one?"

"There isn't a tiller in the shed. Odds are there wasn't one available for this mower. You'd need something heavier for this job anyway."

I was sitting astride this machine, having steeled myself to this task, symbolic or not, and I was stymied for lack of a tiller.

Will said, "I have one."

"Oh. Why didn't you say so sooner? Can I borrow it?"

"Doesn't quite work like that. It attaches to a tractor. I could bring the tractor and tiller over and till the ground."

I shook my head. "I should've just told you to do that the first day we discussed it. I never really had a choice about that, did I?"

Ridiculously frustrated, I wanted to cry.

"Kara?"

I nodded but couldn't bring myself to look up at him.

"If you don't mind . . . while we're here, I'd like to tell you what I see."

I frowned. "You see? What?"

He waved his hand, encompassing the whole backyard area. "We'll till all this and lay sod top to bottom except for a large circular plot in this upper area. Imagine a huge circle. The outer ring will be the flowers. Any flowers you want. If you want annuals, they can be easily reached and replanted in that spot. If you want perennials, wildflowers . . . whatever. The inner circle will be azaleas. They stay green year-round and will be planted such that the early bloomers will give way to the midseason bloomers and then the late bloomers. We can plant those by quadrants or in rows. Do you follow me?"

Without waiting for an answer, he said, "Think of it like a medallion in the middle of the yard. English garden type. And around it, the grass lays like a green carpet. We'll restore some of the terrace effect that's eroded so you'll have flat, level areas for chairs or yoga or whatever, but smooth out those terrace-type earthen steps on each side along the woods' edge. It'll make for a better walking experience. More user friendly for your visitors."

A medallion? English garden type? A better walking experience on the sides?

"Thank you, Will." I pushed my hair back behind my ear, trying to refocus. "Maybe with a fountain or statue in the center?"

He nodded, but not looking at me. He was looking at the yard space, the growing space. Envisioning—I could see that now. Now we were both staring at that spot as if this were a real thing, already done.

He said, "Got it. Good idea."

"Yes." I could see it too.

"Whichever you prefer. You might want a sprinkler set up for the garden anyway, so a fountain recycling the water would make sense."

I stared, feeling the picture grow in my head and before me, feeling almost like Will and I had some sort of idea pipeline shooting visions back and forth between us.

"It will be a wonderful memorial to your father." In a soft voice, Will added, "That's what you're wanting, right?"

"It is."

"And it will serve your other purposes too. Art classes, meetings, or whatever—in the same spot. On hot days, you have the more private, shady nooks in the woods."

"Yes," I breathed, my fingers tight around the steering wheel. He saw it. Will understood what I was creating.

"Will?"

"Yes, Kara?"

"Do you mind if I share my doubt?"

"Not sure what you mean, but go for it."

I kept my eyes focused ahead. "I already told

you this was an impulsive idea. It isn't as if it's been a lifetime dream for me to open a creative place, a retreat for women."

"Not only women."

This time I turned and glanced at him. "I was imprecise. Men and women. Though I think this will appeal mainly to women, don't you?"

He shrugged. "You probably have a better idea about that than I do."

"Honestly? I haven't a clue. Just assumptions. I've been working on a business plan and even spoke with a CPA, but I feel like I'm learning on the job—a fairly high-stakes, costly experiment. Failure would be . . ." I faltered.

"I am encouraged. I'm even optimistic at times, but this endeavor doesn't come with a guarantee of success. I don't want anyone to think I'm something I'm not."

"You are tough on yourself."

"I try to be honest."

Will said, "Honesty is fine, but what you're really doing is overthinking."

I gave a small, slightly rude laugh.

"You're alone too much."

That jolted me. "Not much I can do about that."

"What I meant is when my sister is alone too much, she starts chewing over stuff. By the time anyone knows she's even close to worried, she's tied up in knots over a 'nothing' thing."

"Oh, I see. Seth said I should save big decisions

for morning and then spend the rest of the day focused on getting the job done."

"Smart."

"Do you know him? Seth Albers?"

"Sure, I know Seth. Not close friends. He was a few years ahead of me in school. But yes, I know him. Good guy."

It had felt important to bring up Seth. To put his name, if not his person, right here between us. Between? That was silly. With us, rather. Just to declare that Seth was in my life whether he was on-site or not. Nothing was going on between Will and me except a growing friendliness. Nothing wrong with that.

I said, "Maybe your sister and I have that worry thing in common. For me, though, I think I'm not busy enough doing physical work. I hire people to do the actual labor. I am writing the project and business plans, but"—I flexed my hands—"it's not the same. In fact . . . this will sound foolish, but I'm drawing a layout of the property, like one of those maps they sell in tourist areas with landmarks and restaurants and such on them."

"Yeah?"

"If I like how it turns out, I'll hire someone to execute the final work."

"That's a great idea for your guests. For advertising and promotion too."

"I agree, assuming it turns out, but what I really want to do is . . ." I looked at my hands, palms red from gripping that wheel. "I want to *do* something."

"Like what?"

"Mr. Blackwell is working on the wallpaper. You're handling the yard. Nicole is working with the attorney and the county, getting all that together. I feel as though I'm on the outside looking in." I shook my head. "I'm sorry, Will. Didn't mean to share all that."

"No problem." He held out his hand. "Let's take a walk."

My hand reached toward his automatically, and our fingers touched. I froze. "A walk? Where?"

"Show me what's going on inside."

"In the house?"

"Moore's working in there now, right?"

"He is."

"Then let's go see."

"Why?" What was Will up to?

"Show me what he's doing." He held his hand palm up. He didn't grab my extended hand but waited for me to complete the connection. I did.

I clasped his hand and immediately moved to climb off of the mower. We were holding hands for a purpose. Courtesy on his part. Convenience on mine. I refused to acknowledge how natural, how right, it felt to hold his hand. As soon as I was off the mower and onto my feet, I released his hand and took mine back.

"Thank you," I said.

"You're welcome," he answered.

We walked together up to the porch and into the house. I was rubbing my hands together. Nervous? But why?

Mr. Blackwell heard us coming. He looked up. "Hello, there, Will. How're you doing?"

"Fine, Moore. How are you?" He gave the wall a close look. "Cleaning this paper? Looks good."

Mr. Blackwell nodded across the foyer toward the parlor. "Chip's in the other room prepping that paper for removal."

Moore. Will called him by his first name so easily. We were all adults here. Why was I having such a hard time moving this older man into first-name status?

I tried again. "It's looking really good—" I stumbled before giving in and finishing up with, "Mr. Blackwell."

He fixed me with those dark eyes and heavy brows. "You should call me Moore, too, miss. Simpler."

"Of course. And you'll call me Kara."

Will and I exchanged some sort of glance. I was tempted to look longer, but he'd already broken eye contact. He was scanning the foyer and the parlor and the area around us.

"So it looks like that paper over there is coming down. Dining room paper stays. What about the living room?"

"Sitting room. I use it as a living room, but it

was introduced to us as a sitting room, so that's what I call it."

"Sitting room."

"That paper is coming down."

"Paint?"

"Yes. I haven't decided the colors yet." I shrugged. "So many decisions to make."

Chip passed us with a nod and went out the front door. Will walked into the parlor. He stepped over a roll of plastic and stared at the wall and at the fireplace.

I said, "The fireplaces are all blocked. The work looks clumsy, poorly done, in my opinion."

"What are you going to use this room for?"

"The parlor? A place for guests to sit and read. Small group meetings."

He gestured around the room as he said, "I'd paint the walls gray. A light to medium gray. Install bookshelves on this wall. White with white trim. Keep the rest of the room simple—gray and white—except for the books on the shelves, and maybe a nice rug. If you like murals and want to improve the look of the fireplace, I have a suggestion for that too."

"What?"

"What for which part?" he asked.

"Both. What's the suggestion?"

"A fire screen painting."

Will's appearance might be a bit tamer than when we'd first met, but he didn't even vaguely resemble my idea of an interior decorator. Puzzled and curious, I gave him a long look, saying, "You've surprised me."

"Why? Because I have an opinion about whether to paint or paper?"

"It's more than that." He was being deliberately obtuse. "Your suggestions were so specific."

"I probably saw a picture of a room like that in a magazine ad or something. It stuck in my head. No mystery."

I felt his mental or emotional pushback. I'd trespassed, but he'd invited himself into this, hadn't he? Had, in actuality, invited me into his imagination. I respected that. I knew these walls would never be gray. Maybe a grayed blue, or a bluish lavender. But I wouldn't say it while Will was in the act of imagining. That would've been about as rude as a person could get.

I prompted him to continue. "And in that magazine picture, a scene of some kind was painted on the fireplace?"

"I didn't explain it right. I saw the white bookcases on a gray wall with the wall showing through. You have to build it right, though, or the shelves won't support the weight of the books . . . anyway, the fire screen paintings weren't in that picture. That's something different. It's not painted on the actual fireplace, but it's a painting framed in an antique fire screen that sits in front of the blocked area." Suddenly, he was patting at his pockets. He pulled out his phone. "Here it is."

He was scrolling through his photos in no time—no awkward fumbling for apps or hitting the wrong thing and blowing it up. He said, "Here. This."

He handed the phone to me. I took it.

The photo was small and hard to see in detail, but the painting was situated in front of the fireplace. I could barely make out the fire screen frame that held it, but the intent seemed clear. The painting itself was abstract—a mishmash of colors and textures.

"Beautiful," I said, handing the phone back to him. "I'd love to see them in person."

"I can arrange that."

I nodded. "Are they done locally?"

"Yes." He looked a little embarrassed. "Actually, I have a personal interest."

A personal interest? In what? Who? My breath caught in an odd way, but Will didn't notice.

"My sister, Brittany, paints them. Your interest will give her a real mood boost." He waved his hand. "But don't feel committed or anything. There's no obligation. I appreciate you being willing to consider them."

"Is this the same sister that overthinks things?"

"It is."

Will and I walked through the foyer and down the hallway. My brain was busy. Dad had said something about choosing our color scheme based on one special or unique item. Dad had suggested using the blue vase or even my delphinium needlework piece to build the rest of the decor in the sitting room, and that would help guide the decorating throughout the foyer and into the parlor. Decorating had never been Dad's thing. He was just being logical and using the process to reduce the world of possible choices.

"Thanks for sharing your ideas."

Will nodded. "Not sure I did anything much, but if so, I'm happy it helped."

"I think you did it on purpose."

He smiled. A shy smile. He brushed his hair out of his face. I recognized a defensive gesture— and just like that my hand shot up, and my fingers pressed against the scar on my temple. The thin ridge of flesh was in my hairline and not terribly noticeable, but . . . I pulled my hand back. Maybe Will wasn't just shy. Maybe he had damage too. Most of us did. Some people dealt with it better—or hid it better.

I added softly, "You tried to help me think, instead of just operating on feeling. Is that what you do with your sister? When she gets lost in overthinking?"

"No credit here." He started toward the kitchen door, then turned back. "I'll let Britt know you're interested in the fireplace screens. Maybe I'll bring a couple with me tomorrow?"

"Perfect," I said.

He nodded. I let him go without me.

His eyes had been bright and interested, and I'd almost touched his arm but had pulled my hand back quickly.

It occurred to me that I knew very little about Will. He had some mystery about him. And a pleasant sense of humor.

"You okay?"

Moore was up on a tall ladder. A sponge was in his hand, like he'd paused midaction as he cleaned the paper. I was standing in the foyer, staring at nothing.

"I'm fine. Yes."

"You look relieved. Must've made some decisions?"

"I think so. I've had trouble getting into rhythm with this project."

"Sometimes ideas need to simmer awhile. Good for stew, tea, wallpaper removal, and even certain decisions. Each in its own good time."

"Truth, Moore."

"Yes, ma'am, Kara."

Chapter Twelve

Will was bringing his sister's paintings over this morning. He'd said *probably,* but I knew it was definite. My heart quickened. After washing up and dressing, I went downstairs for my coffee and paused to consider how those fire screen paintings might look in place.

The paintings could look less compelling in person. Could I be honest with Will? Dad had always said not to do important business with friends or family because it was too damaging to the relationship if anything went wrong.

No, Kara. This will be good. And if it's not, you'll be honest with Will. You'll have to.

Yesterday had been a good day. I was still feeling it this morning. What I wasn't feeling was foggy. Was that the recipe? Have a good day and fill the empty nights with expectations of more good things to come? I was doing that. I warned myself not to let that become a new trap and an excuse to backslide when days weren't good.

Will arrived, but in a car this time instead of in his work truck. When I opened the door, he looked up and waved, indicating I should stay on the porch. He opened the trunk and lifted out two wrapped forms about the size of largish paintings.

"Need any help?"

"Thanks, but I've got it."

I held the door wide for him to enter. He set one package down in the foyer, leaning it against the wall. For the other, he removed the brown paper. I caught a glimpse of color and pattern as he arranged the unwrapped painting in front of the parlor fireplace. I moved closer for a better look. At first glance, the tiled effect reminded me of ancient Greek or Roman mosaics, but the subject was flowers—wild, exuberant flowers, with a Grandma Moses feel. The painted white grout between the tiles gave it a 3-D realism look that contrasted oddly with the folksy style. It drew my hand like a magnet; I wanted to touch it. All I could think of was if you mashed Monet with a Roman mosaic, this would be the result.

"It's lovely."

"Thanks."

"Brittany is a talented woman."

He flashed that smile. "I'll let her know." He pointed at the painting. "Imagine that painting in a black iron frame with feet from an antique fire screen."

"Repurposed?"

He grinned this time. "Yeah."

"In a gray or blue-gray room with white trim." I saw them, the colors in the painting, echo right across the hallway. Those bits of bluey lavender would transition right across the foyer from the parlor to the sitting room. I glanced at the second package, suddenly feeling almost hungry in my eagerness to see it.

Will's large, rough hands delicately unwrapped the brown paper, unfolding it slowly, perhaps hesitantly.

Would I be disappointed? I held back, waiting.

Until he dropped the paper away.

No tiles here. Color, yes, but in a landscape scene. It was done in an aerial view but then pulled into an almost globe shape, but only a section of the globe. The distortion was at first glance almost dizzying, but then as the brain processed it, it settled down, and the landscape became less disorienting but more compelling. Hypnotizing.

The paintings touched a chord in me. I felt a magnetic pull. "I've never seen anything quite like them."

There was that slight glow on his face again, as well as a reserve or hesitation I couldn't read.

"Does she paint for a living, or is she in school?"

"She isn't in school right now. She's . . . in between things at the moment. Living with our mom." He paused. "She's had some tough breaks. This could give her a new . . . focus."

How much could I ask about his sister without being rude? I didn't know.

"You'll frame this one too? With the fireplace screen frame?"

"Sure. She paints them to fit the frames we've collected at thrift and secondhand shops. We've even got one that's three panels—like an old Chinese screen—that sits on the floor under its own power. Without feet, I mean."

"I really love these, Will."

"I'll get them set up in the metal framing and bring them back over."

"I suppose it would be overkill to put one at each fireplace?"

"Not necessarily. Also, there are other options. You can do simpler images or cover them in fabric or wallpaper or even combinations like an old-fashioned collage—it could work in the right room."

"Will, thank you. I think I've found my decorating direction, the anchor. I appreciate your ideas and"—I waved my hands at the fireplaces—"these." I stared at the first one again. "You'll ask Brittany how much she wants for them?"

"Happy to."

"In fact, why don't you bring her over, and she and I can chat about this? I'd love to meet her."

Will scratched his cheek. He looked uncomfortable. "About that," he said. "She's not very sociable. I wish I could say she'd come, but . . ."

"It's okay. Truly. She's an artist, and she's had tough times, as you said."

"She was in an accident last year. A rollover. It has limited her physically in some ways. She has trouble getting past that."

I wanted to cry out, *I understand. I was*

in an accident too. I'm still getting over it.
Remembering my own trauma, I nodded. "Then we'll give her a little space for now. Maybe later, after we open, we can feature her along with local artists and artisans? I don't know what kind of event that would be, but I'm open to what makes sense. Perhaps she'll even get to the point where she'll teach a workshop for guests who want to paint."

Will drew in a quick breath. "I hope so. I don't know." He added, "I told her about you."

"About me? You mean about wanting to see the paintings?"

"That you'd been in a serious accident. I don't know much about your accident. You don't talk about it, but I know you were injured and hurt your leg. To look at you, no one would ever know."

I almost laughed. In a sudden, unexpected rush of warmth, I reached out and touched Will's hand. "That's because you didn't know me before, or even during the recovery. I'm only just now becoming Kara Lange Hart again—but a better, upgraded version, I hope."

Will was staring at my hand on his. Self-conscious but feeling oddly unrepentant about it, I slowly withdrew mine. I'd been about to make a joke about being Kara Version 2.0 and thought better of it. Better to drop the chatty stuff and stick with business.

"I'd love to meet her if that's good with her, but

only if she's okay with it. As for the paintings, does she have more? I mean, just in case I decide to use one or two upstairs?"

"She doesn't always finish her paintings, but if she sells some, it might encourage her. These are the two I thought would work best."

He'd paid attention. And had shown excellent taste. My hands wanted to stray again. I clasped them together.

"Will, you are a puzzle."

"In what way?"

"You work hard out there in the heat and the bugs and the 'cautions' that could be hiding anywhere out there in the wild—in the wilderness—and yet I've seen creativity in what you do. An instinct for design. But interior design suggestions? You surprise me."

"I like physical work. Not knocking down trees for the sake of knocking them down—but making the most of outdoor living space and trying to do it in a way that's healthy for the plants."

"I never realized all that was going on in your head when you were hacking at the overgrowth."

My words sounded awful, judgmental, and limiting—I cringed even before I finished saying them—but Will just grinned all the broader and stood a little taller.

He said, "People who work outside are usually more in touch with nature than they get credit for. It's our workplace. Can you imagine going into an office every day, year after year, if you despised it? People tend not to get that. I'm used to the attitude. As for the inside stuff—even a guy can have an opinion on paint colors."

As quickly as I smiled, Will looked aside. I thought of that shyness. We'd seemed to be past that. Maybe not.

He stepped away, and then suddenly he turned, asking, "You like the idea about the garden in the backyard, right?"

"The medallion garden? Yes, I love the idea."

"If you don't mind me suggesting something else?" He grimaced. "I hope you don't think I'm trying to run up the bill."

"Of course not."

"When we're done cleaning the front acreage and getting the parking area the way you want it, would you be interested in walking paths? We can improve the path along the creek. Make it a better user experience, plus safer. You might consider bike paths too."

He must've seen the instant resistance on my face. Walking paths? Maybe. Bike paths? Sounded like a huge insurance liability to me. This was a retreat, not a . . . a . . . I couldn't think of the right word. A resort? A health club? Well, it kind of was. But in a quieter, more cerebral, creative way.

"Just a suggestion."

"It was a good suggestion. Sorry, I went away

again . . . woolgathering. I'm not sure about the bike-path idea, but improve the walking path? Yes, that would be good. In both directions along the creek, I think. We can talk about it more later?"

"Sure. I'll get back to work."

"Thank you, Will." I walked out to the front porch with him.

"No problem. The tractor and tiller will be here this afternoon, and we'll do a proper job on the backyard." He nodded, grinned, and turned away and strode off across the yard and around the side of the house.

That grin was different. He was more comfortable with me now.

And me? Yeah, I was comfortable. Too much so?

I laughed. I was, in truth, alone too much. And I was too grateful for Will's presence to risk screwing that up.

I felt reenergized. By the evening it had faded to a warm, fuzzy feeling—the belief that I could do this. Not overnight, and not without worry, but so long as I didn't let it overwhelm me, I could. I gave Will credit for that thought. Just as I gave Seth credit for the good advice he'd given me about making decisions.

I was sitting in a chair on the front porch in the growing twilight.

The phone was on the armrest—for once near

at hand—and I checked the time again. Could I call Seth and not risk interrupting an important meeting? I wanted to hear his voice. Sometimes I missed him more than usual . . . and tonight was one of those times. It was probably late enough, and, I reminded myself, he'd let it go to voice mail if he couldn't take the call now.

I wouldn't mention Will to him. No need. This was just about me and Seth.

He answered the video call right away. He looked good, as usual. A bit distracted but smiling as he greeted me with, "Hey, Kara."

"Hey, yourself. Is this a good time?"

"Perfect time." He squinted at the phone screen. "Are you sitting in the dark?"

"On the porch." I asked, "Are you busy?"

"Not at the moment. I'm waiting for a couple of coworkers. We're having dinner with a client. Until they come to get me, I'm all yours."

All mine. The warm fuzzies continued.

"I wanted to thank you. What you said about making decisions only in the morning? It was brilliant. You are brilliant, Seth."

He laughed. "Not brilliant, but occasionally I learn from my own mistakes, at least well enough to share it." He paused, then added, "I hope you'll remind me of my own words of wisdom when I backslide."

"Do I hear tension? Maybe a little stress? Is it the job?"

"The job has challenges. I've always worked on my own, even when I wrote columns for the newspaper. As long as I met my deadlines, I could work any time of the day or night. Jobs like this—very office centric—tend to blur that line between job time and personal time."

"But when you're able to work from here, that may improve. They promised you could, right? When that happens, you'll get some freedom back." I wanted him to say yes.

"That's true, but things are pretty dynamic around here—ever moving and changing. I confess that sometimes I'm on board with it—like an excitement junkie."

"That's a good thing, I guess."

"How's it going for you? You look amazing this evening."

I touched my hair and flipped it back over my shoulder. The evening light was kind to me. I was glad he'd noticed.

"Things are going well, Seth. Really well. I got off to a rough start, but now the project is showing tangible progress. I'm excited about it."

"Fantastic, Kara. Super. When you have doubts, and you will, remember that's just a stumbling block. Imagine doubt that way, like an empty can in your way, and kick it—kick it right into the next county."

I laughed. "Sometimes you're funny, sometimes just silly. But thank you for making me smile."

"I hear them in the hallway. I have to go, but listen, Kara: I'm coming home soon to check on Mom and Maddie and all that. When I do, you and I are finally going to have that date."

"I'll be here. Oh, Seth, I have so much to show you. Real progress."

His name was being called, and the voices of several people were audible in the background. They were laughing and chatting.

Seth said, "Gotta go, Kara. Talk to you soon."

Silence.

"Bye—" I stopped. He'd already disconnected. His face . . . his smile . . . gone in a heartbeat. I was jolted. I didn't blame him for hanging up, but I was jealous of those people he was having fun with, even if it was for work.

Darkness had fallen now. I continued sitting. I hadn't turned the porch light on, and no lights were on inside, so the only light available was whatever the heavens cared to share.

I wished Seth were sitting here with me. Tonight, with the insects calling and the fireflies playing hide-and-seek among the pines, this felt like peace. It wasn't permanent. Peace could never be perfect as long as we humans were so imperfect. I missed Dad. He'd never been much of a conversationalist, but he'd been there for me. At times his lack of emotional warmth had frustrated me, but I'd never doubted him.

I felt similarly about Seth. He had confidence

and loyalty. Right now, his absence was disappointing, but I trusted him.

I had encouraged Seth to find a job he could embrace, where he could use his skills. He'd written columns for the newspaper in Richmond until the paper had cut that out of their budget. Since then, he'd been living in Cub Creek with his mom, helping with Maddie Lyn. Even I could see he'd fallen into a rut because he'd wanted to do his part and help his family.

I'd stuck my nose into his business and encouraged Seth to find a job in his chosen field, one that would inspire him. Had I done that because I'd felt I should be getting out into the world again instead of hanging here with my father?

Yeah, I thought I had.

Seth's job offer had come through while we'd been holding Dad's memorial service.

The offer had been an exciting one. I'd urged him to take the chance even though I truly wanted him to stay, to help me through that awful time. The employer had wanted Seth in LA immediately. Seth had been caught in a quandary. In fact, he'd offered to put off the new employer and stay here to help me through the grief. I'd told him no. I'd told him to go because it had been the right thing to do. I'd told him to go so he could come back to me all the sooner.

I smiled at the phone and ran a finger along the sleek plastic casing. He'd return. And when he did, he'd be amazed at how much I'd accomplished.

Would Will be gone by then, having moved on to another job site?

That thought made me sad. But the reality was that people came into our lives and left our lives.

Niles. Victoria.

Niles, *me,* and Victoria. Victoria claimed she'd known him first—had known each of us first. She seemed to think it gave her special status in our lives. Maybe it had for a while. But Victoria had never found her own, separate life. Instead, she'd followed Niles and me to Northern Virginia after college.

Why had I allowed these memories to intrude? What if tonight was the night I gave in to the little voice that whispered I'd already proved I didn't really need the pills—that I could take them or leave them? I'd already proved I could *leave* them, so I could go back to taking them anytime I wanted. No problem.

It was a thin line between a poor choice and a good one.

The meds were still in the drawer. I hadn't disposed of them.

Not all addictions were physical. Maybe certain addictions, or even bad habits and other crutches, were opportunistic . . . like weeds, ready to fill the empty spots and choke out the opportunity for better ones.

· · ·

There were several vehicles parked in the driveway the next morning. Will's truck, plus another truck and Lon's sedan. At least, I thought it was Lon's. He tended to drive a variety of vehicles. Moore's van wasn't here today, but Chip was unloading a tarp from the back of his own truck. He looked up and waved. I smiled and returned his greeting. "Door's unlocked. Let yourself in."

"Will do."

"I'll be out in the carriage house if you need me."

Will and his crew were working around the property, but no one was in sight as I followed the path with a light step. I was feeling good about the project and pleased to add another pill-free night (despite some moments of temptation) to several in a row.

The shady coolness of the carriage house, and the sense of mystery and untold stories in its ambience, drew me. Most of the wild growth had been cleared away, the electric line had been connected, and the mustiness was almost gone—I found it enchanting. Full of promise. Plus, Will might be there. I had ideas I wanted to discuss with him.

The doors slid open smoothly on newly oiled runners.

I stood in the open doorway, my hand against

the gray stone, and allowed my eyes to adjust to the darkness inside.

As the interior took form and its dirt floor and beams and stairs became recognizable, I imagined potter's wheels and maybe easels filling the open space. They would need to be movable or at least spaced right to keep the area flexible for multiple uses. It was all running through my head: the visions, the setups—I could almost see the women who'd be using the equipment. Maybe a few men, too, as Will had reminded me. And of all ages. Some bent over the pottery wheels. Some standing in front of those easels.

What else? I didn't know. The loft areas above might be great writing spaces or reading havens for individuals. Garret-like. Maybe with a small desk and a chair, plus a comfy chair in the corner.

I was standing there, staring above at the light coming in through the high windows and imagining that comfy chair, when a voice came from behind me—and every good feeling inside me came to a grinding halt in a jarring crash as Victoria said, "Hey, there, Kara."

Chapter Thirteen

In disbelief, I turned toward her voice. Victoria. She was wearing black slacks, an off-white blouse, and her favorite heels. A large rectangular package was in her arms. She hugged it to her chest almost like a shield.

My stomach lurched as I put one hand on the nearest object—the wooden stair railing to the loft above. "You aren't welcome here, Victoria."

"I know that."

"Then why are you here?"

"Because I need to talk to you about what's going on between us."

I shook my head. "There's nothing between us, and I don't care what you need."

"You do care. You wrote."

"I wrote, and I made it clear in my note that I didn't want anything more to do with you. Ever."

"I read between the lines. The subtext. I read that you were uncertain, maybe even regretted what had happened the last time I was here. For both of us, for our peace of mind, we need to have this conversation. Calmly. Privately. To clear the air." She paused and added, "I wrote you back."

"I told you not to respond to my note."

"Did you get my letter? You did, didn't you? I

can tell by your face. But you didn't open it, did you?"

I ignored her question. "You came here last week."

She opened her mouth to speak, then closed it, placing her chin lightly on the top edge of the package she was clutching. "I came to face you, to have this conversation. I lost my nerve. I left."

"Yet here you are today." I tried to sneer as I spoke.

"I didn't cheat with Niles. You know that. I know you know, because if you believed I had, then you wouldn't have written to me at all."

My jaw ached. I wanted to reach up and massage the joint, but that would be a gesture of weakness.

She said, "I may not have handled the situation in the best way, but I truly was trying to get Niles to clean up his act and talk to you honestly. I was trying to play along and cajole him. You know how he could be. He never took criticism or instruction well. But my intentions were good."

"Go away, Victoria."

She crossed her arms. "I know that you don't want to hear this. It's easier, more comfortable, for you to believe that I'm the villain and that you were wronged. But when it came to you and Niles, I was trying to be a friend to both of you."

I shook my head and looked away. I stalked past, moving quickly out of the carriage house and toward the terrace and back porch. I was too close to losing my temper.

She was right on my heels. "Wait, Kara. Please. Talk to me."

My arms were as tightly crossed as they could be and still allow me to breathe.

"Get away from me." My voice was low and harsh, and I turned my back to her again. I'd reached the terrace. Not much farther to the house.

"Please, Kara. They fired me."

That stopped me. I refused to look back at her. "None of my business. Not my concern."

"Well, it wasn't exactly a firing, but it was the same thing. You know how it goes. The layoff with a severance? Not a great severance, but something. I gave up my apartment in Northern Virginia, and I'm moving back to Richmond."

I threw back my head and laughed. An ugly laugh. Where had I learned it? No idea. But the sneer was real this time as I turned back toward her.

"Nowhere to go? Oh, but Kara is so stupid and naive, right? You thought you could make up with me. Did you think you could weasel your way back into my home? You were a guest before, but you'll never be a guest here again."

"No," she protested. "I don't want to come back here. Well, I would, but only if you wanted me to. And I couldn't stay long even then because I have to find a job, and there's nothing out here in the country, as you know."

Oblivious. Sheer self-centered, oblivious arrogance. There were no other words that could come close to describing Victoria. And yet we'd been friends, once upon a time.

"I'm sorry you lost your job. Maybe you should've tried harder. I recall you lied to your boss to get out of work more than once."

"Ouch. That was to attend your dinner party right after you and your dad moved in here. To be here to support you." She shook her head. "And again when he died. To be here to help." She squeezed her eyes closed. When she opened them, she tried again. "You're still angry. I understand. You want to hurt me because of that. Go ahead. I goofed big-time, and I'll accept whatever fault you need me to." She held out her arms and extended the package toward me. "I brought a gift. Call it a housewarming gift, an apology, or a peace offering."

With the unfortunate timing that could only be achieved by sheer bad luck and perfect innocence, Will entered the electric, rarefied space between Victoria and me. I saw his face change as the charged air hit his flesh. His shoulders went back. His hands were suddenly open and ready. Whatever he'd intended to say was forgotten.

"Is something wrong?" He looked at me when he asked it.

I forced my aggression down, mentally pushing it away. This ugliness didn't need to be on display for others. Not to anyone except Victoria. And she'd soon be gone.

"Not a problem. We're good."

Victoria interjected, "Are we? I don't think so." But she kept her voice soft.

Again, I saw Will react. He was picking up on more than could be seen and heard. "Are you sure?"

I nodded and forced a small smile. The smile felt false, but it was all I could manage. "We're fine."

"Okay, then." He looked doubtful. "Call out if you need me. I'll stay nearby."

Victoria looked astonished as Will left us. She said, "Unbelievable. Doesn't he know that you're the dangerous one?"

"Dangerous? I've never touched a hair on anyone's head in anger. I don't even like to squash insects."

"There's a lot more to dealing out pain than fists, Kara. People admire you. They see you as a role model. But when they fail—fall short—one look from you, and . . . they know they're done, banished from your life forever."

"I'm not the one who caused the problem, Victoria. That's all on you. On you and Niles, too, maybe. But not me. Don't try to shift the blame. I refuse it." I crossed the terrace and climbed the steps to the porch. Without pausing,

I went straight inside the house, closed the door, and locked it.

Taking a quick second to stop and breathe, I then went to the kitchen window. Victoria was standing out in the yard and staring up at the house. She looked . . .

I tried to pin the word down. Sad? Annoyed? Arrogant?

Not my problem. I just wanted her to look *gone*.

Over the next couple of hours, I peeked out the windows, but casually, so Chip wouldn't wonder. He was a quiet, pleasant young man who focused on his work and showed no curiosity. I was glad the confrontation had happened in the backyard. Chip wasn't even aware of it.

When I was finally convinced she'd left, I began to relax. I was shaky, though. Too much adrenaline. I didn't feel good about what had happened, but I was pleased I'd controlled myself. I'd held my ground.

I wished I'd seen her drive away so I'd know for sure.

Will's truck and a car were still parked out front. There'd been two cars, aside from mine, out there earlier. One now. Lon was still here, so the car was probably his. Neither of the cars had looked remotely like Victoria's, but one was gone, so Victoria must be too.

As I pulled my hand away from the window, I saw it was still shaking. Surprised, I tucked my hand under my arm and hugged myself. My phone rang. It drew me away from the window. I was grateful for the distraction.

Nicole said, "I want you to meet some people."

"Who?" But I already knew. "You're talking about those craftspeople and such?"

"Are you okay?"

"Of course. Why do you ask?"

"Your voice sounds odd. A little . . . I don't know. Just odd. Strained."

"I'm fine."

"Good to hear."

"The more I learn, the more I realize how much I don't know."

"Then let's work on that." She hung up.

She hadn't said when. Maybe that was just as well given my present mood.

Will came to the door a short time later and knocked. "Is everything okay?"

He meant Victoria and the scene he'd walked into. I knew that.

"Yes, everything's fine." I smiled to show it was nothing. I shifted the focus by changing the subject. "It's looking good outside. I'm thinking I might want a picnic area. You know, like with a table and a grill, over there under those pines near the parking area."

"Excellent idea and easy to do. But I was

talking about your visitor today. I wouldn't have told her where you were if I'd known there was a problem."

"I thought she'd come around to the back on her own."

"She was on the porch. She asked if you were home. Sorry if I put you in an awkward or unpleasant situation."

"No, Will. You did right. She and I . . . we're old friends, but we had a falling-out a while ago. You couldn't possibly know that."

Relief relaxed his expression. "Yeah, that happens. Friends fall out and make up and all that."

I shook my head, but kindly. "I don't think we'll ever make up. I'm sorry you were caught in the middle, even a little bit."

Will smiled. It lit up his face. "Well, if you're okay, then I'll head off. Lon too. We'll see you in the morning."

"See you then." I smiled, waved, and closed the door gently, then leaned against it, feeling drained.

After they left, the only car in the driveway was my own.

I faced the empty house. Sometimes it felt open and full of potential. A house of dreams. At other times it felt claustrophobic—full, but full of emptiness crowding out the good stuff. The house didn't change. It was me. I was the variable in the equation. And right at the moment I was emotionally exhausted.

• • •

I prepared a simple supper, and after eating I went out to the front porch and saw a car had returned.

Will had said they were leaving. And the vehicles had all left.

Uneasiness rolled over me. My stomach clenched, and my supper, though light, felt like a brick.

I was overreacting. *Get a grip, Kara,* I told myself. *You're overthinking this.*

Seconds passed. Then a minute, and then two. During the time I'd been standing out here, I hadn't heard a breath or a step except my own. There was plenty of light left in this summer day. It was possible that one of Will's guys had returned to finish a task or two.

I walked softly along the porch, scanning the grounds. No one. Nothing.

Coward, I called myself. *Chicken. You know what this is about. Victoria.*

I descended the porch steps and went to the car. I looked in through the side windows. It was older but very clean. It was empty except for a duffel-type bag on the back floorboard and a coffee cup in the cup holder between the front seats.

The birds were surely singing, and the squirrels must have been scampering through the tree boughs, but I heard none of that. I was focused solely on where Victoria might be hiding.

Hiding? No, not hiding but lying in wait. She was like those annoying little dogs that set their teeth into your pants leg or your ankle—not big enough to do real damage but beyond tenacious and annoying and given to causing pain.

She must be in the carriage house or down by the creek. I paused in front of the open carriage house doors and found her.

"Have you been here all afternoon?"

Victoria shook her head no. "I left. Before I reached the interstate, I turned back. Stopped in Mineral for lunch and then did some sightseeing. It's a nice town." She shrugged. "I decided it would be better to wait until everyone else was gone for the day before trying to talk to you again."

When I didn't answer, she added, "It's all looking really good around here. Much better than when I was here last. It seems a lot different, too, with Mr. Lange . . . not here."

"I don't know what your game is, Victoria. But this time when you leave, don't come back."

Victoria looked down at the package she was holding, the same one she'd had earlier. She stripped the wrapping from it and held it out toward me. It was a huge book. I could read the title from where I stood: *Wildflowers of America.* It was a coffee-table book, a picture book of glamour shots of flowers. Victoria was gripping it almost like a weapon, which it kind of was, because as she walked toward me holding the book up, she wielded it against me, but with words, not physical force.

She said, "You claimed you knew the names of the wildflowers. Do you remember?"

I stared at her. Had Victoria lost her mind?

"When I came here to visit the first time—before your father died," she prompted. "You said you were learning the flower names?"

I shrugged.

"But you didn't, did you? You didn't even try to identify them and learn about them, though you claimed to admire them so much."

"I already knew a lot of the names. Remember my needlework?"

"There were more types of flowers out in the yard than you ever stitched. When I asked you about it that day, you lied. You weren't even trying to learn them."

"It was none of your business. Still isn't."

"*I* learned their names." She held up the book. "See? And I was going to show you which flower was which so you could replant."

I waved my hands at her and half laughed in disdain. "Are you insane?"

Victoria ignored my attitude and answered only the actual words. "No, I'm not insane, but I'm smart, and I know you well. You loved those flowers for their beauty, but you would never have bothered to find out about them—about them as individual flowers. Pretty flowers. They made you feel good and had a nice story to go along with them. But what about them? The flowers?"

Despite myself, I asked, "What about them?"

"They have identities too. Some need more sun. Some require more water. You wanted to compartmentalize them like you do people."

"You *are* insane."

She pulled the book to her chest and hugged it. "I was never more than that to you. A fill-in-the-blank friend. Just an anonymous living thing, someone you didn't need to trouble yourself with overmuch. Being friends meant something different to me than it did to you. I was always more your friend than you were mine, and that's the truth. So here's your book." She held it toward me again.

I kept my arms crossed.

"Take it."

I stayed as I was, trying hard to keep my anger within my control. She'd give up. She'd go away.

"Take it, darn it. Take the book. I bought it for you. It's yours. I have no use for it."

I refused to be drawn into her madness. I tried to think of the cruelest thing I could say—something calculated to shut her up and force her to leave. "The wildflowers are gone. You should be gone too. Go find your own life instead of trying to live mine."

She gasped, but more in amazement than in

hurt. She said, "Are you kidding me? I have more life in me than you'll ever dream of." She shook her hand at me, but with her pinkie finger raised. "More in my little finger! And do you know why? Do you have any clue?" She slashed the air between us with a rough movement of her hand. "No, you don't, because you wear so much protective gear that sometimes you're barely sentient."

"Barely sentient? Really? Frankly, I'm surprised you know the word and how to use it in a sentence."

"I—I . . ." She fisted her hand. "People think I'm arrogant and unempathetic. They think I'm like that bull in the china shop, but I'm not. I'm a force of nature. That's what I am. I forge my way through life, and sometimes it's clumsy, and I make mistakes . . . but you? You are so afraid of moving forward that you're almost paralyzed."

She glared at me but rushed onward without waiting for a response. "Even now, I want to talk about this, and you're so desperate to stop me that you will do or say almost anything to make me shut up, give up, and go away."

"Talk about it? Fine. Why don't you talk about my husband's arm around you and your arm around him and how you both had those drunk-happy goofy smiles on your faces?"

Her voice dropped low. "You mean those pictures in my phone?"

"Of course."

"I already explained about those, Kara. Niles and I were just laughing. No more than that. Please. I was telling him to talk to you about the problems in your marriage. To talk to you and be honest. We were drinking. Not hard liquor, but we were a little tipsy. Stupid, maybe, but I was trying to be the best friend I could to both of you."

"And that didn't involve telling *me* that Niles was cheating with one or maybe more women? Even aside from the dishonesty—the treachery— what diseases might he have brought home to me? What about his partners? Did they know he was married and that I was in the dark? Did you know I—" I broke it off there. I'd said enough. I couldn't say the next words. She didn't need to know about the miscarriage.

I closed my eyes and tried to count to ten, to control my breathing, but before I could, more words burst out. "I lost more than love and trust. I had dreams for our marriage, for our future— of us together. Our future. Our family. When you found out what he was doing, instead of telling me, you went to him. Did you truly believe he'd come to me and confess all? That I'd forgive him and we'd move forward? Ha. Not likely. No, you went to *him*. And you can tell me from morning to night—you can assert it until you are breathless and die of suffocation—that you weren't thinking, hoping, he'd turn to you, and I won't believe you. I suppose I can give you credit that you didn't cheat with him, but you did cheat on our friendship in ways that are unacceptable to me. You're right: I don't give a damn about you. When I look at you, all I see is my lie of a marriage, the death of my hopes and dreams. I see lies, Victoria. You. You are the living embodiment of the lies that killed Niles, nearly killed me, and stole my hopes and dreams."

I turned away and ran to the house. I'd exposed myself—and unnecessarily. I'd abraded my emotional wounds, so recently healed, but the flesh was tender, and now it was burning and screaming again. My head pounded, and lights were flashing in the backs of my eyes. I'd thought all that leftover crap, the physical manifestations from the accident, were gone—what I'd called the light-and-sound show. The accident that had taken Niles's life and nearly my own had left those artifacts behind in place of my lost child. It all flooded back now. Summoned by Victoria's reckless self-centeredness.

I headed straight up to my room. The early-evening light, still strong, streamed in. I flinched. The light hurt my eyes. Sharp pains shot through my brain. I rushed to the nightstand. This time it wasn't about being alone or needing to sleep. This was flooding, overwhelming pain. I opened the drawer and grabbed a pill bottle. Twisting the cap off, I spilled the pills onto my palm and grabbed one of the white ones—the strongest ones. I tossed it into my mouth knowing I couldn't dry swallow it, and I headed for the bathroom, drinking water straight from the faucet, choking and coughing when the powder still clung to the back of my tongue. I drank some more.

Did I think I could outrun it? The headache? The past? Mistakes? It didn't work. The pain in my head grew worse. My thigh seized up, and even the long-healed injury to my arm chimed in.

I returned to the drawer. I knew better than to take a second pain pill, but desperate, I took it anyway, and then a blue one. Not much more than an over-the-counter sleeping pill, I told myself. It would add that little extra push to the white pills to get me past this.

Whatever that burst of frantic energy had been, possibly adrenaline, it was easing. My breathing had slowed, and my heart felt steadier. I stood at the top of the stairs, which looked hazy and seemed steeper than usual. I flexed my leg to ease my thigh—I needed to find my cane. Holding the rail, I limped carefully down the stairs.

The headache . . . the thigh . . . this was no more than a minor setback. A result of an emotional shock to my system that would soon pass.

Downstairs, especially here in the front of the house this late in the day, the light was dim. The wood floor, the wood paneling, it all seemed to ground me to my surroundings in a secure, reassuring way. In the cool dark of the sitting room, I stretched out on the sofa.

I tucked the throw pillow under my head, then pulled the sofa blanket down. I didn't need the blanket because the air was chilly but because I needed to hug it to me, to cover my face and curl my body around it. In that semidark cocoon, I heard a car engine rev and then the sound of tires against the dirt-and-gravel driveway and knew Victoria was gone.

Good riddance.

Keeping my eyes closed, I tried to empty my mind of noise and light and ugly words. I heard the smooth, even tones of Seth's voice telling me to make decisions only in the morning. After the morning, it was work, work, work, but no decisions. No questions. No doubts. I heard Will's voice asking me if he'd done wrong to help Victoria find me this afternoon . . . and talking about medallions and gardens.

Good thing Seth wasn't here. He would be very disappointed in how I was handling this. I didn't want to see Niles either—my cheating, now-dead husband. And I certainly didn't want to see Victoria.

I wanted to see my dad. No, he hadn't been perfect, but he would've helped me as he always had, to the best of his ability. Who could ask anyone for more than that?

• • •

In my half sleep, I felt the gentle pressure of hands on the blanket where it was stretched, entwined around my arm and over my head. Even in that half-dream state, I didn't believe they were real hands but rather more of a wished-for comfort. I was an adult, a grown woman. But still young. And my life was empty. Alone.

Empty. Alone. Those thoughts didn't even feel like my own. More like shared thoughts, shared experiences—like those hands—and as whispery as that sensation had been and as swift as their absence, those thoughts, too, felt like something left behind, perhaps in haste, and abandoned.

I tugged the blanket down, freeing my face and arms. There was no sense of anyone else here. Just me. I rolled over and pushed myself upright, scouring my face roughly with my hands. It felt a little numb. Definitely cotton mouth. A small wave of nausea rushed through me. A medication hangover. The headache was mostly gone. But I was utterly embarrassed by my weakness and my fear.

It was pitch dark. What time was it? How long had it been since I'd shrieked at Victoria and fled into the house?

Because yes, in all honesty, I had shrieked and fled. Victoria had been right—I would've done almost anything to make her go away, to avoid reliving bad memories over and over. I greatly resented that she'd made me say those hard words and hadn't left on her own. If she had, we could each have moved on with a little dignity.

I stood too quickly, and the world flipped; I fell, hitting the wood floor hard. After a long moment of rolling nausea and shock at my legs failing me, I pushed myself upright, keeping my hands flat against the floor.

More of those pills, and I might've had a bigger problem. Overdose seemed too strong a word, and yet here I was . . . sitting on the floor where I'd fallen and trying not to puke. A new low. How proud my father would be. How lucky I was not to have a witness.

I tried to orient myself amid the ladders and tools. They looked foreboding in the dark, almost like they had secret identities I wasn't supposed to see. The light around me was weak, but enough starlight filtered in to show me the general outlines of the chairs and other furniture. The floor was hard and cold. Dad and I were supposed to have shopped for rugs together. He'd written it on his list, and then he'd put it in his pocket along with a stubby little pencil that looked like it had come from a golf course.

I rubbed my eyes. This time I stood slowly and carefully, testing my legs. I was okay. I steadied myself against a wall. A dull headache and a touchy stomach remained. There was no clock here in the sitting room, and I'd left my phone somewhere. I was hopeless about keeping track of it. Maybe it was a subconscious desire *not* to be in touch or accessible to the outside world. I'd intended that thought as a silent jest but shivered, suspecting it was truer than not.

Was it the middle of the night? Early middle or late middle? Bracing myself with a hand against the wall, I trudged along the hallway to the kitchen. I pulled the fruit water from the fridge. I didn't need a glass. I stood there and drank it straight from the jug. It dripped down my chin and onto my shirt.

Not like me, I kept thinking. And then I'd think, *Just like me.* This was me in the middle of the night in a vast, empty house after yet another angry encounter with my one and only old friend. *Former friend.*

I'd been willing to do or say whatever it took to make her leave me alone. And I'd run to that drawer and those pill bottles. So willingly. Maybe even eagerly.

The nausea rolled through me again.

I slid down. The back of my shirt snagged against the rough doors of the lower cabinets. I continued holding the pitcher and didn't spill it, but it was a wonder. I felt as boneless as a puddle. Was this my lowest point? Could I go lower?

Probably. I didn't want to find out.

I pushed my hair out of my face and wiped my wet chin against my forearm.

Self-pity? Guilt?

How much of what Victoria had said was true? Some of it. Did that mean I was in the wrong? I asked myself, Did it matter?

Dangerous, she'd said. But if people saw something in me that wasn't there—something that gave me a . . . a presence that they misunderstood—then that was on them. Not me.

Not my responsibility.

I rubbed my eyes. I wanted to sob. I wanted the pain, the hurt, to build to the point where I could release that pressure, but it wouldn't happen. My crying time was past. Assigning fault was a fool's game. I had to find a way to move on, but Victoria . . . she wouldn't let go. Right and wrong and common sense didn't seem to play much of a part in it.

She'd said she wanted to apologize, and she'd waved that stupid book at me. I understood she wanted forgiveness. She didn't need forgiveness from me or anyone. Forgiveness was meaningless. You still had to live your life one way or the other.

Stuff happened, and you just had to find a way to move on. Right?

Seth had said to make decisions only in the morning. Before or after that—ignore them. I repeated that concept like a lifeline and gave myself permission to put any questions or introspections aside until true morning arrived. I was done in.

The clock over the stove said morning would be arriving in a few short hours. It was after three a.m., and Moore Blackwell was going to be here around eight.

I groaned. Why was it that some people attached a weird sort of virtue to beginning their day so soon after dawn? Barbaric practice.

The fruit water was working its hydrating magic. I felt it reaching my brain and the cells throughout my body and drank more. At first the nausea increased, but then it rapidly subsided. After a few minutes my mouth and throat felt more acceptable. I made it to my knees and then to my feet. I left the water jug on the counter.

My phone was on the top of the piano. I set the alarm then and there. In the morning, other than by the purplish circles under my eyes, no one would know how truly dark my night had been—unless I overslept and the wallpaper crew couldn't get in or the kitchen renovator was locked out. Will might even have a question about the work outside. Three hours or so of civilized sleep in my bed instead of crumpled up on the sofa wasn't much, but it would have to do.

As I turned toward the foyer and the stairs, I heard a tiny squeak from outside. It sounded suspiciously like the bench.

I stood in the dark and listened. Hearing nothing more, I walked softly to a window facing the porch. The night outside was well lit by moonlight and starlight. I stared out and saw a large shape move on the bench.

A bulky figure. But so like a dark shadow that I wouldn't have been able to distinguish it if the figure hadn't moved.

Victoria. She'd never left.

I wanted to pretend I hadn't seen her. I was too tired. I needed to go upstairs and get some sleep. Ignore her. Take care of myself. I could deal with her later.

I flipped on the porch light, opened the front door, and stepped out.

Victoria had squeezed herself into a cramped sleeping position on the bench. Various clothing items were half-pulled across her, and a mostly empty duffel bag was abandoned on the porch floor. After a quick scan of the scene, I shook the bench. Hard. Victoria stirred, and the clothing covering her shuddered and slid. She rose up on her elbow. Her dark hair was in tangles. The yellowish glow from the porch light gave her flesh a sickly cast.

"What?" she said, startled and pushing the hair from her face. "Oh. You." She pushed herself the rest of the way upright with a loud groan. "Don't yell," she said. "I have a headache. And a neck ache. And an everything ache. I also have a broken car."

I tried to process her last words. "Broken?"

She was sitting upright now. She rubbed her

hands over her face. "I was leaving yesterday after . . . after our talk, and the car stopped halfway up your driveway. I called a repair shop, but no one could come check it out until today. I walked back here thinking to ask for help, but you never came outside, and frankly I didn't have the nerve to knock on the door." She dropped her hands and fixed her stare on me. "I sat here to wait."

"On my bench."

"Where else? Nothing is within walking distance around here."

I gave a long, disgusted look at the clothing that was now spread from her to the bench and the floor.

"It wasn't cold," she said, "but I had no protection from the gnats and moths and mosquitoes and other things I don't want to think about. I was their banquet. So I pulled all this stuff out to cover myself with."

I knew what I must say but couldn't speak the words aloud. They lodged in my throat. Instead, I went to the door, held it open, and gestured silently and begrudgingly toward it.

"Seriously? Do you mean it?"

She waited only a second before apparently deciding that my wordless response equaled assent. She grabbed up the clothing, snagged the duffel bag, and hastened inside. She paused at the foot of the foyer stairs and looked at me.

"You know the way." I hoped my face expressed the distaste that I might not have conveyed strongly enough in my tone.

She looked away but climbed the steps. She did know the way. Apparently she even knew the way to get invited into the house.

Not fair, Kara.

Had her car really broken down? Would she have slept on the hard, cramped bench if she'd had a choice? Why not sleep in her car?

Because I wouldn't find her there and feel pity . . .

I might be foolish, but I wasn't stupid. Not generally.

She could leave in the morning—either in her repaired car or by begging her mother or brother for a ride. In the meantime, however stubborn I could be, this was the middle of the night, and I was too exhausted to fight.

Chapter Fourteen

Things did look better come morning. I was up early enough—just barely—to grab a shower and dress before any of the workers arrived. I would waste no time fretting over Victoria. There was no need for me to even speak to her. She'd be gone as soon as her car was moving—whether under its own power or being towed.

I'd done the decent thing. I'd helped her without having to forgive her or even be kind. Just the basic courtesy of helping someone in need. She might have been a stranger. And that was how I chose to think of it.

Despite the awful night and some lingering ill effects—a slight headache and a touchy stomach—my heart was lighter. It made no sense, but I went downstairs feeling pretty good about things.

And found the front door already wide open.

The floors had long been covered with tarps and paper, and the scaffolding felt almost like a house fixture. I didn't recognize the young man carrying a ladder inside. He smiled cheerfully, deposited the ladder, and waved before ducking back out. I thought he must be working for Moore.

Looking at the gear, hearing men's voices outside, I stood on the last stairstep, assessing.

No one had been able to get inside before without me unlocking the door and inviting them.

And then it hit me—Victoria. She'd let them in.

Victoria was surely already up and out—probably at her car with, or waiting for, a mechanic. I walked down the hallway toward the kitchen. I needed coffee. I caught the aroma of it wafting past me on its way out the open door.

It was already brewing. It smelled wonderful.

Victoria again.

I was pouring myself a cup when Moore Blackwell joined me.

"Coffee?" I offered.

"No, ma'am. Swore off it a couple of years ago. The caffeine amps me up too much, and I don't see the point in the decaffeinated brew. Gave it up when I gave up smoking."

"Really? That must have been a difficult time."

"Expect it was. Perhaps more for my wife than it was for me." He gave a short sandpaper-sounding laugh. "When it's convenient, let's take a walk and talk about where we're at with the wallpaper?"

"Now is fine."

"Are you doing well?"

I frowned, and then it cleared. "You mean about my father?"

"Yes, ma'am. I know the loss isn't as fresh as it was, but I don't want to be tripping any live wires, if you know what I mean."

"No worries."

"Glad to hear it. If you need to avoid certain topics or whatever, just give me a wink, and I'll veer off."

My lips twitched. A wink? I wouldn't laugh, though the image of me winking at this tall wrinkled man with his gravel voice to warn him away from sensitive subjects just about tickled me into fits of laughter. How long had it been since I'd had a good laugh?

The unexpected. The ironic. I'd always had a taste for it. I'd be able to laugh at myself, too, once I got back into control of my life.

Moore said, "Dining room is done. Chip is about done with the parlor paper. He'll float plaster over what can't come down without damage. You'll never know the difference." He pointed at the sitting room. "We're about to start in there. Unless you've changed your mind about it."

"Take it down."

"Those vignette scenes are nice. If I can save some larger pieces of it, might you want to use those in some way? Maybe frame them or such?"

"I love that idea, Moore. Anything else, I'll be working in that room for a while. Just yell."

I shut myself into the middle room. I felt safe here. Safe from what? From emotional upheaval and fights and whatever else might come at me. The morning was half-gone before I wondered again about Victoria. I got up to stretch my legs and walked out onto the front porch.

The morning air was still fresh, but it would be a hot day. My car was parked over to the side. Mr. Blackwell's van was parked nearby, along with a truck. Likely his assistant's vehicle. No Mitchell Landscaping vehicles. No Will.

What of Victoria? She wasn't around. Nor was her car. I presumed she'd gotten it fixed somehow, or it was somewhere up the drive, disabled. Should I check? In fact, had I picked up the mail yesterday? I didn't remember doing so. I could take a walk and check the box. And maybe find out what else was going on.

I slipped on my shoes and set out.

Her car was up around the curve, pulled off to the side on a slightly wider stretch of the drive, far enough over that the other vehicles had been able to get past without incident. Victoria was leaning against the side of the car, her back to me, and talking to someone who evidently belonged to the work truck that was pulled up close to hers—almost nose to nose. That person was hidden by the raised hood.

I recognized the truck—Will's—as Victoria laughed.

Darkness stirred in me, an upwelling of raw emotion, even bigger than the anger and resentment I'd felt before. Like an ancient tide it came, with frustration, resentment, anger, jealousy, and dark impulses rolling up before it. I didn't recognize these feelings. I didn't *want* to recognize the ugliness hiding in that morass of emotion. Shaking seized me, and I felt powerless to stop what was about to happen.

Chance in the form of Mel saved me from awfulness I could never have taken back. Mel drove toward us, slowing as she reached Will's truck and Victoria's car.

The shaking grabbed me again and ran the length of my body. I pressed my eyes tightly closed as I breathed in deeply. I discovered I did have control, after all. It had been me, all of it—the darkness, the anger. All parts of me. My knees felt weak, and I crossed my arms tightly.

Was I jealous of Victoria interacting with Will? Probably flirting with him? Not that alone. There was a history of things she'd done.

A tiny voice in my head whispered that my logic was flawed.

"Kara?" Mel called out. "Can you come over here?"

I walked. An ordinary response to Mel's request, but it felt unreal laid over the top of what was still stirring inside.

Will caught sight of me and waved in my direction. His smile was bright and open. Victoria half turned and saw me. For a brief moment I thought a smile was about to appear on her face, too, but as I passed her, her expression changed, and she backed away. I kept moving.

When I reached Mel, she put her hands on

my arms. "You okay? You're white as a sheet."

"Am I?"

"I brought this for you." She handed me a covered casserole dish. "If you aren't going to eat it right away, go ahead and freeze it."

"Yes, ma'am."

"What? You aren't going to argue?"

"Not today. Thanks, Mel."

Will walked away from the car, leaving Victoria standing there. He asked, "Are you okay? You're pale."

I forced a smile. "I didn't sleep well last night." I nodded toward Victoria and the car. "She has a problem."

He nodded. "Maybe we'll get lucky and I can fix it here and now."

"Maybe so."

Mel said, "Get in the car. I'll give you a ride home." She kept hold of my arm until I was securely in the passenger seat. I was still holding the casserole. As she settled behind the steering wheel, she said, "You want to tell me about it? What's wrong?"

"No. Nothing, I mean."

I felt passive. Maybe in shock. I was afraid that if I put a foot wrong, that dark ugliness would swamp me again. Would overwhelm me. I hadn't thought I was capable of so much . . . hate.

And that wasn't Victoria's fault.

So much of it . . . I must've spent a lifetime

accumulating it, tucking it safely away. Thinking that was good enough.

At the house Mel got out of the car with me. She took my arm again as we walked up to the porch. "You gonna be all right?"

"I'm fine, really." I gave her a polite smile.

She squinted at my face. "I don't think so. Maybe go lie down for a while? I can stay, if you need me."

"That you, Mel?" Moore Blackwell called out as we walked inside.

"It's me, Moore. How're you and Sheryl doing?"

I took that opportunity to get away. I said, "Bye, Mel. And thanks." With a quick reassuring smile, I gave her a hug and disappeared down the hallway with the casserole. I closed the door to the kitchen, put the casserole on the table, and sat.

Maybe thirty minutes later, Victoria walked into the kitchen. I'd spent the time trying to recover my calm, to know that I was in control of my life and no one else.

I was also responsible for my life. In charge, as Seth might say. I couldn't blame anyone else for what happened in it.

As pleasantly as I could, I said, "You didn't need to come back to the house." My voice sounded wooden.

Her smile faltered, as did her voice. "I wanted

to thank you for your hospitality and give you an update on the car."

I stared at her. "Okay."

"Will's a really nice guy, isn't he? He tried but couldn't figure out what was wrong. Maybe the alternator. At any rate, he has a friend with a tow truck, and he's getting him to tow my car into his service station."

"Okay."

She cleared her throat. "I'll catch a ride with the tow guy when he arrives. I'll get out of your way."

"Okay." But this time, the repetition of my stoic *okay* grated. I added, "That's good."

She nodded and tucked her curls back behind one ear. "When I lost my job, I traded my other car in for this one." She shrugged. "Smaller payment and cheaper upkeep, presumably, yet it's already broken down and needing repairs. Hope they're not expensive." She flashed a nervous smile again. But she lingered.

What more was she expecting or hoping for? I kept silent.

Finally, she said, "I'll wait on the porch."

I looked away. Victoria walked back to the front of the house.

A few minutes later, the kitchen guy arrived. Victoria must've let him in, because I looked up from where I sat at the kitchen table, and there he was, carrying some odd pieces of cabinetry that hadn't arrived with the rest. He said I could stay and wouldn't be in the way, but I was still in that state. That nothing state. I excused myself and went out to the terrace and planted myself there instead. I felt like a hostage. I was also the jailer. If I had the key to escaping this nothingness, apparently I'd lost it.

Will came around the corner of the house and stopped when he saw me there. He came over. "Sorry for the delay."

I crossed my arms. "No worries. You were doing a good deed."

"Still angry with her?" He raised a hand. "Sorry, not my business."

"No, it isn't." I looked away, shaking my head. "I apologize. I'm in a mood this morning. Might be coming down with something."

"I hope not. Do you need anything?"

"No, I'm sure it will pass."

"I wanted to let you know that I wasn't able to help her much. Unless my cousin Mack can figure out the problem on the scene, and I doubt it since I couldn't, then"—he shrugged—"it looks like a tow-and-repair job." He nodded. "But he'll do right by her. He should be here anytime now."

"Good." I added, "That's excellent news."

He gestured toward the creek and the woods. "Lon and Derek have been working on the creek path." He gestured to his right. "Instructions were to trim back growth and try to smooth out the path where possible without losing the natural look. Take a look when you have time and let me know if we succeeded."

"Sounds good." In fact, I loved the idea, and I was sure I'd feel excited about it again eventually. When this empty feeling passed. Talking to Will . . . his steadiness . . . his manner was calming. I wanted to prolong the encounter. "Maybe we should add a bench along the way, just in case someone wants to rest or pause for a while to listen to the birds?"

Will grinned. "Wooden and rustic?"

"Exactly."

"Your color's a little better now. Can I get you something? Maybe something to drink?"

"Thanks, no. I'm feeling better."

He turned to leave.

"Will?"

"Yes?"

There was an expectant look on his face. Again, I was struck by the change to his appearance. It made me doubt my memory of him from the day we'd met. Maybe I hadn't been paying adequate attention.

"Thank you for helping Victoria," I said.

"No problem." He turned away, and this time I let him leave.

It would be strange not to have Will around, but that day would come. I'd miss his . . . handiness. Dad had been excellent in business but hadn't been handy. Niles certainly hadn't been. But Will was, and he was pleasant to have around too. I felt selfish. He'd had a life before me and Wildflower House. His sister, for instance. He'd mentioned his mother and a grandmother too. Maybe . . . a wife? No, somehow I knew there was no wife, but shame on me for not asking him about his life.

At some point the work here would run out . . . but not yet. And he'd started planning out the new wildflower plot. I thought of it as a memorial. A private memorial that would mark events and feelings in my life that most would never be aware of. Will had called it a medallion. I liked the sound of that.

"Kara?"

With a jolt I turned to face Victoria. Her duffel bag was at her feet.

I asked, "Did the tow truck arrive?"

With a tiny hitch in her breath, she said, "It did. He came. He towed." She shook her head and spread her arms. "I'm sorry. I intended to leave with the tow truck, but he had a helper with him. No space for me. He's towing the car to his brother's garage, and they'll let me know what's wrong. Fingers crossed, it's a cheap, easy fix."

She shrugged and paused, perhaps hoping for signs of a thaw from me. I couldn't give them to her.

"So anyway, the repair guy will call me with the

news one way or the other. I'm going to call my mom and see if she can drive out here and fetch me." She paused for breath. "I apologize that I'm still here. I'm trying to work this out. The thing is I don't know how I'll be able to prevent her from wanting, expecting, to say hello to you. She doesn't know about our . . . difficulties. I can tell her you aren't home. That should work if you'll stay out of sight when she arrives."

Stay out of sight? Hide from her mom? How ridiculous would I allow this to get?

"When do you expect the garage to call?"

"This afternoon, but I don't know for sure."

"Fine. If they haven't contacted you in a little while, give them a call for an update. You can call your mom then, if you need to."

"Well . . . but if the car is ready today—that's if I get super lucky—I'll need a ride over to the garage."

"Then go ahead and call her now, or maybe Will can take you." I turned away to hide my face.

I heard Victoria running up the steps to the porch and then the screen door shutting behind her. Not long after, the door opened again. Victoria.

"Mom is visiting her sister in Hampton." She breathed in and out sharply.

I looked away. I wouldn't offer. I'd already allowed her into my home. No more. "Then I guess you'll have to wait until you can get a ride with Will or one of the other landscapers into town, or maybe call a cab."

She looked stunned. I stood and walked away without another word.

What would my mother have said about my behavior?

Not a clue. She probably would've smiled blankly and patted my hand and gone back to staring at the window.

What would Dad have said?

He'd ask me why I was being such a jerk. But then he'd always liked Victoria. He'd say, *If you want Victoria gone, then why not expedite it? Give her a ride to wherever she needs to go.*

I'd already allowed her to stay, not only overnight but while she was waiting for the tow truck.

Yeah. I was quite the generous spirit, wasn't I?

I hadn't been able to confront Mom about her lack of mothering. With Dad I'd pushed about certain things but had never told him where he'd failed as a father. So why was I so determined to punish Victoria for relatively minor wrongs?

Did it matter that I was in the right? Sometimes you went overboard, so far beyond reason that it was hard to find the way back, at least the way back with dignity.

I was determined. I was in control. Most days. Today . . . maybe not so much.

My head ached again, and my thigh hurt. I reached the bench and the creek. My cane . . . where had I left it? Should I blame Victoria for the return of the pain? Was she responsible for everything that had gone wrong in my life in recent years? Where was my responsibility?

I stopped and pressed my hands to my temples. The ridge of scarred flesh was there. Another reminder of Niles and failure.

This was killing me. This iron control. This denial of expression.

And who was asking me to hide what I felt?

Only me.

I bumped into the bench and gripped the back tightly.

Victoria said softly, "Kara?"

"What? Are you following me?" The words burst from me. "Can't I have any peace from you?"

"Kara. Please listen to me. You're wearing me down. I'm close to giving up. That's your plan, right? Ignore me or insult me until I vanish?" She whispered, "I don't altogether blame you, but you are wrong. You *are* wrong."

I gripped the back of the bench so hard that I thought my bones might snap. I didn't speak.

"Tell me this," she said. "Let's keep it basic and simple. Do you believe I cheated with Niles?" She paused, then resumed. "Even if I considered it, at any time in my life, I never acted on it."

I controlled my expression, but I couldn't keep contempt from my voice. "Do you want a gold star?"

"You are angry at me because when I understood what he was doing, I went to him instead of coming to you. I didn't tell you right away, and you feel I betrayed our friendship. That I was disloyal."

"You did. You are."

"Maybe. I think we will have to disagree on that, but I concede that I should've told you when I found out. I shouldn't have waited, hoping that Niles would be honest with you himself."

"That last day, the day I told you to leave, you said it was my fault."

Victoria grimaced. "That was anger. I'm sorry for that too."

I opened my mouth to speak, and Victoria said, "Wait. Please. I want to say something else, and you might want to kick me out—again—when I'm done, but since you care about honesty . . . in a way, it *was* your fault."

I felt that red-hot anger rising, wanting to rush right up into my face and heat my cheeks.

"Because you are strong. A strong personality. Always contained and always in control, but fierce when crossed and sometimes scary. You know that old saying about keeping one's mouth shut and that everyone will think you're smart until you open it and prove otherwise?"

She shook her head and held up her hands. "Wait. That isn't what I'm saying. You're smart. Very. But it's that calm, stoic personality you project. It's a little scary at times but also attractive. It attracts people. They read into it what isn't there. Even I didn't understand that until I met your dad and got to know him a little. You are strong. You are in control. But not necessarily because that's how you are. Rather, it's how you had to be to keep your life together. People like Niles never understood that. He was attracted to you because you had what he lacked. Steadfastness. Courage. Focus. He didn't understand that a partnership like marriage required him to have strength too. He didn't get that he couldn't ride into his future using you as a crutch. Not that he thought he needed a crutch. But you know how he was. He got by on flash and charm. On personality. And maybe that's what attracted you to him."

She shrugged. "I'm sorry. It seemed clear in my head when I was thinking it through, but I'm saying it all wrong."

There was a very long pause. I held my thoughts, my own angry words, inside, where they churned and slashed within me. The air around us grew sour and bitter.

Victoria said, "So that's it? Is that all you've got for me? Fine. Let's just forget it." She crossed her arms. "I'm going to slip away and call the

repair guy and do some begging. Excuse me."
She left.

My lower lip trembled. I was glad I'd been able to hide the hurt, the pain, until she'd gone. What a mash-up that explanation had been. Nonsense. Except I did know what she meant. And she wasn't all wrong.

I needed air and movement to dispel the awful miasma Victoria and I had created around us. Will had said something about working on the path. I could check that out. Maybe Victoria would be gone, one way or the other, by the time I returned.

I fled, as I'd fled from her in that confrontation in the carriage house. Was I fleeing from Victoria or from this box I'd trapped myself in?

Victoria had said I would go to almost any length to not allow someone a second chance. A second chance was one more opportunity for hurt. Better to focus on other things. Inconsequential considerations. Decisions that didn't need to wait for morning light. The best kind.

Once in the woods, I paused to catch my breath and massaged my thigh. I would never be free of the past if I didn't find a way to let it all go. All of it. All the way back to my early memories, including my mom.

Toss out the old junk. Make new stuff. Cultivate the stuff I wanted in my life. Like adding that bench along the creek path. A small thing, but a nice touch. Forget the old painful stuff. Instead of walling it in, wall it out.

Much nicer to think about a new bench. Who could dispute the value of a convenient resting place along a forest path? Not me. Not the imminently reasonable, well-controlled Kara Lange Hart.

Kara, whose good opinion, once lost, could never be regained.

Pride and Prejudice, right? Hadn't Darcy said that?

Okay. Call me Darcy. I felt the smile trying to twitch up the corners of my lips.

Admit it, Kara. You've gotten so lost in ugly you've also lost sight of common sense and fair play. And forgiveness.

Was it as simple as that? Really?

Maybe. But it was risky. People hurt people.

I'd survived hurt thus far, hadn't I?

Mostly.

Maybe the biggest question wasn't about forgiveness itself but rather about who needed to forgive whom.

Overwhelmed again, I limped along to the sound of the creek and the birds and thought about the bench—much more pleasant to think about than other recent events.

The path followed along the creek for a long way before it diverged and turned inland toward the old Lange property where Dad grew up. I was pretty sure Will's crew would not have cleared the path that far. I wouldn't want them to. Dad had owned that property and had left it undisturbed for personal reasons—not all of which he was able to verbalize. Now I owned the property and had no idea what to do with it, but I didn't want it as part of the retreat. For the guests, it would be no more than a curiosity—a fallen-down house they had no understanding of, no respect for the personal history around it. I should clear the land, I thought. Clear it out and erase its past. Maybe salt the ground or something. Maybe pray over it, wishing peace to the memories made there and forgiveness for the mistakes of those who'd dwelled in that spot.

There was that annoying word again—*forgiveness*. I swatted it away like a gnat.

All of that flitted through my mind. I saw a few butterflies lighting on bushes along the side of the yard and dragonflies touching down on the surface of the creek, on the sides of the creek, and on a fallen, half-submerged branch. With the people gone, my walk was peaceful.

Along the path, I saw obvious cuts to greenery where branches and sticker bushes had been trimmed back and other improvements. The larger trees, the oaks, were farther back from the path, but their branches arched over, crowding much of the overhead view with only peeks of blue between the boughs. Near to the path and back with the oaks, the pines with thick trunks rose high. The heavy layers of bark were decorative.

Where the rocks nearly blocked the creek, I stopped to consider. There'd be space for a bench here if we cleared away some of the scrubbier brush. Perhaps room for even a discreet gnome or two?

This was the farthest I'd gone along the path before. And I'd never gone alone. I was pleasantly surprised by the feeling of peace and of quiet that wasn't silent. I heard a gobble in the woods. Maddie Lyn's turkeys? I'd always been a city girl. Turkeys, living and breathing and gobbling in my woods, instead of beheaded and frozen in the grocery store, seemed way too exotic.

Signs of path clearing ended abruptly. The path beyond, the woods ahead, had a different feel altogether.

Was it the quality of the light? The accident, now close to two years past, had left me with an extreme sensitivity to light; bright light, especially artificial light, could give me a vicious headache. Oncoming headlights in the night brought up the fear and horror of the accident. My response to light had been so much better since we'd moved out here, as if that wildflower field, bathed in light and color, had rewired my brain's perception of—perhaps fear of—bright light. I'd been overwhelmed, in a dazzled way, by the sunlight, the flowers, the colors, the reflections on the creek that first day. Strains of music had found their way out of my memory and had played in my mind as naturally as breathing. The experience had been euphoric, like standing in the midst of a colorful rhapsody—or maybe existing as part of lyrical color itself. As I stood here now, on this path, I remembered that first day, and I tried to hug the memory, the joy of it, to me, because I sensed that I must be near the Lange house now.

I thought of the day when Dad, only a kid himself, had come home and the twins hadn't been there. Laura and Lewis. Old Mr. Lange had refused to explain. Only said the little ones were gone and not coming back.

As bad as that was, my guess was that the worst part for my dad, a teenager at the time, had been the helplessness, the actual inability to force his father to acknowledge or explain. No power. No ability to force or punish. Dad had been an outsider in school and in the community. No wonder he'd left.

By the time he'd been an adult and had had some means of looking, he'd hit dead ends. And speaking of dead ends . . . I cringed, remembering how it had hurt him to tell me that he'd borrowed cadaver dogs to search the property, afraid that his father had gone too far and committed an unspeakable crime. He'd even hired a private detective, but no luck.

The old house must be near because the shadows hung more heavily. I heard no birds singing or squirrels in the boughs overhead.

I spied a path—or the hint of a long-ago path. I stepped over a downed tree, avoided getting my foot caught in a hole, and then ducked to pass under a low-hanging branch. I could see the debris from the house, maybe even a slice of roof through the greenery, and tried to move forward. Something tugged at my shirt. I turned in a rush, and it snagged my sleeve. It was a sticker bush, huge and grabbing at me. I felt a burning pain as a thorn penetrated the fabric and cut my flesh.

"Ouch," I said and struggled to escape until a voice behind me froze my movements.

"Stop. Hold still."

Chapter Fifteen

Arms wrapped around me—real arms. I knew instantly that they were friendly, and in the next heartbeat I knew they were Will's.

I tried to turn toward him. The thorns dug into my arm more deeply.

"Hold still, Kara. Let me untangle you." He proceeded to do exactly that, carefully disentangling the thin green branches with the big nasty thorns from my arm and my shirt.

"Ouch," I said again. "Sorry. Thanks for helping."

He shook his head and grinned. "I'd say *my pleasure,* but . . . ouch," he echoed. "That one got me." He held the longest branch aside, saying, "I think you're free now."

I stepped away from the bush. "I am. Thanks again. How'd you come to be here?"

"Pure chance. I came to check on the work and heard you yelping."

I frowned. "Yelping?" Didn't sound very dignified. More like a needy puppy.

"Calling for assistance, then?"

"Yes, that's better. Thank you for responding."

Will looked beyond me and then around us, curious. "We didn't plan on clearing the path this far out. Did you want us to? I'm not sure where your property line is out here."

"Not this far out, no. We're somewhere near the property line between Wildflower House and the old Lange property."

"That house I see back there? Is that where your dad grew up?"

I was surprised. "You know about that?"

He shrugged. "That day when your father was telling Jim Mitchell about the yardwork he wanted done, he mentioned growing up out here. Jim made some kind of connection between his last name and a Lange family that used to live out in this area."

"Seriously?"

"It wasn't a big thing. Just a short piece of a longer conversation, and then you came outside and joined us." He looked aside.

That quick look away reminded me of how Will had been around me early on. I didn't want to go back to that. I wanted to see his eyes and his smile. I said, "Thank you for telling me, Will. It's a complicated thing—my dad's early life."

He nodded in the direction of the collapsed house. "This place has a sad feel. Like a shadow over it. If he grew up here, then I don't wonder that he wanted to forget it."

Will Mercer. Hearing him, being so near to him, made me a little breathless.

"Will you walk me back to civilization? In case

I need to be rescued again?" I said it lightly. I wanted to keep this improved mood wrapped around me.

"Yes, ma'am, Kara." He grinned again.

"So," I asked, trying to sound casual, "are you familiar with the Lange family?"

"No, I'm not. But everyone around here—other than the newcomers—seems to be related to everyone else in one degree or other."

"Really?"

"Yes. That's a hazard, or blessing, of living in the country. Everyone knows everyone else's business, but likewise, they tend to keep it all between themselves. It's a great place for secrets."

I wanted to think about this. Maybe when everything settled down, when Victoria had finally moved on and the renovation was closer to being done, I'd ask around. But how would my dad have felt about me discussing his family business with strangers?

Will and I stopped to discuss the bench location, but otherwise our walk was mostly silent. When we reached my backyard, I thanked him again, but the heaviness in my heart seemed to have returned. I had to go back into my house whether Victoria was there or not.

As soon as I entered the house, she saw me. "There you are. I wondered where you'd gone. Kara, please wait." She followed me down the hallway. "I'm sorry," she said. "It's bad news."

I swung around. "What now?"

"My car. It needs a part. The service guy explained what was broken, but . . . well . . . I hate to say I don't understand cars and engines, but I don't. Whatever the thing is, he needs to order one. It will take a day to get to his garage. I need a place to stay tonight."

That feeling I'd shared with Will . . . I wanted it back. I couldn't continue to argue. No more for now. My unyielding stance seemed foolish anyway.

"Okay. Stay."

She rocked forward on her feet in a movement I interpreted as relief or even encouragement. I didn't want her to read too much into my concession. But I also was starting to feel like a bully, belaboring our differences when, in the end—after my pride and ego were out of the way—how much did they matter anyway? Would I show kindness to a stranger? I hoped so. Did I have to keep this going with Victoria? Being kind didn't mean that I forgot she'd made a grave error as my friend—or that I had to pretend I'd forgotten. Allowing her to stay another night didn't mean we would go back to our old relationship.

Victoria said, "Mind if I fix us a bite? I don't want to push you too far, but we both have to eat. I noticed there were a lot of frozen casseroles in the freezer."

"Sure. Okay."

"Do you have a preference which?"

I shrugged, a hard shrug that may have warned her I was struggling with this.

"Never mind. I'll choose. They all look good."

I walked out.

That feeling of unreality seized me. A shift. Like a shift in time, in thought. I'd felt it the day I'd walked around the side of the house and had seen the wildflowers. It had been a permanent shift, and I'd known, even if I hadn't acknowledged it in that moment. The same thing—that moment of shimmery reality change—had happened on the day Dad had died. No going back. I'd blamed the whims of fate. Why was I feeling it now?

I was in the middle room. The door was firmly shut, and I was staring at the framed photograph of the turn-of-the-century women posing on my porch.

Time. It recurred every second. On and on. And each new second was an opportunity to do life better. Or worse. Unless you were too busy mourning the past seconds to see the opportunity—or the danger.

There was a wall in my mind. A barrier. It kept me safe—the basic me—when life tried to throttle me. But sometimes it was hard to see around it. To see life on the other side.

I exited via the side door, the one that was next

to the servants' stairs, and walked along the path to the carriage house. I paused in its dim, cooler air, but it didn't speak to me. I wandered down toward the creek, keeping to the woods' edge and the shade. I slipped into one of the nooks that Mary Forster had created.

A short path led to a narrow bench. There was room for only one person to sit here. This nook was simple and solitary. An unsullied carpet of leaves from autumns past indicated that it was seldom, if ever, visited.

I emptied my mind. I needed to cool my brain. I needed to not care so much about things because that caring cast me into turmoil, and I kept losing my way forward.

Breathing deeply and slowly, I closed my eyes. I concentrated on the feel of my breath coming into my lungs and going out through my nostrils. Over and over. I kept the rhythm and focus going for as long as I could and then opened my eyes.

Everything looked the same—the same trees and low-hanging boughs, the green leaves thick and varied from the many different types of trees that grew in my woods. My woods. I didn't feel it as ownership but as more of a caretaking. The bark on the larger trees created an amazing texture. I'd noted that on the path earlier, especially regarding the pines. The oaks had a shallower, tighter bark, and . . .

I choked, then smiled. One of the oaks had a

nose . . . eyes with heavy brows . . . a smiling mouth. And nearby was another.

The features fit in so well it took me a moment to translate what I was seeing. It was one of those plastic sets that could be purchased anywhere and attached to trees. I'd always thought they ranked on the tacky meter near pink flamingos and garden gnomes—a tackiness level I admired and appreciated more each day.

Mary had left her mark on the grounds of Wildflower House. I'd been trying to leave a mark, too, but I felt surrounded now, invaded. Victoria. Seth, who wasn't here. Will, who was.

I made excuses for him, but I was disappointed in Seth. I would have liked to have a frank conversation with him, but I'd never learned how to criticize or complain in a positive way.

"Kara."

Victoria.

"How did you find me?"

"I called you from the back porch. You didn't respond, but I saw you go into the woods here." She went silent, then started again. "I wanted to tell you supper was ready." She rushed forward, gripped the armrest of the bench, and dropped to kneel on the ground. "I'm sorry," she said. "I never meant to hurt you. I know I did, and I wish you'd forgive me. I could promise never to mess up again, to be the perfect friend, but you know me—I *am* that bull in the china shop, and so often

I don't think things through. Forgive me, Kara. I won't be underfoot all the time—I promise—but I need you to forgive me so I can forgive myself."

Her entreaty hurt my heart. I wouldn't sob. I had no tears left after all those that I had shed for my father—and years before for my mother—and yet my face was wet. So was my shirt. The salt taste was on my lips. I stretched my sleeve to reach my eyes and mopped at them, at my cheeks.

"I'm sorry, Victoria—" I nearly choked saying the words, but I meant them. I did.

"No, you have every reason to be angry. I don't blame you, but I need to fix it somehow."

I shook my head. "No, I mean *I'm* sorry. I don't have the right to withhold forgiveness from you—to prevent you from being able to forgive yourself. That wasn't my intention . . . not on purpose, anyway."

"Oh, Kara. I know that. You had enough bad memories and didn't want to add more. Remember, I told you I know you. Maybe even better than you know yourself. But I don't want an apology from you; I need your forgiveness. That's all."

My shoulders slumped. I wanted to pull them back and sit up straighter . . . but I was unable. "I'm so tired of being angry."

"Then don't be." She laughed, and I was shocked. She said, "But you will because that's part of who you are. Learn to let it go. Vent when you need to. Neither of us is perfect, but we each have value. Even our imperfections have value."

I snorted. "I'll have to think about that one." I nodded. In a more serious, sincere tone, I said, "I believe you, Victoria. And I forgive you. I do. Truly."

After a long moment of silence, she said, "Thank you, Kara."

Her eyes lit up, and her expression brightened. Apparently restored to her usual energy level, Victoria said, "Supper is ready. It's getting cold."

"Heaven forbid," I said, cringing in mock horror.

She laughed and jumped to her feet. "It might take a couple of days for that car part to come in. Maybe it would be okay if I need to hang around here a little longer?"

I felt a frown—a wondering frown—forming on my face. Had I just been played? Then Victoria laughed again and blurted, "Who put a face on that tree? This place—your Wildflower House—is the most unexpected place. Like its own peculiar universe."

With a sigh, I said, "I'll join you at the house in a couple of minutes?"

"Oh. Sure. No worries. I'll put the lasagna back in the oven, but don't take too long because it will dry out. I made a green salad too. Your salad dressing was out of date, so I threw together an oil-and-vinegar dressing. Hope that was okay. See you shortly."

She left. I looked back at that face on the nearest tree. Was it laughing at me? I didn't think so, but I could almost believe that I saw it wink and grin.

Victoria had set the table. Mel's lasagna was hard to beat. The green salad was a nice touch.

I'd forgiven her. I felt it in my heart. But I didn't have much to say. It was that whole shift thing. I wasn't a flexible person. I'd had the same problem with my dad after we'd had a difference of opinion. I'd felt wordless for a while, but it would pass. At least I could look forward to a better relationship. Maybe not perfect, but a restoration of a level of friendship.

But Victoria wanted to chat. Maybe she didn't quite trust my forgiveness yet. She kept throwing out comments like a test and then checking my face.

"How nice of Mel to prepare all this food for you."

"Uh-huh," I said as I chewed.

"The freezer is stuffed. If it's all from her, it's a wonder she has any casserole or baking dishes left."

She couldn't know about the dishes Mel had already taken home, but I could see why Victoria would say that. I kept eating.

After a few more attempts at conversation,

Victoria lapsed into silence too. But the silence between us wasn't hostile; it was almost companionable.

After we'd cleaned the kitchen, I said, "I can't invite you to stay here indefinitely. You know that."

"I know. I couldn't stay anyway. I need a job. There isn't one out here that will pay me enough. I'll get an apartment near Mom. Something short term. But I'd like to help you. I promise I won't overwhelm. Maybe we never really knew each other before, Kara. Or maybe we did, and we're not those people now. We've changed."

"Do people change? Can they?"

"At least in terms of how we understand ourselves, others, and the world—yes. And really, what else is there?" She stared at me. "Please invite me back whenever—if you need help with a project or just to talk. You know we both enjoy that. Things change, but I don't think that ever will."

I smiled. "It's good to have you around again, Victoria." I pushed the last bits of salad into a small pile on my plate. "In fact, I have some ideas about things I'd like to do around here. Maybe we can mull them over a little?"

"Anytime, Kara. Just let me know."

Seth called the next afternoon. I was standing at the window watching for Will with my phone in my hand when it rang and Seth's face appeared on the screen.

"Hi, there."

"Hi, Kara. I'm working on arranging another trip home. This one will be for us. I'll take another stab at convincing you to come out and visit me here, but I promise you this time we'll have our date."

"That's great, Seth, but do me a favor?"

"What's that?"

"No more surprises. Let's actually plan a date and keep it."

"I agree. We'll do it right this time."

I smiled at my reflection in the window glass. "Thank you."

"You sound different, Kara. Is everything okay?"

"Oh, sure. It's just that I miss you. I wish you could be here to share the project, and the progress, with me."

"I doubt I'd be much help, to be honest. This is really your thing, right? I want to encourage you and support you, but I have my own work to do."

"Of course. I just mean that when it comes to choices and decisions and all that, it would be nice to have another opinion." And someone to celebrate with when it was going well. And someone to commiserate with when it wasn't.

"I have to go now. I'll call when I have details about when and where. Talk to you soon."

"Soon, Seth."

Not a satisfying farewell. I was left with the feeling that our potential as a couple was slipping away fast.

Had Seth changed?

Had I?

I hadn't known him all that long before he'd left. But it was likely his priorities would change along with his new work situation. Why wasn't I angry?

Victoria had been right when she'd said I'd get angry again. It was my way. Sometimes I got angry first and asked questions later.

Was I learning to let it go? Maybe. Or . . . maybe it was that the degree of caring equaled the degree of distress. I missed Seth, right? Sure. But not like I had before.

It was a shocking realization. I didn't know quite what to make of it.

"Almost gone." Victoria spoke from behind me, startling me.

"What?" I spun around.

She flipped her hair back over her shoulder, tugged at the collar of her white shirt, and gave a big shrug. "Me." She gave me a long look before adding, "Took a little longer than expected, right?"

Her expression was wistful. Maybe a little regretful? It moved me. "Almost gone, you said? Not forever."

"No, not forever." She smiled and moved with

a light step to where I stood at the window. "And not until Will is ready to leave. He's packing up his truck, so I think it's almost time. Sweet of him to give me a ride to pick up my car." With a tiny change in tone, Victoria added, "I hope you're okay with that."

I turned away, pretending I didn't know what she was talking about. Just before our big blowup, I'd seen her being very friendly with Seth. And then I'd seen the pictures of her with Niles. Jealousy was an ugly thing—and pointless. Especially pointless when it came to Niles and Seth, who were grown men and responsible for their own decisions, including the poor ones. But Will seemed different somehow. A good guy. An honest man. Maybe only because he hadn't let me down yet?

I said, "That's perfectly fine. I'm sure he doesn't mind." I added in a lower voice, "He's a good guy."

"What's that?"

"Nothing."

But she'd heard after all, because she said, "What about Seth? Is he a good guy too?"

With a dark look, I said, "You have a lot of nerve to ask me something like that."

"So we're good, but not that good? Not yet?" She gave a short, sharp laugh and picked up her bag. "It's all good, Kara. Give it time."

I almost smiled. Her jokes sometimes came

with a dig. But she had a knack for hitting the mark.

She walked past me but stopped at the door and said, "I think it comes down to patience. I'm good with persistence, but I never learned patience. Maybe I don't have the genes for it." She shrugged. "By the way, I've got a line on a good job. Not the kind of salary I made in Northern Virginia, but then it costs less to live in Richmond, so it works out." She gave me a last look. "It all works out, Kara. Some things can't be forced. People just have to remember that."

Chapter Sixteen

A week later the kitchen contractor said, "We'll be done in here in a few days."

It had been a much longer project than I'd anticipated, but the white cabinets, plentiful and spaced properly, and the white, lemon-tinted walls with melon trim were fresh and eye catching. The results were well worth the inconvenience. With less enthusiasm, I looked at the stacks of dishes and foodstuffs and pans piled in the pantry and on the dining room table and thought restocking would be a more enjoyable task if shared with a friend.

I telephoned Victoria and said, "I could use your help."

"Whatever you need."

She sounded eager. I felt a little guilty.

"It's not an emergency or anything. If you'd rather not or you're busy, just say so. The kitchen renovation is almost done. Sometime next week I have to put the bits and pieces back together. Wouldn't mind some help, if you're willing? We can have dinner, if you're interested."

"Just tell me when. I'll be there."

"I'll let you know." I added, "Don't risk your job to help me." Odd, I thought. I'd never say such a thing to anyone else. On the other hand, Victoria was one of a kind. She was sometimes her own worst enemy. I laughed. I could say the same of myself.

Victoria would help me tackle the job of restocking the dishes and pans and all of that assorted stuff. She'd throw her energy at it—a level of energy that sometimes caused issues, but that energy was also her strength. I missed seeing it. Putting the kitchen back into good working order felt like a good opportunity to share some time together, too, and make a step toward restoring our friendship.

The dining room wallpaper restoration was complete. The paper removal / wall plastering in the sitting room was getting close to done. We'd soon be ready to paint.

The parlor wallpaper was long gone, and plaster had been floated across the walls to smooth the surface. Moore's helper had painted the room a silvery blue gray. The walls were now dry, and Will was ready for his newest project, inside the house this time.

"You're a carpenter too?" I'd asked him when he'd offered to build the bookcases.

"I am, actually. Pretty good at it." He'd spanned the wall with the measuring tape and noted the length on a notepad.

"A man of many talents," I'd said with a smile.

"Good with my hands generally."

He'd already turned away to take another measurement. I stared at his back. Had he meant that the way it had sounded? Or had I colored the meaning of his words with my own?

If I could've thought of something clever to say, I might've, but I couldn't, so I'd said, "Good to know," and left the room quietly. I'd stopped in the foyer and looked back. And caught him looking too.

We'd both smiled.

"Build me some fabulous bookcases, Will Mercer."

"Yes, ma'am."

A few days later, Will arrived with the boards and a saw. He set the saw up in the front yard and carried the boards in and went to work building the bookcases.

I said, "Victoria is coming to help me with the kitchen later. You can join us for supper, if you'd like."

"Sure," he said, hardly looking up.

He was busy marking a measurement on a board. I got out of Will's way with a remark to call me if he needed help and went to the kitchen, thinking I'd get a head start while waiting for Victoria to arrive. But I didn't get much done because I returned to the parlor many times to peek at Will's progress.

I tried to be discreet and not disturb him. When he was outside cutting, sanding, or painting the boards, I stood at the window, knowing it was unlikely he'd see me. I also took the opportunity to imagine how the parlor would look when it was done. The fresh gray paint, the crisp white semigloss finish of the trim and the fireplace, the fireplace painting that would sit on the hearth in front. I had some pretty things to set on the shelves, like my embroidery books and Victoria's gift, *Wildflowers of America*, but I needed more books.

"Excuse me," Will said, carrying a finished board back inside.

I moved. I knew I was underfoot, but in my head a weird comparison was in progress. Will and Seth. How did I feel? If they went away, who would I miss the most? Did I have feelings for Will? Could I trust them considering how easily I'd fallen for Seth? And not knowing how I might feel about Seth when he returned . . .

"Seth is coming back soon," I said.

Will said, "Yeah? That's nice."

Why had I said that? "Not to stay. He'll be home for a few days this time. A little more time to spend with his family."

"And you too?"

"Sure."

Will shrugged. We were having a conversation of shrugs and intonations. Victoria, if she were here, would surely read a ton of subtext into it.

"Excuse me," he said. "I'll get back to my work."

On one of my stealthy ninja trips up the hallway, Will said, "All that tiptoe stuff is distracting."

Oh.

"You can trust me to do the job right, I promise."

"No, it's not that. I wanted to see how it was going but didn't want to disturb you."

He paused in fitting a long board against the corner and gave me a dark look. "No? Well, you are." He shook his head. "If you want to see what's going on, just walk in. It's okay."

"Sorry."

"Don't be sorry. Nothing to be sorry about." But his dark look didn't ease.

"Okay. Well, I'll check back in later. If you need anything, yell."

He nodded and turned away. He'd gone from friendly to grouchy, and I saw I'd gotten on his nerves.

"I'll get out of the way."

"Kara?"

I stopped and turned back.

"Yes?"

"If you have a moment, I could use your help after all."

"Sure. What can I do?"

"Steady this board? The wall isn't exactly a right angle, and I don't want the board to move out of position while I secure it."

"Of course."

"Right here," he said. "Put your hands here."

"Got it," I said, glad to be able to help.

My hands were supporting the board at about shoulder height. Will moved close so he could screw the board to the wall. When he worked on the screws midway up, his head was near, and I had a clear view of his dark hair and neat part. His shirt pulled tight across his back and shoulders.

It was a short moment. An easy task.

"Okay. You can let go now."

"Are you sure?"

"Yes, it's secure now."

I released the board and stepped away, stepped on the edge of something, and nearly toppled. Will grabbed me by the arm, steadied me, and then released me without remark.

I still felt his hands on me, as if they were still catching me. He had a speck of sawdust in his hair. I wanted to brush it off.

"Kara? Something wrong?"

Not Will's voice. Victoria's. She had arrived.

She gave an awkward little laugh as she darted quick looks back and forth between Will and me. "Door was open. Hope you don't mind me just walking in?"

Will's face was a little flushed. My own cheeks felt hot.

"He's building bookcases."

"Yeah, I can see that." But she sounded non-committal.

I said, "Will, if you don't need me any longer, I'll get back to work?"

"I've got it from here."

"Fine, then." I tugged at the hem of my shirt.

With a sideways glance, Victoria asked, "Did you forget I was coming over?"

"Will needed me to steady a board for him—that's all. If you need more help, Will, just call me." He nodded, and I turned to Victoria, saying, "Let's get to work. Everything is out of place in the kitchen and the dining room. It's a mess."

I got her into the kitchen quickly before she could say more. She cast a long look at the dishes and pots and mixing bowls stacked on the table and the counters, and the foodstuffs from flour to lentils to canned goods, which occupied every empty space between. Victoria went around the room examining the new quartz countertops and the oak cabinets. She walked into the updated pantry closet, saying, "Nice. Very nice."

"What a difference," she said in a normal tone as she came to stand near me. Then she lowered her voice and asked, "What was going on in there? You had red cheeks and a look . . . I thought for a moment there that I'd . . . well, interrupted something personal." She grinned. "Did I?"

I glanced down the hallway. Will wasn't in

sight. I closed the kitchen door gently. "No. Of course not. I was helping him."

"Keep your voice down."

Victoria was telling me to keep my voice down . . .

I said, "Then stop saying outrageous things. Don't tease. It isn't nice."

"Whatever you say." She spoke in a normal voice, but then her body shook as if she couldn't contain herself. "Okay, I'm taking a risk, but I'm going for it." She raised her hands, as if to direct or ward off. "I'm just saying this outright. I don't know where things stand with you and Seth, but it's okay to have more than one boyfriend. It's different from being officially committed to someone. You can date two different guys at the same time. Or people can. Honestly, I'm not sure *you* can. But you *can*. It's allowed."

"Date two? Seriously, Victoria. Right now, I'm not even dating one." I picked up the plates and kept working. "Besides, I have a feeling it's different in small-town America. I think people are less anonymous here than in a city."

"Do you still see Seth as having boyfriend potential? I know he's long distance for now."

I struggled with the answer. Things once said stayed said. I bit my lip, then released it. I admitted, "He's long distance and looks to be staying that way for a while."

She waited, apparently expecting me to say

more. When I didn't, she asked, "Can that work for you?"

"He wants me to fly out there and visit him. See LA. See California."

"Go." Her face lit with excitement. "Why not? Go check it out."

"I don't think so."

She stared at me, not speaking, but I could see her brain was full of words that wanted to be said. I gave her credit for not blurting them out.

I said, "I think he needs time to find out whether the job, the faster-paced life he's living now, is what he truly wants for his future."

"What about what *you* want?"

"I want to stay here."

"So it's a case of here or him?"

"Potentially."

Impulsively, I covered my face, but only for a moment. I looked at Victoria and asked, "How am I supposed to know what's real? I care about Seth, truly. I looked forward, so much, to him coming back to stay, but now . . ."

"Now you'd rather be building a bookcase?"

I gasped.

Victoria smirked. "I'm good, aren't I?"

"Seriously, Victoria. I don't know what to do."

"Then don't do anything. Not right now. Give it time. Seth isn't here. Will is. Get to know him."

I stared at her. She made it sound so reasonable.

She said, "And thanks for not biting my head off. I appreciate that."

I put my arms around her in a wordless hug. Neither of us spoke. When I stepped back, I touched my lashes. "Allergies, I think."

"Probably. So hey, let's get to work."

"Yes, please." I was delighted to change the subject. "I've tried, but I can't seem to focus."

With a sly look she said, "No joke."

"Stop it. He's shy, Victoria. Please don't tease him. Or me. It's cruel."

"Shy?" She held a stack of plates. "Might be he's just shy around you. But don't mind me. I've been wrong before. I'll finish putting the dishes in these cabinets and the utensils in these drawers. Why don't you set up the pantry?"

Victoria had never been able to resist being nosy or teasing. I found I didn't mind so much. I reopened the kitchen door in case Will called for help, and we both got to work. In the middle of our concentrated effort, Victoria said, "Do you have an official start date? A grand opening date?"

"Not yet. I'm thinking I won't officially open for business until spring."

"Spring? That's months away. Practically a lifetime."

"Downstairs is coming along nicely, and the grounds, too, but I have a lot to do upstairs, most notably adding in bathrooms." I picked up the boxes of pasta. "There's still lots to do before I'm ready for overnight guests."

Victoria stepped down from the stool. She came over to me and put her hands on my arms. "You can do this, Kara. I have no doubt whatsoever. And you don't need to wait until spring. Get your feet wet first with day activities. Work your way into it and build your expertise with each experience."

I must've opened and closed my mouth a dozen times before finally giving the words voice. "I swore I wouldn't whine. Wouldn't give in to fear. But what if no one wants to come here? No one." I looked away, embarrassed.

"You are mistaken about that, I promise you. For now don't panic; just be you, Kara. It will be wonderful." She grabbed my hand and pulled me out of the kitchen and down the hallway. At the foyer table she released my hand and opened the drawer. She looked at me with a question. "Where's the picture? Where are the women?"

"In the middle room. Sorry, I mean the project room."

"What room is that?"

I took a deep breath. "Come with me."

We stopped just past the grand staircase.

"I never noticed this door before, Kara."

I opened it, as I had with Nicole, and invited her in. "This is where I work on the business stuff. The business plan, project plan, and all that."

Victoria entered. She bypassed the stacks of papers and the computer on the table and even ignored the framed photo that was still atop the bookcase. She stopped directly in front of the large white paper taped to the wall.

"What is this?"

"A map. A fun map. You know, just something for marketing, maybe. I'll have a professional do the final, polished version and get it printed properly."

She leaned into it, closely examining the nooks, the special spots like the picnic area and the carriage house. I was pretty sure she didn't miss anything on that paper.

"Did you draw this?"

"I did. It's rough."

Victoria laughed. It didn't resemble Nicole's sedate chuckle in the least. She laughed so loudly that I wanted to muffle her somehow, but she did it herself, putting her hands over her mouth. When she removed them, she whispered, "Now I get it."

"Whoa. Wait." This was too much like Nicole's reaction but magnified.

"No, seriously," Victoria said. "I wondered why you were doing this whole creative retreat thing."

"Apparently everyone was."

"Hold on, Kara. *Just listen.* I *love* the idea. I'd do this"—she waved her hands to encompass the house—"this retreat thing myself if I had the opportunity. But that didn't explain why *you* were."

"What?" My reliable default, cynicism, came forth to protect me. "Please don't go on about the artist thing. That's what Nicole said, but frankly, I'm drawing a map. That's all it is. It's helped me get the business details worked out."

Victoria snorted. "Sorry. I'm trying not to laugh, so I'd appreciate it if you'd be a little less oblivious."

I was angry now. "Oblivious? Me? I deal in reality."

But Victoria ignored me. She said, "Nicole is right. You have talent. You are an artist."

"It was never part of my life, Victoria. Never. An artist creates art. I never have."

She pointed at the map. "Again, you're missing the obvious. But let me say this: If you are an artist, then you are. The only choice you have is what you do with it." She lowered her voice again, so low that I had to listen very carefully to hear what she said. "You, Kara Lange Hart, couldn't settle for a paint by number or even a little happy doodling. You are building an entire retreat. You aren't going somewhere to learn art. You are bringing the artists and creatives to you." She stepped back and said in a more normal voice, "I was always impressed by your strength, your resilience, but I never realized you were building your own world.

"You are creating the world you want to live in. You'd darn well better use it to its fullest, or you'll hear about it from me." She picked up the picture of the women. "Look at them. Look at their faces. They've waited long enough."

Abruptly, she exited the project room with the photograph in hand.

"It's a picture. Just a picture," I said to her retreating back, in a sudden rush of panic.

She stopped in front of the foyer table. "Hang it."

"I will. I'll get it taken care of."

"Hang it now. And hang the samplers too."

I waved my hands. "No, listen. I'm not procrastinating. I don't have the right hardware. A nail isn't enough. Not with these old walls."

"I can hang it for you," Will said. "I have the hardware."

He had joined us in the foyer. I'd forgotten he was nearby. How much had he heard? Now I was trapped between Victoria on one side, holding the frame, and Will on the other, holding a hammer.

Accept help when it's offered and available? That sounded like advice from Dad. Did he feel nearby this time, as he had when I'd tried to hang it before?

"Where do you want it?" Will asked.

I pointed to an area on the wall. "Hang it right there. I want the needlework frames to be on either side of it." I pulled them out of the drawer.

"I've never seen these," he said. His curiosity and question were implicit in his tone.

"I stitched them right after Dad died. I intended to hang them here with the photo, but I . . . I hadn't gotten around to it."

I shot a look at Victoria. She met my eyes and grinned.

"No time like the present," Will said.

Victoria held the photo up against the wall. "How's this?"

I touched her arm. "Just about perfect."

"And when we're done, I'm going upstairs and doing you a huge favor by packing away your dad's stuff."

It was a long, almost endless moment of silence. No one breathed. Not even Victoria. Finally, I spoke.

"I appreciate the offer. More than I can say. But it's something I have to do for him myself."

"I'll do it with you. I'll help you."

"I'm not ready yet. I'll let you know when I am."

Victoria threw her arms around me in a quick, ferocious hug. I would've returned it, but she'd already backed off. I gave her a smile and took her hand in mine. I said, "Thank you."

Will finished hanging the second needlework—the one that read,

Wildflower House
You are welcome to thrive here.

I felt overwhelmed. Tears stung my eyes again, and the tightness in my chest felt like a fist. If my commitment had been less than 100 percent before, it was now in full force.

The sharp grief I'd experienced in that second week after Dad's death had apparently returned, piggybacking on the emotion of the moment. I pressed my hand to my chest, willing the crying not to start.

Victoria put an arm around me. "Are you okay?"

I nodded. "I'm fine." But my words were broken, and I said, "Going for a walk."

Victoria called after me, "Need any company?"

Will asked, "Are you okay, Kara?"

I waved them back, unable to speak.

I stood on the porch, clinging to the railing. This was my perch and my view of my kingdom. A tear slid down my cheek. The kingdom I was building? My world, per Victoria? I almost laughed and then choked on the tears. I let them roll, not in grief but in gratitude with a fillip of wistful nostalgia. The wildflowers were long gone. Will, with a tractor and a tiller, had plowed under the muddy chaos the hail had left behind. Most of that area was being restored to lawn, and grass was already growing, but Will had sectioned one area—the medallion—like pie slices around a central circle. A statue of some sort would occupy the middle, and evergreens like azaleas and rhododendron would fill in the interior sections. The outermost sections would be for wildflowers, not the invasive kind but the ones that had to be planted and tended. I'd thumbed through Victoria's book and suggested sweet alyssum and sweet william. Will had his own ideas. We had plenty of time, he said. He'd prepare the beds now, put in the azaleas, but wait until spring to get the flowers going.

What excellent good fortune had brought Will Mercer to my door? Another tear wet my cheek. And it had brought Victoria back. She'd been a blessing. And then there was Nicole. She'd gone out of her way to support me, to help me. A lot like an older sister might have done.

I pulled up the hem of my blouse and mopped at my eyes. I was midsniffle when the door opened behind me.

Will said, "Kara. I'm sorry to disturb you. Are you okay?"

We seemed to repeat this scene, and on this porch, regularly. He always showed up when I was in the grip of some emotional storm. I smiled through the teardrops on my lashes and turned to look at him. "Don't mind me. I'm fine. And I appreciate your help, Will. I'm grateful."

"Well, don't speak too soon."

No, I told myself. *Don't assume the good stuff is about to blow up and get messy. Don't.*

"Okay? What is it?"

"Someone's here to see you."

"Who? Should I be concerned?"

"No. Maybe yes." He grimaced and shook his head. "It's my mom's cousin. I told my mom that I was building the bookcases. She must've mentioned it to her cousin. She's here and wants to see . . . and she has something for you."

"Has something for me? Who's your cousin?" But in that moment, I already knew. "Not Sue Deale?"

He nodded.

I said, "She's the heir. She inherited the house and the contents." I pressed my hand to my cheek. "Oh, but you already know all that. Did you know she's already brought other items like the piano and the dining room furniture back here?"

"Yeah, I know. Believe me. The whole family knows how unhappy her husband is about her hoarding ways. This is a little different, though. It's not about furniture. She brought you something else."

I couldn't read Will's expression or tone, but he seemed concerned. I asked, "What is it this time?"

He smiled with encouragement. "Come see for yourself."

I dabbed at my lashes with the back of my hand. "I got all emotional. Do I look awful?"

"You look beautiful."

My heart skipped a beat at the words, at the

way he said them. For a moment the world came to a stop.

Victoria's voice called from inside, "Kara? Come here, please."

Will held the door open for me. I preceded him inside but waited for him to join me on the walk back up the hallway to the front of the house.

Victoria and Sue were chatting in the foyer, standing near the parlor door. There was disorder, but since Will was doing most of the messy work out front, it didn't look too bad, and enough shelves were up that it was easy to see how gorgeous the effect of white on soft blue-gray walls was going to be.

Sue said, "Hey, there, Kara. How're you doing?" She gave me a close look. "Your eyes are red and puffy. Are you having allergies?"

"No, I'm good. I'm fine."

She made a noise but didn't question my red eyes further. She pointed toward the parlor. "You need some color in that room."

"What did you have in mind, Sue?"

"I've got touches of color for you. How about books on those shelves? Colorful bindings?" She shook her head. "Before you say no, take a look. These books would be perfect here. They'll give you exactly the look you're going for. Vivi told me all about it."

Will said, "Vivi is my mom. Vivian."

Sue took a quick step around me and stopped

in front of the picture and needlework we'd just hung. "I knew I was exactly right about selling this house to your father and you. This parlor is perfect, Kara. Perfectly perfect." She shook her head. "That paper in the parlor was nasty dirty, so I'm glad you yanked it out."

She stopped in front of the sitting room fireplace. I'd put the first fire screen painting there and felt a small thrill as she stopped to admire it.

I said, "We have another that will go in the parlor."

"Wonderful. Amazing." She looked up and spied Will. She said, "I've seen these or something like them before, haven't I?"

"Will's sister paints them."

Sue made a humming noise and shook her head. "Poor girl. How's she doing, Will?"

He said, "She's doing better."

She moved on, pausing in the wide opening between the sitting room and the dining room. "You kept the dining room paper," she exclaimed and clapped her hands in delight. "It looks so good!"

"Moore Blackwell did a masterful job of cleaning and repairing it."

"I've always heard how talented he is with such things." She added, "The paneling glows, and the fixtures sparkle. This house hasn't looked this happy in a long time. Excellent work." Then she caught a glimpse of the renovated kitchen, so we had to inspect the new cabinets, counter, and flooring. She oohed over the island and lighting fixtures and went positively ecstatic over the sliding barn doors that opened onto the pantry.

"Amazing. Just amazing. When your daddy wanted to buy this house, I knew it was fate. Small world and all that. He never knew the Forsters, of course. They lived here during the years he was off in Richmond." She hardly paused to breathe. "My, my, but I never dreamed he could turn it into this. Oh, but that's your touch, right? The Langes were never fancy people, and Henry, insofar as I knew him, was all business. This, though—this is beautiful. You have a gift, Kara. An eye for art." She pressed her hands over her heart. "My cousin Mary would've adored this."

"Sue, please, did you know my father? Before he bought the house, I mean."

"I remember him as a boy. Standoffish. Kept to himself. But there was a certain sweetness to him. And he was a hard worker. It was too bad about his family."

"You're talking about his parents. My grandparents."

"Well, yes, that's true. You didn't know them, if I'm right. Your daddy kept a lot of distance between himself and his father."

"Yes."

"They've been gone so long. I hadn't given them a thought in decades. No one did. Especially since Henry left so young and didn't keep in touch with anyone. Most people wouldn't know anything about them. The county has grown so much hardly anyone knows anyone else around here anymore."

I had other questions. Did I dare ask them? I didn't doubt she'd be talking to other people. I needed to think about it first before blurting out stuff about my father's siblings and asking what she might know.

And Will. What about Will? He was related to people who might have known the Langes long ago. I glanced at him, but he was busy moving boards around.

Sue added, "The boxes are on the front porch. Any books you don't want, feel free to give away. I can't bring myself to part with things, especially family things, but I can certainly understand you might not want all of them. Just don't send them back to me, if you don't mind."

"I understand. If I can't use them, I'll find them new homes."

"Thank you, dear. I just can't dispose of . . . well, you know. My Joe thanks you too."

I escorted Sue out to the front porch. There were six cardboard boxes stacked near the bench.

"I picked out the best books—the ones I thought you might enjoy and would look particularly fine on the shelving. I know well enough that when I die, my kids will toss all my stuff, unless they can find a way to make money from it. So I hope these will be good for you."

I was astounded. "This was a lot of work, Sue."

"Ah, well, I didn't mind a bit."

I followed her to the truck. Her husband was seated in the driver's seat. He gave me a courteous wave and nod.

"Thank you, Sue." I meant it.

She said, "One more thing. The red book at the top of one of those boxes is an old school textbook. Keep an eye out for that one. The schools used to sell or donate old textbooks when they were being replaced. I forget how I came to have that one, but I put it in the box especially for you."

She paused with her hand on the truck's door handle and looked back. "I almost forgot," she said. "My book club has a meeting next month. I was hoping we could hold it here?"

I panicked inside but did my best to keep my expression impassive. "I don't think the house will be quite ready."

"Oh, goodness, I'm sure it will be lovely. It doesn't have to be perfect. Just a midday meeting. A few ladies. We'd love to sit in that parlor of yours and discuss our monthly selection."

A couple of hours? Sitting in the parlor? Not really official or anything . . .

I took a leap. "Okay. Sure. We can make that work."

Sue smiled, her face lighting up. "They'll be so pleased. I told them I knew the perfect place, and when I told them *where,* they were so excited." She cocked her head and winked. "I told them I had an *in* with the owner of Wildflower House."

"They knew the name? Wildflower House? Nicole did tell me people are calling this the Wildflower Property."

"Oh, sure. You betcha. Nicole's been talking it around. I love all the great things you're planning for this place. Mary would've been over-the-moon thrilled. Folks around here have always just called it the big old house where Mary and Rob Forster used to live. So much simpler to say Wildflower House." She put one finger in the air, almost like an antenna. "Oh, and don't worry about food. We'll bring our own. You won't mind if we use the kitchen, will you? Just to heat up the casseroles? If we should bring our own plates, just let me know."

I tried twice before actually managing to speak words. "That will be fine. And I have plates."

"Let me know what the fee is. Our little club is small, but we have petty cash set aside for such things."

"Fee? No fee. We aren't officially open for business yet. It will be my pleasure to host your club meeting here."

Sue beamed.

This time she joined her husband in the truck,

and as he put the vehicle into drive, Sue waved merrily.

Okay, I thought. *It's okay. Calm down.*

Victoria spoke from the open doorway. "I'm proud of you, Kara. That was perfect. And it's a great way to dip your toes into the pool." She laughed. "To christen the new life of this old house—Wildflower House—and its fresh start." She went directly to the boxes and started moving flaps aside.

Had Sue and Victoria discussed the book club meeting while I was on the porch? Maybe, but I wouldn't ask. The decision was made, and it felt like a good one.

And as Sue had affirmed, the house was happy.

Victoria said, "Oh, hey. What's this?"

I looked over to see her examining the binding and the inner pages of a book, an old book by the look of it.

"Davy Crockett," she said. "Printed in 1834."

"You're kidding." I leaned closer to see.

"Not kidding. Serious. Too bad about the water spotting." She set it aside and picked up another. "A history of England from 1912. Gorgeous cover."

Will came over and sniffed. "They smell old."

Victoria looked at me. "Didn't Sue say she put a red textbook in one of the boxes for you to see?" She held it out to me.

A red textbook. A large math textbook that

reminded me of middle school math books from a long time ago.

I laughed. "Maybe she thinks my math skills need refreshing?" I flipped the cover open and saw a name scrawled partway down a list pasted inside the back cover. A record of who the book had been assigned to. Other names preceded the most recent, and that last name, the childlike writing faded and smudged, was Henry Lange's.

In my shock, I must've made a noise, because Will asked, "What's wrong?"

"See this? This is my dad's name. His handwriting. A kid's writing."

Will took it and looked closer. "Now that's cool. Must've been his book. When the books would be retired or replaced, the schools used to give the old books away." He went to hand it back, and it fell. My heart fell with it as it hit the hard floor—and then stopped altogether when a folded paper slid out from between the interior pages.

I knelt to retrieve both. The note on the paper, written in an adult's hand, read, *Ann—Make sure Henry gets this back.* I unfolded it and found a photo.

Dad's memories at Wildflower House had been made with the family who'd lived here before the Forsters—the Bowens. Dad had done yardwork for them and felt welcome at this home . . . this house we now called Wildflower House.

The photo was an old Polaroid type. It had faded but was still compelling. I stared and gasped, and my knees went weak. My dad. He couldn't have been more than twelve or thirteen. He was posed with a woman and a little boy. I was certain it was the Bowen family. In the darkest days of his young life, my father had pretended that these people were his family, that he lived there—here—with them.

His youthful face glowed with pure joy—joy that I'd never seen on his face in all the years I'd known him.

My heart hurt. My eyes burned. I took the book, the note, and the photo. I fought the urge to run. I forced myself to say, "Could you excuse me for a little while?"

"Go," Victoria said.

"Let me know if you need anything." Will's voice trailed away as I ascended the stairs.

I was sorry to be rude, but I needed to hide for a while. I went to Dad's room and shut the door behind me.

Some time passed. Maybe an hour. A soft knock sounded on the door. Victoria said, "Kara? You okay?"

I opened the door. I knew my eyes were swollen and red.

"You poor girl," she said. "Is there anything Will or I can do to help?"

"No, I'm fine, truly. Grief is a process, right?" I

tried to smile. "I appreciate you both, but I think I'm done for the day."

"Will's worried about you."

"Tell him I'm fine. Tell him thank you and I'll see him tomorrow." I pointed to my eyes. "I'll be myself again by then."

"Why don't I put together a meal for us?"

"Thank you, Victoria. Mind if I take a rain check on that? Besides, I owe you a meal for your help today. We'll plan something special."

"Are you sure?"

"Positive."

She gave me a hug. "Call me if you need anything."

"Victoria?"

She stopped midturn. "Yes?"

"Thank you. For everything."

She grinned. "My pleasure."

Chapter Seventeen

Dad had lied to everyone, including me, about his early years. Outright lied.

After Dad and I had moved to Wildflower House, he'd taken me to the long-derelict Lange property and confessed he hadn't been born in Richmond but instead in Cub Creek. After his mother had died and the twins, Laura and Lewis, had vanished, he'd run away from his father. Tall and self-assured for a fifteen-year-old, he'd worked odd jobs in Richmond until he was of legal age, and then, gifted with a strong, single-minded will, he'd built a successful business from the ground up. He'd been wedded to his job more than to his wife. He'd nurtured his business in a way that he'd never had the capacity to nurture me.

Dad had withheld information about my mom that I had a right to know—not maliciously but because discussing it was too painful. I'd known he loved me, and he'd shown it in countless ways. I'd trusted him and depended on him even after I'd known about the lies.

How much had he not shared? Lots, probably. That was his prerogative. I'd wanted to question him more. I'd thought we had time yet.

Sue had sparked my curiosity again. Her remarks had reminded me that while I'd been busy restoring the house and setting up the business, there were paths not followed. As Mel had pointed out, time was busily erasing sources of information, just as it had taken my dad.

Suppose I did have family out there?

Lately it seemed as if my mind, my very world, was expanding. Possibilities were finding their way into it—and finding fertile ground.

I would have liked to ask Sue if she knew what had happened to the twins, but she was a gossip. If I talked to her about it, everyone else would soon know everything I'd told her.

Case in point—Sue had known I had new bookshelves in the parlor before they were even finished. Small town. Small world.

What would Dad have done?

He'd shared with me what he'd chosen to. I respected that. Should I now toss out his desire for privacy by opening his history up to the speculation of others?

I'd told Mel, of course, but she'd keep my business private.

The next morning, before the day heated up too much, I followed the creek path, admiring the improvements Will's crew had made, including the bench that was now in place. Very rustic. It would be a pleasant spot to rest or contemplate. Today, I kept walking.

When I reached the thicket of sticker bushes—and the thorns Will had helped me escape—

I sidestepped them. The house was just beyond.

It had collapsed in on itself long ago. Out here alone, I didn't want to go too close lest I fall in an old well or cellar.

What troubled me and had haunted my dad was the missing children. He'd been too young and powerless to force the issue with his father back then, and without the little ones to protect, he'd had no reason to stay.

How would I even begin to search for them?

I could do a DNA test and see if someone showed up as a match online. It was a long shot, but it would be easy to do and discreet.

Dad had left this land untouched over the intervening decades. He hadn't interacted with his father otherwise, but he'd kept the taxes paid and had kept the property intact even after his father's death.

Until I found his brother and sister or discovered what had happened to them, I felt like I should do the same—leave it undisturbed. At least until the day when I could accept there was no point in searching further.

Someday this debris must go, and the land must be restored. I couldn't change the past, but one day perhaps I could write a new, better future for this sad place.

Chapter Eighteen

I was home from my hike by midday, had changed into fresh clothing—cotton capris and a roomy T-shirt—and was in the parlor sorting through Sue's books when my cell phone rang. Mel's name popped up. I answered.

"Hi, Mel."

"Is Maddie there?" Her voice was almost hoarse.

"Mel? Are you okay? What's happened?"

"Maddie was right here, but I can't find her, and I'm afraid to wait. If she's not with you, then I'm calling the sheriff."

"Take a deep breath. Tell me, when did you last see her?"

"I don't know. I mean, I do know, but I was watching TV, and she was playing with her dolls. I must've dozed off. I have new medication for my joints. Maybe it made me drowsy. I woke, and she was gone. I didn't think anything of it at first, but then I couldn't find her."

Her words faltered. "The back door is unlocked, Kara. I'm certain it was locked before. I think Maddie went outside while I was napping."

"Don't panic, Mel. Calm down." I told it to myself also. Panic wouldn't help anyone. "Mel, let's think about this. Maddie was in the house and went out via the back door, so she probably wasn't taken or picked up by someone."

"Oh, my good Lord. My sweet Maddie."

She sounded so different from her usual self that I was afraid she might have a heart attack or a breakdown. Heaven help me if Mel collapsed. Such things could happen. After all, my dad had had a stroke. "What I mean is maybe she fell asleep in her playhouse or something like that."

"No, I checked everywhere."

"Take a deep breath and call the sheriff—that's a good idea. I'm heading outside to check the grounds. If I don't find her, I'll follow the path to your house." As I spoke those last words, a shot of light, brighter than any I'd experienced postaccident, sliced through my head. They'd been common after the accident, but not for a long while. This sharp stab almost blinded me. I grabbed the tabletop as my legs went weak.

"Kara? You there? What's happening?"

"I'm fine."

"You moaned. Loud."

"I'm okay. Just a sudden headache. Worry, of course." I shook my head and rubbed my eyes. "I'm hanging up now. I'll keep my phone with me, and I'll call you as soon as I know anything. You call me right away if she turns up where you are. Maybe you should take a look up and down the street. Maybe check with the neighbors."

As we disconnected, I wondered if my legs

would hold me. I stood gingerly with my hand still on the table, but my legs felt solid again. That shot through my head was gone, leaving only a low, dull ache.

I slipped on my shoes. With my phone clasped in my hand, I stuck my head out the front door and yelled Maddie's name. I didn't expect her to be on the porch, and she wasn't.

I closed the screen door but left the front door open in case she did show up. I wanted her to have safe access into the house. Then I rushed down the long hallway and out the back door. Calling her name, I hurried to the carriage house first. It seemed unlikely that she'd be there, but it was closer than the creek and the paths and quick to check. I wasn't panicking. We'd find Maddie, and she'd be fine. I repeated those words over and over under my breath just to prove it was true.

As I headed downslope to the creek, I called loudly, "Maddie Lyn! Where are you?" A nearby bird squawked and took wing. A bunny jumped from its hiding place and hopped away.

No one answered my call. I picked up speed, thinking of the bridge crossing Cub Creek.

She wasn't at the bridge either. The railing was hanging at more of an angle. I stood trying to assess the likelihood that Maddie had been here. Might she have turned back home? I ran across the bridge and to the tree trunk Maddie had stood on when she'd shown me the carved initials. I stopped there. I was almost back at Mel's house. Mel would've called if Maddie had shown up there, so I started back. By the time I was nearing the bridge again, my feet were dragging a little. But maybe because of that, because I was going slower, I saw what I'd missed the first time—a yellow hair ribbon caught low where the railing joined the footbridge. I gasped. My stomach rolled over as I spied small footprints in the muddy bank very near the water, and a longer skid of upturned mud showed those feet had slipped. The sagging railing would have been within reach of a child, who might have grabbed for it as she slid into the creek.

Fear gripped me. I called out, "Maddie!" Without hesitation, I stepped into the creek and began wading downstream. The water was cold, and the footing was treacherous, but staying on the path would've risked me missing her because of the undercuts and the low growth along the banks.

The dark water came only to my knees, but I stumbled over rocks and other hard, rough objects. The water wasn't deep—not deep for an adult but more than deep enough to drown a child.

I ran—or tried to run—and I stumbled and fell, but I got up and kept going until I'd waded up the creek far enough to reach my own yard. I paused and looked. No one was in sight. There was only the empty bench and the big house up the slope. No sign of a child or anyone.

"Maddie," I yelled again. I'd been calling her name regularly to no effect. I hoped that she'd returned home and this effort, this crazy, ridiculous search, was unnecessary. My phone was surprisingly dry—unlike my clothing—and any moment now Mel was going to call, saying it was all a mistake, that Maddie had fallen asleep behind the sofa or in her playhouse.

I was counting on it.

Seth, Maddie, and I had been here at this bench on a sunny day shortly before my dad had died, and before Seth had left for California. I'd been sitting on the bench when Seth and Maddie had come running along the shoreline sailing their boats. Their appearance that day had lifted me out of a very sad state. We three had had so much fun chasing and retrieving those boats. I'd gotten wet that day, too, as had Seth when he'd jumped in to help me to my feet and out of the water, and Maddie had jumped in just for fun.

Suddenly, I knew exactly where Maddie was.

Grabbing a low-hanging branch, I used it to pull myself up onto the bank and solid ground. I'd lost a shoe somewhere, and my foot was bleeding, but only a little. From here I'd go by the path. It was faster. And this time I was less worried about checking the underbrush.

I ran along the path calling her name. I even imagined I heard my name called faintly, and I paused for a brief moment and listened. Nothing. My imagination. And so I ran again, and it wasn't long before I saw the new bench. I slowed. There were the large rocks in the creek where Maddie's boats had washed up and been caught. And there was Maddie, sitting atop the biggest rock.

Relief filled me as I stood on the bank. Maddie was crying a little, and I saw a bloody knee and a few other scrapes, but that was it.

Calmly, I asked, "How did you get onto that rock all by yourself, Maddie Lyn?"

She hugged her legs. Her lips squinched up, and she buried her face in her arms.

"Stay put, Maddie. I'm coming over." But first I called Mel.

She answered immediately. "Yes?"

"She's here. I have her. She's fine."

I heard a ragged breath from Mel's end.

"I'll bring her back shortly." I disconnected and put my phone on the bench. I didn't have a pocket, and I needed both hands to cross those rocks. I wasn't as confident in my nimbleness as Maddie was in hers. I was glad to be wearing capris. They were drenched but not as heavy and restricting as wet denim would be. I left my remaining shoe on shore for better footing.

I made it. The rocks were warm from the sun, but the creek water wasn't. It felt cool and good—a relief mixed with other relief. I settled next to Maddie. She was wearing a yellow cotton sundress, and it was as wet as my clothing.

"Did you fall into the creek?"

No answer. I stared at her stoic face with its wet, streaked cheeks, and my heart hurt. I plucked at my wet shirt and pants in a way I hoped was funny. "I'm wet, too; did you notice?"

Still nothing.

My phone rang over on the bench. I presumed Mel was ringing me back, but I ignored it. I couldn't reach it from here.

"You scared your Grammy by going off on your own. Did you know that?"

A small nod.

"Why did you leave her?"

She shifted her arm and her face. She looked at me sideways, and then I saw she had something green in her hand. A small plastic boat. It was one of the boats I'd seen the day she and Seth had floated them down Cub Creek.

"I wanted to go sailing."

"Alone? I think you know better than that."

"Yep." She ran the back of her hand against her nose.

"You know Seth isn't here, right? If he was, he'd love to sail with you, but he isn't."

"I know."

I was reassured by her attitude. She wasn't fantasizing. She'd had a goal and had overestimated her ability to handle it herself. Scary in its own way, but not unexpected at her age.

She sniffled. "I fell in. Grammy will be mad I messed up my dress."

"Nope. Grammy doesn't care about the dress. Grammy is worried about you." I poked her with my finger. "You."

My phone was ringing again. I looked over, wishing I could read the screen from here, but the mystery was quickly solved as Will came around the curve in the path. He was holding his phone. When he saw me, he disconnected.

"There you are. I saw you rushing past, but I was up at the house. Were you wading? You didn't stop when I yelled." He gave Maddie and me a longer look. "Maddie wasn't with you before. Why are you both wet? Did I really see you climbing out of the creek?" He noticed the one shoe. He picked it up, puzzling at it.

"Don't ask," I said. "I won't be needing it."

By now, he'd stepped from the bank over to the first rock. He read something in my face, and I saw his own curious, almost alarmed expression grow gentle.

"Well, you ladies look very comfortable here, but I am surprised. When I first saw you, I thought I was seeing mermaids. Just two mer-maids sitting on a rock in the middle of the day."

I glanced at Maddie. She was looking at him, staring.

He scratched his head. "What's her name? The name of that mermaid? I could've sworn that's who was sitting next to you, Kara."

"I think the mermaid you're thinking of is called . . . Wanda."

He shook his head. "Doesn't sound quite right."

Maddie said, "Ariel. That's me."

"Are you?" Will gave her a big bright smile. "Well, Miss Maddie Ariel, would you like a hand off that rock?" He held out his hands. "In fact, I've never assisted a mermaid from the creek."

Maddie giggled. She was back. My heart eased but not my worry.

"Just a sec, Will. Maddie?" I touched her arm. "You know you can't play at the creek without a grown-up, right?"

"I know. Uncle Seth and I sailed boats. I found my boat. It wanted to go sailing."

"Promise me you won't go off again like that, and never to the creek, alone."

"I promise."

"You already promised Grammy, but you did it anyway. You can't do this again until Grammy says you're old enough. Understand?"

"Yup." She pushed wet hair back from her face. "Yes, ma'am."

"Well then, Miss Maddie Ariel, let's go see Grammy. You owe her a big apology."

"I'm sorry."

"You'll have to tell her that yourself." I shifted

331

to help her stand and kept a hand on her. "I'll help you over to Will."

She made the transition easily. Meanwhile, I was awkwardly making my own way across the rocks. By the time I made it to shore, Maddie was holding Will's hand and hopping a little, laughing at my old-person awkwardness, which I exaggerated for comic effect. Will grinned broadly as he took my hand and helped me onto shore.

"Where to, ladies?"

Maddie said, "Mermaids!"

"Mermaids. I stand corrected."

"To Grammy's house," Maddie said. "She's waiting for me."

We saw Mel approaching before we reached the bridge. Maddie ran to her. Mel was immediately on her knees hugging her granddaughter.

"Don't ever go off like that again." She kissed Maddie's face. "Never do that."

"I promise."

Mel nodded, and more quickly than it would take to say it, she gave my wet clothing a second look, realized Maddie's dress was damp, spared us a quick smile, hugged her granddaughter again, and pressed her face into the child's silky hair.

Love, I thought. It was all about love. Guilt, responsibility, duty, betrayal, and too many words and concepts to name were all rolled up into that one simple word. Not to mention receiving love and the fear of losing it. And the need to give love—and having someone in your life who was pleased to receive it.

Will and I walked back to Wildflower House together.

"Thank you for your help," I said. "Maddie misses her uncle very much."

He nodded. "Seems like a lot of folks miss him."

His remark seemed pointed, perhaps directed at me, but before I could respond—or choose not to—he added, "That's a good thing. It'd be sad to leave and have no one notice."

My imagination, then? "That's true," I said. "What about you, Will?"

"Me?" He shrugged. "Nah. I don't miss him much."

"What?" I saw him grinning, and I groaned. "That's not what I meant. I mean you. Your family. I don't know much about your life."

He smiled. "My family is as brilliant and as messed up as most. That's what makes them worth knowing."

"I love how you say that."

"Anytime you want to hear more, I'm happy to share."

Was it the words? The tone of our voices? A teasing quality in our interaction? One of us, or maybe both of us, had steered this conversation into interesting but risky waters. Too soon, I cautioned myself. I wasn't ready for this.

I put extra space between us. We walked the rest of the way in silence, each with our own thoughts. I hoped his were more pleasant than the mash-up going on in my head. I liked Will. I liked Seth. Seth and I had something going, right? Potential, certainly. And Will?

As we neared the house, we stopped.

Will cleared his throat. "Speaking of leaving, Jim asked me to take a look at another job, a big one, that he's got coming up, and he'd like me to check out a couple of others."

"You're leaving me?"

"Let's be up front here, Kara. You can't keep thinking up projects, and I can't continue suggesting projects so I'll have an excuse to be here."

"Is that what we've been doing?" I looked down at my wet clothing to avoid his gaze. "Yes, I guess we have." I frowned and then stared him in the eye. "But every one of those projects was important. Look what we've built here. And don't you dare say *we* didn't build it. I couldn't have done it alone."

"It was my pleasure to be part of your project, Kara."

"We aren't done yet."

"Aren't we?"

Undercurrents, other meanings, swirled around us. Victoria might enjoy them, but I didn't.

"Don't talk that way," I said.

Will said, "Lots of talk, but neither of us is saying what's really on our minds." After a long moment of silence, he asked softly, "How's Seth, Kara?"

I was struck silent, but my brain churned furiously. I tried to think of something clever or witty or diverting to say. I failed.

Will took my hands in his. "Be honest, Kara. Tell me what you're feeling. If I'm wrong, if you don't feel the way I do, then I'll back off. Just say it."

Instinctively, I tried to pull my hands from his. Will looked at me, then released them. I stepped back, but I couldn't bring myself to walk away.

"Do you have an understanding between you? An unofficial engagement or something like that?"

"It's not that simple, Will." I shook my head. "Long-distance relationships aren't easy. He's caught up with the new job. I encouraged him to go." And I'd said I'd wait for him to come home, hadn't I? I'd told him I'd be here when he did. I felt confused.

He gave me a long look, stepped toward me, and gently touched my cheek. His fingers rested there for a moment before tracing the curve of my jaw and the length of my neck.

"Will?" I whispered.

"I understand. You should talk to him. I won't bring this up again until you tell me you're ready, but please don't take too long figuring it out. Life goes on, Kara. It doesn't wait. We don't want to miss our chance." He took his hand away. He said, his voice low and steady, "I won't be here tomorrow—nothing to do with anything except Jim asking me to check out those new jobs—and I'll be back to work on the medallion garden, but if you need me or need anything, call me. Anytime."

I let him leave. He walked around the side path, and I put up a hand to wave, expecting him to look back. He didn't.

No point in denying I felt something for Will. I should've figured things out with Seth before now. I'd thought I had time.

I wished Will had kept his feelings secret a little longer, because I didn't know what to do.

My heart was racing. I pressed my hand to my chest.

Forgetting my thigh and the possibility of falling flat, I chased after him. Maybe I could catch him. Maybe—

The driveway—only my car was there. A thin cloud of dirt hovered over the drive. Will was gone.

I showered off the creek water and changed into shorts and a fresh shirt. I stood in front of the mirror and examined my face.

Will's fingers on my face, my neck . . . my skin

felt different somehow. Still oddly tender.

I'd known that he had feelings for me. Seth had feelings for me too. I believed that, but how deep were they? I cared about Seth. I cared about Will.

We were all living in the midst of change. Life was constant change, and sometimes our lives were shuffled and redealt despite our intentions. No wonder we got confused.

Patience, I told myself. *Don't panic, and don't rush because you're afraid.*

Back downstairs, I stopped in the foyer and stood in front of the photo. Each of those women, from the youngest in white dresses and black stockings to the older women in dark, heavy-looking gowns, had a story. They'd had heartaches, embarrassments, and fears. I hoped they'd had laughter and triumphs too.

I hoped they'd been able to laugh at those embarrassments and fears. I hoped they'd found love.

Seth had brought me that framed photograph from Sue Deale soon after we'd moved in because he'd known I'd love it. Victoria and Will had helped me hang the photo and the samplers because they were my friends. I was glad. The photo, the samplers, the piano, and all the rest belonged here at Wildflower House. And so did I.

That night when I went upstairs to get ready for bed, I opened the nightstand drawer and pulled out the prescription bottles. The remaining pills rattled in the plastic containers.

Heaven knew my brain was dizzy enough tonight with thoughts of Seth and Will flashing back and forth in my head.

I looked at my bed, the covers, the pillow. I'd been sleeping well lately, but if I didn't have these meds on hand . . . I felt the pressure in my veins increase ever so slightly, and the beat of my heart thudded faintly but noticeably in my temples. My breathing rate increased. A low hum began in my ears.

For me, these pills weren't the problem—I was the problem. I was lucky, unlike my mom and others who had a physical dependence on a substance. I'd gone for days now without taking them and had experienced no ill effects.

So I didn't need to worry about it, right?

In fact, it made sense *not* to toss them. If I didn't have a problem and *could* toss the last ones, then I should just go ahead and finish them up over the next several days. *Finish them and be done.*

As I pressed the cap down and twisted it off, I felt a telltale easing in my heart rate, and a sense of well-being flooded me . . . a feeling of "This is good." I tilted the bottle, and one pill slid onto my palm. I didn't have water handy.

But . . .

After a very long moment, I upended the bottle,

and the last pills joined the first. I did the same with the other leftovers. I closed my fist around them.

In the near dark, I descended the stairs. Moonlight backlit the stained glass window, and I could see my way. I exited through the kitchen and walked out into the backyard. The ground was so familiar to me that I didn't hesitate. The slope was wide open down to the creek. The bench was a dark silhouette, unmoving—a reliable marker in the night.

The grass was damp, especially near the creek. I stood in the moonlight, wanting to make a statement before heaven, for tomorrow and the future, and to do it here, on the banks of Cub Creek, which had flowed through time, lives, and generations.

I was doing it tonight with the wet grass beneath my bare feet and the moon overhead as witnesses. I had to. Because tomorrow came with no guarantees. Life didn't wait.

Extending my arm as far as I could, I turned my hand over and allowed the pills to fall into the flowing water.

I thought of Mel and Maddie and those women from the photograph and so many unknown, anonymous others. In comparison to what they might have experienced or the difficult tasks they'd had to accomplish, this was a nothing thing. This was no more than the giving up of a crutch. Postrecovery, these pills had only been a false protection from life and difficult emotion.

My mother's need had been different, and perhaps stopping had not been an option for her—I couldn't judge that, but I understood it better now. I was grateful that for me it was a simple fix.

Sometimes the simplest fixes were also the hardest—because they required a person to take a chance and get out of her own way.

And for once, that was what I'd done.

Chapter Nineteen

Come morning, my perspective had shifted. I was done with being torn between feelings for Will and Seth. Both were good men. I wouldn't torture myself about it, especially when there were more important things to consider. In fact, worrying over two grown men when Maddie was the one at risk . . . I couldn't turn my back on that reality. I saw her again in my mind, huddled on that rock, her clothes and hair wet with creek water, missing her stand-in father.

I called Seth.

Was I doing the right thing? Did I have the right to interfere? To, in effect, tattle on his family?

I had to, regardless.

He answered, and I asked, "Is it a good time to talk?"

"Kara. Yeah, it's good."

"This is awkward, Seth. I apologize up front for calling about it."

"What's up? Is something wrong?"

"Yes, I think so. I'm worried about Maddie."

"What? Is she sick? Is she okay?"

"You know she's having a really hard time adjusting to your absence."

"I spoke with her yesterday. She sounded okay."

I went silent for a moment. Trying to convey

341

my concern delicately wasn't getting the job done.

"It might be more than that, Seth."

"It's normal for children to take a while to adjust to changes in their lives, but they do. Maddie has lots of love and support. Is there something specific that's causing you worry?"

I sputtered a little, uncomfortable. "Mel isn't getting any younger, Seth. She looks tired."

"Tired? What does that mean?"

"Well, I think it's normal for her age. Keeping up with a young child isn't easy."

"Oh." I heard Seth breathing. Finally he said, "I spoke to Mom yesterday. She told me about Maddie's adventure, but she said everyone was fine. I can't believe she'd take a risk regarding Maddie Lyn."

"She'd never allow Maddie to be put at risk, but she might overestimate her . . . personal bandwidth . . . her energy. Did you know that Maddie has run off on her own twice now?"

There, I'd said it. Now it was in Seth's hands.

But Seth still didn't get it. "Mom told me that Maddie had gone over to your house a couple of times. We both explained to Maddie that she's too young to walk over by herself. Was there more to it than that?"

Was there, I asked myself? I thought yes. Should I reemphasize my concern about Maddie? I settled for, "I don't want to intrude. Talk to your

Mom and Nicole. Make sure everyone is on the same page, okay?"

"I will." His voice took on a softer tone. "I appreciate your caring and talking to me about it."

"Come home soon, Seth, okay? I'd like to talk to you face to face."

"Soon. And I understand. Phones are great, but it isn't the same. I've decided where we're going to dinner. It's a pretty cool place, and the food is excellent."

He may have heard my sigh through the phone, because his tone shifted. He said, "I've been wanting to talk to you in person, too, so I'll have a better chance of convincing you to come out here with me."

"It's not that simple, Seth."

"For a visit, at least. I know you're busy. Maybe for a week. Just consider it."

I sighed again. Seth gave a short laugh.

"No worries, Kara. We'll talk it out. And I'm glad you called. See you soon."

"Bye, Seth."

We disconnected.

It was left to me to wait.

And what about Will? I was pretty sure he wouldn't be content to stay in the friend category. So maybe he was waiting on Seth too.

The next day, Nicole called. "I'm bringing Hannah Cooper over to meet you today and to get a look at the carriage house. Maybe in about an hour?"

"Looking forward to it," I said. And no time like the present. I was counting on Hannah's involvement even though I'd yet to even meet her. I knew she was the most well known of the local artisans we were hoping would engage with us for our someday guests. Plus, that vase . . . its artistry intrigued me. When Nicole called out from the front door, "Kara?" I came up the hallway to see her and a slim woman with blonde hair at my front door.

I opened the screen door, saying, "Welcome. Please come in. You must be Hannah?"

"I am."

She offered her hand. I shook it, saying, "I'm pleased to meet you. I'm sure Nicole explained what I'm planning here at Wildflower House."

"She has. It sounds interesting."

"I'd love to show you the carriage house and get your thoughts on how we might use that space for pottery and ceramics. I want to use it for other things, too, like maybe painting, but I was hoping you could look at the space and help me understand what I don't know enough about to ask reasonable questions. I want to maximize the space."

"Happy to." But she wasn't looking at me. She'd stopped in the sitting room and was standing at the fireplace mantel.

"The blue vase? Nicole gave it to us as a house-warming gift. It's beautiful."

Hannah smiled at me. Her face lit up, and her blue eyes deepened. "I'm glad you like it."

"How could I not? It's amazing. I've never seen shaping and glazing done quite like that. Maybe one day you'll tell me the secret?"

She gave me a sharp look and then visibly relaxed. In a teasing tone, she said, "We all have our secrets. Sometimes they are better kept than shared."

"Truth," I said.

Hannah cast a wider glance around the room as we moved from it back into the foyer. She paused for a long moment in front of the photo of the women before turning back toward me. "I'd love to see your carriage house. And if you don't mind, I'd love to see more of the house too."

"Of course."

"You probably know that I grew up not far from here. Cooper's Hollow."

"Yes, I do. You're still in the area, right? Near here?"

"Still in Cooper's Hollow." She smiled. "I never wanted to live anywhere else."

"Perfect, because what I'm hoping to arrange is a place where local artists and artisans can work with groups who are visiting here, depending upon their interests."

Nicole said, "And more than clay and painting.

Local talent and specialists. If someone wants to bird-watch, we can certainly find someone who can provide that instruction. I know a local man who's a chess master. My yoga instructor can teach classes. My friend Dierdre has a massage table and will travel."

I stepped back, physically and emotionally. "Not a spa, Nicole. Birds, maybe, but . . ."

Hannah laughed. She touched my arm and said kindly, "Don't limit yourself and don't limit your world because you're worried about overreaching. Open the door to your world, and see what shows up." Her gaze shifted below the mantel, and she smiled. "Who painted the fire screen paintings? They are perfect."

"Do you know Will Mercer?"

"I don't believe so."

"He works for Mitchell's Lawn and Landscaping."

"I'm familiar with them." She looked curious. "They're into fine art?"

"Oh, no," I said. "Will's sister, Brittany, painted these. He introduced me to her work."

The three of us walked through the house. Hannah remarked, "I grew up nearby but never had the opportunity to come in here and satisfy my curiosity. My grandmother knew the Forsters in their younger years . . ."

"My father grew up in the area, too, but left when he was young. The Langes?"

"Sorry, no," she said. "I don't recall them, but we didn't get out much. We kept to ourselves, mostly . . ." She trailed off, and we walked outside to the grounds. She went silent as I opened the wide doors to the carriage house. I went in ahead of them and pulled the chain to give us light.

Throughout the tour and now in the carriage house, Hannah carried herself with grace and contained energy. When she spoke, her hands moved as if crafting the words and phrases—as if the internal music of sculpture ran through her clear to her fingertips. I found myself watching her speak and listening to her tone and word choices and totally missing what she was saying. Dad had always spoken in even, controlled tones. Hannah's voice and cadence were almost magical. But her hands . . . I understood why she chose to express herself with them, albeit via clay.

Hannah said, "If you don't mind, I'd like to share what you're planning here with some of my friends. See who might be interested."

Hannah Cooper believed in this project. I did, too, but to have this kind of help offered . . . it was humbling. And uplifting. That was the thought that remained with me after Nicole and Hannah left.

What she'd said about leaving the door open and seeing what showed up . . . that idea lingered with me, teasing me. I laughed. I certainly did leave my door open most every morning, literally, for the fresh air and the breeze and the morning sun. Maybe I could do it emotionally, too, and grow more confident in my ability to deal with whatever walked into my life. And whoever."

Chapter Twenty

Seth called two days later to say he had his plane ticket.

"We're going to Tavern on the Rail for dinner. You'll love it. Great food and ambience. A special kind of place. Not too dressy. I'll be on your doorstep at six sharp on Friday. Nothing will get in our way this time."

"I'll be here." I disconnected with a smile.

Dressy. Not too dressy. What did that mean anyway? The restaurant was in the country, so no diamonds or sequins, I joked to myself. Plus, there was more to this date than a dinner. I would welcome Seth and see where it went from there. Whatever worked out between us or didn't, I considered him a friend.

I hadn't seen Will in two days, and before that, I'd seen him only in passing, delivering some plants and enriched soil that was now piled in the area intended for the medallion garden. I trusted Will. He was a valued friend.

I didn't want to lose either of them as friends. For more than friendship? I had to give Seth a chance—or at least be honest with him face to face. It was hard to walk away from a relationship I'd put so much hope into.

A simple dress, sleek and flattering to my

thin build, seemed a good choice. Might as well maximize my few good features, I thought, and I laughed again, but the sound had a nervous edge to it.

Come Friday, his knock on the front door was punctual and crisp. It echoed up the hallway. I was already in the foyer, ready and waiting—also punctual. I opened the door, trying to play it cool, but couldn't stop myself from throwing my arms around him and hugging him. When I stepped back, only slightly embarrassed, Seth smiled at me and said, "You look amazing."

"So do you," I said. "I mean, you look amazing standing in my doorway. It's been too long, Seth."

"Don't brush off the compliment, Kara."

I allowed myself to preen a bit. It had been a long time since I'd dressed up for pleasure, for anyone. Not since the disastrous anniversary when Niles had died.

"Come in, Seth." He did, and I closed the door.

He walked past me, crossing through the foyer into the sitting room. He stopped in the wide opening between the sitting room and dining room.

"You left the wallpaper up in the dining room?"

"Moore Blackwell worked on it for days and days." I flipped on the chandelier. "What do you think?"

"This looks great. You've made it work—

mixing the old and the new. Nicole told me it was beautiful."

"She did?"

"I see Hannah Cooper's blue vase in here, and it echoes the blues in the parlor. What's this?" He'd stopped in front of the fireplace. He looked back at me. "Who did these?"

"Will Mercer's sister, Brittany."

"Really? You said he works for the landscaper?"

"He does."

"Well, these are nice. Very nice."

"Beautiful, actually. Brittany is very talented. Let me show you the kitchen remodel."

He walked with me into the kitchen and gave a low whistle. "Wow. That kitchen was so awful." He laughed. "I heard you say that yourself. But this is . . ."

"Perfect? Gorgeous?"

"Perfectly gorgeous." He turned to me with a serious look. "You've done great. Nicole thinks you're almost ready to open for business."

I drew in a hard breath. "Not quite. Nicole is an optimist. We still have to deal with the sewage field and adding the small bathrooms upstairs, and it will all have to pass inspection."

He frowned. "Are you still worried about it?"

"Worry? I think it's more about dealing with reality. Some things are worth tackling, and some aren't. Unfortunately, we don't always know ahead of time which is which." I touched his arm. "I'm firmly grounded in reality. Not the businessperson my dad was and not the emotionally driven, hidden woman that my mom was. I'm somewhere in between." I laughed. "And now I'm discovering I have a bit of an artist in me. I can't imagine where that will lead."

"You are you. Just be you, Kara."

"And you should be you, Seth."

He looked at me for a long moment. "I want to be honest, Kara."

"Me too, Seth. I think we should talk."

"I thought maybe after dinner, but . . . I don't know. There's something in your face, your eyes."

I nodded. "What are your plans for the immediate future and long term?"

He looked away, then back at me, and he shrugged. "I like LA. I like the city."

I nodded. "I know."

"We've had something special between us from the day we met. You feel the same, right?"

"Yes."

He sighed. "Come out there, Kara. Come see the city. I'm torn between being there and here. I can't keep making these quick trips every few weeks."

I looked away. I took my emotional temperature by the rate at which my heart beat and found my answer. After a deep breath, I said, "Then you should stay."

"I can't." He shook his head. "I have to be back

before Wednesday. I have a big client meeting that day and—"

"No. You should stay *there*. If returning to Cub Creek was the answer, you wouldn't feel torn. You'd just be planning how quickly you could make it happen."

He stared at me.

"In fact, you didn't come back this time because you wanted to. Or for me. Did you? You came because you felt you had to, not because you wanted to."

Seth said, "It's not that simple, Kara. A big part of my life is on the far side of the country. It's like a whole different world—and one I'm discovering that I'm pretty successful in."

"Then I'm happy you've found success, Seth."

"You don't sound happy. I'm doing the best I can to take everyone into consideration."

I heard his swift intake of breath. He looked me in the face and leaned toward me.

"Kara, the current situation is confusing for me too. I care about you. I wouldn't hurt you for the world."

"The best way not to hurt me is to be honest. That's all you owe me, Seth. Just care enough to be honest."

"I'm not sure I want to return to Cub Creek." He watched my face. "At least not now."

He waited. I did too. What was there to say?

"You don't look surprised," Seth said.

"I'm not. Not really . . ."

"We hardly had a chance to get to know each other before our lives turned upside down." He paused before adding, "At one point I didn't believe you could really make this dream into reality here at Wildflower House—but you are; you have. It astounds me. Maybe it shouldn't. Maybe it just shows how little I truly knew you."

"Or know me."

"Kara."

"It's okay, Seth. It really is." I rested my hands lightly on his arms. "Nothing stays the same. No moment stays static. We had a moment. We just didn't know it was a moment in the midst of change. Maybe if we'd been together, changing together . . ."

"You encouraged me to find a job I loved. You told me to go for it."

"I did. I would do it again. It was the right thing. I still believe that."

He nodded but didn't speak for a long moment. "I guess time will tell how things work out for us?"

"Or won't work out." I pulled my hands back. "I think we already know the answer, Seth. I don't mean to sound hard, but I'm tired of waiting. Waiting on what my husband wanted, waiting to see what my dad decided, waiting . . . waiting on my mom to come back home and put our lives back together." I clenched my fists. "I did, you know. I stood at the windows watching for her. I cut school to search the area on foot, looking for her car."

He frowned. "Your mom died. She couldn't come back."

"Two years after she left, yes, she died. But that's not my point. I waited on everyone and never fought back, not for myself. I tried to fit myself in everyone else's life, their needs . . ."

"Kara, I never asked for you to do that."

"No, Seth, you didn't. I volunteered it. I have always taken the second seat. I've always ridden shotgun throughout my life. I want to drive for a change. I want to do what I want to do with no regard for anyone else. And I don't care if it sounds selfish. It's simple honesty."

He opened his mouth a couple of times but then closed it. He was thinking. I could almost see his brain working. Finally, he said, "Don't get mad. I'm just gonna say it outright. You do sound selfish, but I think you've probably just spoken the truest words anyone has ever uttered. Everyone feels that way at some point."

"Seth, distance doesn't work for me. I want to share my life with someone in real time."

As we stared into each other's eyes, it felt different. Our dynamic had changed along with expectations. Had almost vanished. I saw a man. Seth. Someone I liked well enough to be a friend to, who'd been kind to me when I'd moved here, but whose shortcomings were his own. His flaws required no action, no cover or explanation, from me.

I asked, "What about Maddie?"

He looked away. "It isn't that I don't want her in LA with me, but it would be irresponsible. When she's older, having her in my care will be more workable. Maybe then . . ."

My heart broke a little for Maddie and also for Seth. One day he would look back and question his choices. But that would be on him. Not me.

"Good luck, Seth. I hope the job continues to be everything you want it to be."

"Come and visit me there. Stay. Get to know the area. I want Maddie to visit too. It's a long trip but just a flight away."

"It's okay, Seth. Truly. Go. You don't owe me anything."

"Los Angeles is a fantastic place. A place you should experience before you dismiss it."

I shook my head. "I won't be flying out there. I'm pretty busy here."

Seth stood, and I stood with him. He put his arms around me, and I returned the hug, but it was a friendly hug. A wish-you-well hug.

"Goodbye for now," he said.

"Goodbye, Seth."

He left. I locked the front door behind him, kicked off my heels, and went out, but in the opposite direction.

I sat for a long while on the bench by the creek. My head was empty. Not in a bad way but in that waiting mode. The lying-in-bed-wondering-why-I'm-awake way. The trees were darkening with night shadows, and the sky was tinged with deep purple. I saw the first firefly lights winking in and out at the edge of the woods.

As night fell, the creek continued to pass quietly and discreetly. Birds called from the nearby trees. Gnomes might be watching, and a deer or two might be hoping I'd leave so they could graze without distraction. Still, I sat, but now I asked myself, Why? What had happened? How did I feel about it?

I'd feared disappointment and maybe a broken heart. Maybe even guilt because I'd almost screwed up again—or would have, if I'd had my bullheaded way. I would've committed the same mistakes as I had before with Niles. Why did people do that? Because it was the familiar path?

But I didn't feel disappointment. And my heart was beating cheerfully in my chest. Nothing broken there.

His friendship and his support—I wanted to keep them, but I also wanted to stay here. Seth wanted a different path. Maybe we'd never been on the same path. Maybe they'd only run parallel for a short time. And maybe part of the attraction, despite everything I'd been telling myself, was that as long as he was away, we could put off commitment. We could avoid screwing it up.

I felt relief. Like I'd had a near escape from a big mistake. A mistake that would've harmed us both.

Seth was doing exactly what I said I wanted to do—living his life in real time, making his decisions without needing approval or permission.

I laughed, and one of the nearby birds settling into the trees for the night squawked and trilled at me. I laughed louder, and a deer on the far side of the creek raised his head, and his bright eyes looked at me in question.

Waiting on me to leave, probably.

I was laughing because, of course, what I'd said I wanted was exactly what I didn't want. I wanted to be my own person, but I also wanted my own person. *My own person.* Not someone to follow or miss but someone to partner with. To dance with. To kiss. To hug whenever I felt like it. I wanted to be with someone who wanted to be with me—not because he had to be but because I was me and he couldn't imagine being anywhere else.

The day after Seth left, I visited Mel. I was apprehensive. When she answered the door, I said, "Can we talk?"

"Come in, Kara." She didn't look too pleased. I noted the shadows were darker beneath her eyes, and her cheeks looked gaunt. Where was the vitality I'd seen only a few weeks before?

"How are you feeling these days, Mel?"

"Slow, Kara. Just slow. Feeling my age, I guess. Have a seat?"

We sat at the kitchen table.

Mel said, "I'm glad school is back in session. Maddie needs to be out among children her own age."

"I'm sure you're right." I cleared my throat. "I've been thinking about something. I hope you won't mind if I make a suggestion?"

She shrugged. "Of course not. If I do mind, I'll tell you straight out."

"I know you will." I gathered my words. *Practice empathy,* I told myself. It wasn't always my strong point, but I could claim more competence with it than my dad. "I was thinking that Maddie could spend afternoons with me. Maybe start off during the week. She can join me after school. That will give you a little time to breathe." I stopped, trying to gauge what she was thinking.

Mel shook her head. "I know what you told Seth—I wasn't up to taking care of Maddie anymore—but remember it's not just me alone. It's me and Nicole. I know Maddie has wandered off twice now, but that's due to Seth being gone. Him leaving shook Maddie's world. But she's adjusting now, especially with school to occupy her."

"I meant no offense when I told Seth." I looked

away and shrugged. "He didn't take my worry seriously, anyway. He thought I was just wanting him to come back home."

"Did you?"

"Did I miss him and want him back here? Yes. But that's absolutely not why I told him. I was concerned for Maddie and you."

"I know that." She picked at a thread knot on the tablecloth. "Do you still want him to come back?"

I struggled with what to say. I had to be honest with Mel, but I didn't want to say the wrong words and hurt her. But I took too long. Mel stood up and walked away.

"Mel."

"Hang on."

She returned to the table with a slab of fudge. She unwrapped the waxed paper. "Cooked this late last night. Had trouble sleeping, and it seemed a good thing to do." She pushed a sharp knife through the chocolate goodness. She put a hefty chunk on a napkin and slid it over to me before slicing her own. I waited as she fixed us each a cup of coffee.

I took a bite of fudge and sipped the coffee. "Mel, I think I've just experienced a glimpse of heaven."

Mel smiled.

"You asked if I still wanted him to come back. I can honestly say I want him to do what calls to him." I took another sip. "When I think about it, I hardly knew him. I liked and still like Seth very much, but I wanted him to be who I needed—not who *he* needed to be." I smiled wryly. "Sorry to be so awkward with words."

"You and that Will Mercer seem to be getting along well."

Will. After misjudging the stability of my marriage to Niles and, more recently, the feelings that Seth and I shared—or not, as it turned out—I was determined not to rush blindly into a new relationship. I had no intention of involving Mel in that.

"Will and I have worked well together, and I like him, but Mel, the reality is that I haven't had much luck with choosing men. I'm not placing any blame or criticism on Seth. He was willing to stay here, but then the job in LA came along. You and I know that staying here would've been wrong for him. Seth and I want different things. I'm glad we found out before our hearts were too committed. As for Will—whatever happens, I'm not going to rush into a new relationship.

"For now, I'd like to help you and help Maddie too. If you'd like to try it. In the evening, you have Nicole for help, but we both know Nicole will always have her head in her business. It's where her comfort is."

Mel shook her head and pulled at her hands.

"But that's the thing—I mean Seth staying in California and you maybe liking Will. Nicole means well and tries, but I can't count on her in that way. Maddie has had her life turned upside down enough. She needs stability."

"There's truth in that. But there's also value in having your eggs in more than one basket." I laughed. "Sorry. Didn't mean to throw a cliché at you. What I mean is it's good to know many people care about you, that if something goes wrong or you lose someone important in your life, others can and want to step in and love you. Stability is important, but nothing's certain. When we least expect it, fate jumps in and shakes things up."

Mel looked thoughtful, but she didn't respond.

I touched her hands, and they stilled.

"Give it some thought. I wouldn't make the offer if I didn't mean it. Over the winter, I'm having construction done upstairs to add bathrooms and also to improve the attic area. I won't host overnight guests until early spring. When it comes to lonely winter days, it will be especially nice to have Maddie around."

I'd managed to get past my growing self-medication problem. For me, I saw that as a personal triumph over fear. But a crutch could be simpler at its core—a basic emotional human need for love such that people settled for relationships not right for them rather than risk being left to live life alone.

I'd done that too. And I was proud of the big steps forward I'd made. I had another problem to tackle—allowing myself to be vulnerable to risk or rejection.

Victoria and I had reached an understanding. Same with me and Seth.

Now there was Will.

I'd hardly seen him since he'd finished up the carriage house and the paths. He'd had other jobs over the past week. Wildflower House wasn't Mitchell's Lawn and Landscaping's only client, and Will was in demand, but I wondered if he was also deliberately staying away. He'd come back today to plant the azaleas he'd ordered for the medallion garden bed. I'd returned home from Mel's on foot, and I stood at the path's entrance watching him as he worked.

I was getting up my nerve to tell Will that Seth had gone back to LA and we were no longer anything more than friends. But suppose Will had had time to reconsider? It had been almost two weeks—really just a little more than a week and a half. But maybe time had already moved on for him. And for us.

Chapter Twenty-One

I walked up the slope toward him. Still several yards away, I stopped and called out, "Will, can we talk?"

He glanced up from where he knelt at the planting area, but then he looked away quickly and focused on brushing the dirt from his hands.

"I talked to Seth," I said.

He looked at me and rose to his feet. "And?"

"Will? Is everything okay? You don't seem like yourself."

"Just say it, Kara. If you've decided to give Seth another chance, just say the words. I'll disappear."

"I—" The words were there in my head, ready, but I wanted to say them right. "I don't know how much you know about me—my history."

"Don't take this wrong, Kara, but I don't care about your history. I know you and want to know you better."

"Of course," I said.

He looked confused.

Surprised, I said, "What I had in mind was a fresh start." I spoke slowly, saying, "A fresh start for us. For me."

By now, the space between us had vanished. As we met somewhere in the middle, I put my hand on his arm.

"Bear with me, Will. I need to say this."

"Okay." He took my hand from his arm and held it in his.

"I thought Seth and I were more than friends. I thought he and I had a future. Don't misunderstand me—he didn't do anything wrong. I saw him as someone he wasn't. That's not his fault. In my heart, though, I knew. I saw the truth coming at us head-on. Seth and I would've been a mistake, and I'm grateful it got sorted out before that happened."

I kept my eyes pinned on Will's face as I was speaking. "I don't want to repeat that mistake with you. I want to know you better and for you to know me. Who we really are. As for Seth, he's not in my life now, other than as a friend and occasional neighbor."

Will smiled, and his eyes—that perilous blue—lit up.

He squeezed my hand gently and then realized the dirt on his hand was now also on mine. He brushed at the bits of dark earth. "Sorry, I've been planting."

I grabbed both his hands and held them securely. "This is Wildflower House. The Wildflower Property." I smiled. "This is Wildflower dirt, and there's none better."

Will nodded. "I agree. Anything else you want to say?"

"No, that's it. Assuming you're still interested, of course."

He said, "I'd like to invite you out."

"A date?"

"A date. You and me. Wherever you'd like to go."

I experienced a sudden rush of anticipation that immediately defaulted to doubt. I was too happy. This was too much like daring fate to screw with my life again.

"Will, I hope you understand I need to take this slow. A lot of things have happened in my life this past year—even before that—and I want to make decisions regarding my life, not just react to change."

"No objection. Slow is fine as long as we're taking it slow together."

"Then I'd love to go out with you. Maybe dinner?"

"When?" he asked.

"Whenever."

Will said, "Then now, but I need to clean up first."

"You look fine."

"No, ma'am. I'm sincere about this. This is a small town, and people may recognize us. I won't have anyone thinking you weren't worth cleaning up for."

That stopped me. He was thinking of me. Concerned about me.

"I can be back here in about an hour and a half. About suppertime."

"Where shall we go?"

"There's a place in Louisa. Good food. A relaxed, comfortable place."

"I'll be ready." I was so delighted, so suddenly energized, that somehow more words rolled out past my lips. "I'm glad you aren't shy now."

Will smiled. "Shy? Maybe a little. But only because I fell for you the moment I saw you. That day when Jim Mitchell and I were talking to your dad about the landscaping work and you came out of the house . . . your face was lit up, and it was all I could do not to say how I felt right out in front of everyone. But we were strangers, and I saw pretty quickly that you had feelings for Seth. With him away so much . . . well, it seemed wrong to move in like that. I was afraid to rush it, that you might shut me out." He touched my cheek. "I'm glad you're giving us a chance."

"Me too," I whispered.

Will had said the restaurant was relaxed and comfortable. I tore through my closet. Jeans or leggings didn't feel like a safe choice. I was getting nervous until I caught sight of my worried face in the mirror.

I untwisted my anxious fingers. No worries. Not for him. Not for me. This was about dinner with someone whose company I enjoyed. Stress and worry didn't fit into that picture.

Will Mercer. Kara Lange Hart. Supper.

The rest was just noise.

He pulled up in his truck, but the ladders and work material were gone. Judging by the water droplets still hiding in the crevice where the door met the truck body, his vehicle was fresh from a car wash. Will had shined up, too—nicely, in fact. He wore a blue cotton button-down shirt with jeans so neat they looked pressed. He must've moved fast.

I stood at the front door as he pulled his truck up to the front steps; slipped out of the driver's seat; came around, beating me to the passenger-side door; and held it open.

"Nice manners," I said, smiling.

"Maybe," he said as he reached out to help me with that big step up into the truck. "Mostly, I can't have you falling out. You might get injured, and we'd have to reschedule supper."

"No way," I said with a mock frown. "You aren't getting out of this so easily. I'm tougher than I look. And I'm hungry."

The view from the height of the passenger seat was almost heady. I glanced at Will, giving him a sharp look, and he grinned. The blue shirt made his eyes even bluer.

I shook my head and focused on fastening the seat belt as Will settled into the driver's seat. "I've never ridden in a truck before."

He looked at me, those blue eyes giving my heart a sharp twang, and said, "Better hold on tight, then."

"What?"

"Joking," he said. "Just joking, Kara. I didn't mean to alarm you." Boldly, he reached across and rested his hand on mine. "Just sit back and enjoy the ride. If I scare you, you let me know."

With his hand on mine, so comfortable yet so new, I was a little scared then, but not in the way he meant. And I certainly wouldn't enlighten him. I might be scared of getting hurt, maybe even of the temptation *not* to take it so slowly, but I wasn't going to allow that impulse to control my choices. *I* was in the driver's seat for that.

Will drove to the town of Louisa. It was a relatively silent few miles until I said, "You know a lot about me, but I don't know much about you."

"What do you want to know?" He tapped the steering wheel. "Born and raised here. I've been out of state a few times, but never to anywhere bigger than Nashville."

"I've never been to Nashville."

"Nice place. Nice countryside between here and there. I have a cousin who works at the Opry part-time. She might get us in backstage with a little notice."

"Seriously?"

He nodded. "But that's not what you want to know. I understand that. There's not much to tell. I have a small place on the other side of Mineral. Live alone. I'm not there much because it seems like I'm always working." He gave me a sideways glance. "Especially over the last couple of months. I wish I could tell you I was smart and educated and well traveled. I can't. I barely made it out of high school and will never sit in another classroom again, not if I can help it. I'm smart, but in other ways. I'd rather be doing than sitting."

"I think my father would've agreed with you. I wish you'd had the chance to know him better." More than that, I didn't say, but I saw in Will that work connection with my Dad—the love of creating something with one's own hand—but more. Creation with a purpose.

By then we were driving along a street in the town of Louisa, a street on which businesses had been operating probably before it had officially become the county seat. Old and restored storefronts filled the block, and in the middle was a restaurant named Obrigado.

"Right there," he said. "Good food and good people."

Will was there at the side of the truck to catch me as I pretty much fell out while trying to exit. He laughed as he steadied me but didn't release me—not right away. He kept his hands on my waist, and I kept mine on his arms, but now it was my turn to feel shy. When he did let go, he moved his hand beneath my elbow in case I needed assistance in stepping over the curb.

"Thank you."

As Will had said, the restaurant atmosphere was casual and relaxed, but the aroma was amazing. My stomach growled, and I would've been embarrassed, but the noise was covered by a man who was sitting on a stool on a small stage strumming a guitar in a jazzy tune. Low conversations hummed around us, and a woman walked past us with a quick "Hi, Will" and a "Take a seat where you like." I didn't miss that extra look, the quick one that she cast back at Will and at me before moving on.

"Over here," Will said. Before we could reach the table, a man came forward and slapped him on the back. It seemed rough, but Will didn't blink. Instead, he grinned and said, "Kara, this is Clay Ward. He's a relative of some degree or other. Clay, this is Kara Hart, who consented to join me for dinner, so I'd appreciate it if you didn't cause any chaos or embarrassment."

"No indeed, Cousin Will. Pleased to meet you, Kara."

I almost giggled as Will urged me forward and we left Clay behind.

Will pulled out my chair. I touched his hand where it was still positioned on the chairback.

He looked at me and smiled, and my heart was happy.

The date had the usual ebb and flow of first-date conversation—but different. It wasn't like conversations with Seth. Will and I didn't speak of favorite poets or the excitement of LA, and besides, Will and I had spent a good deal of time together already. We'd worked on improving and readying Wildflower House for its future, so we had that in common, and it might have seemed a natural topic. But it was different when you were sitting across a small table from each other, hoping you weren't going to screw up an already friendly relationship by trying to take it further than it was ready or able to go. I'd been there, done that already with Niles and Seth. Maybe this was a case of the third time being the charm?

"You said you grew up here," I ventured. "Does that mean your family has been living in the area a long time?"

"Long time. Lots of extended family."

"You're lucky."

"Has its good points and bad points. Mostly good, I guess."

We paused while the waitress brought us a menu and took our drink orders. When she was gone, Will said, "I guess that means you don't have much family."

"Nope. Never have." I thought of Dad and the

missing twin siblings. Not much family, but the possibility of more was out there. "What about your sister? Did she study art in college, or is she self-taught?"

Will looked across the room at the bar. Several people were seated there chatting and eating. He nodded. "She went away to school. To Charlottesville. Studied art, but she had that accident and dropped out."

"Sad. Especially about the accident."

"She'll be okay. She's tough. She just needs time."

"I'm looking forward to meeting her. What about your parents? You mentioned your mom once but didn't really say."

"She's Mom. Vivi. I'll let you make up your own mind about her." He sipped his drink. "What about yours? You lost her when you were young, right?"

This time I looked aside. But only for a moment. I turned back toward Will. "She loved to dance. It was before I was old enough to remember, but Dad told me. And she loved flowers. I have some that she pressed in waxed paper long, long ago. By the time I knew her, most of that—or whatever it was that made her who she was—was gone. I wish I'd known her before she lost herself."

Will stared. He reached across the table and put his hand on mine. "We all get lost from time to time. Just make sure you have the right people around to pull you back into the game when you need them."

I clasped his hand in return. It felt like a moment. A huge one. And it was interrupted when the waitress returned with our drinks.

"Ready to order?" she asked.

I looked at Will, he looked back, and we laughed.

"Sorry," he said. "We haven't decided yet."

"Okay. Just wave when you're ready."

"Got it," he said.

"Wait," I said to her. I did a quick scan of the menu. "The greek salad looks good."

"Yeah?" Will said to the waitress, "Two of those."

She walked away.

I stared at Will. "Seriously? Have you actually tried the greek salad?"

He laughed. "No, I haven't. I'm not too sure what all that stuff is in there."

"Then why did you order it?"

"Because I haven't had it before. I'm more of a beef person, but it doesn't hurt to try something new from time to time." He leaned toward me. "I want to know what you like. If you like greek salad, then so be it."

I felt touched by his gesture and his words.

He continued, "That said, if I don't like it, I'm going back to the catfish dinner next time." He touched my hand. "It's good to be flexible, but it's important to be honest."

I put my hand over his. "We might make a good team, Will Mercer. I'm looking forward to finding out."

Chapter Twenty-Two

Victoria arrived with clothing and a box of small but tempting pastries.

She said, "I'll run up and change real quick. Take the box"—she handed it to me—"and put them on a fancy plate. I'll be right back down." And she rushed up the stairs.

I stood there in her wake, wanting to say that the book club members were bringing their own food. And they were. But I saw what Victoria was intending. Delightful pastries on a crystal plate on the foyer table. Totally unnecessary but indisputably inviting. And I had the perfect little napkins to set right beside it.

I went back to the kitchen to get the plate.

The club members were due to arrive soon. Victoria had driven down to be on hand to help. When I'd called her and asked if she still wanted to participate, she'd said she'd check her calendar and then burst into laughter. "I'll be there," she promised. "I'll be there so you can stay all cool and together. Like . . . what do they call it? A genial host?"

I laughed softly now. We all had skills and talents, all the nicer when they meshed well.

Victoria reappeared in sleek black slacks and a dressy shirt and heels. We'd decided to dress up a bit for the occasion. But not too much. What did one wear when hosting a book club meeting? Was there a preferred genial-host outfit? I didn't have a clue. I settled for a silk blouse and slacks.

She mentioned my mood again as we were setting up the dining room. "You don't seem nervous or anxious, Kara. You are cool, calm, and collected."

"I'm always cool," I replied, folding the napkins and laying one beside each plate.

Victoria arranged the silverware around the table. "You appear cool, but you rarely actually are." She shook her head. "You forget I know what happens when you lose that cool."

I fixed my gaze on her. "I'm not the only one here with a temper."

She waved a fork in my direction. "There's a technique to managing it. Better to vent it regularly than to go nuclear."

I could've corrected her, but I didn't. The reality was that I wore my frustration just below the surface as a protection. And others could sense it, I realized now, but they didn't necessarily under-stand the fear that the appearance of strength was hiding. Yet the wall had been mostly dismantled. I was slower to shut people out. I called that a win.

"Just an FYI, Victoria. You'll find I'm more even tempered now." I eyed her. "But don't test me."

Victoria laughed. "I'm pretty tough myself.

What was it your dad said? That you were resilient? Well, maybe it's catching, because I've discovered I am too."

"What you are is stubborn. You beat me out in that category every time." I shook my head. "Sometimes maybe stubborn is a strength too."

She stopped and stared.

I brushed at my face and my blouse. "What?"

"Something's different." She shook her head. "Not about your outfit, puh-lease. No, this is something else. What aren't you telling me?"

"I have no idea what you're talking about."

A grin slowly appeared on her face, and her eyes lit up. "Is it Will or Seth? You finally went on that date with Seth, right?"

I shrugged. "We talked but never actually went on the date. We cleared the air. We're friends, and we're good."

Victoria clapped her hands. "It's Will, then! You went out with Will."

"Why do you think that?"

"Because there's a difference in your step. I don't know how to describe it. Your step, how you're standing. A general sort of . . . glow." She grabbed my arms. "Are you officially in love?"

"Officially in love? What does that even mean?"

"Don't deflect, Kara. Just tell me."

I sighed. "Not love, not yet, but we did go out. We both agreed to take it slow."

Victoria laughed loudly and threw her arms

around me. She stepped back quickly, though, to smooth our blouses. We both heard the first car arrive and composed our expressions.

The ladies arrived for their meeting a car at a time.

"Didn't Sue say five or six people?"

"She did." Victoria laughed and held the door wide as several women walked in. In the driveway, another car had pulled up, and two more women exited and approached the steps. Someone else had parked in my new lot. Four women climbed out of that car.

I smiled in welcome.

The last person in was an older man. He greeted me pleasantly, and I returned the favor.

Several carried covered dishes. I gestured toward the kitchen, and Victoria, with a reassuring glance my way, left the front door and followed them down the hallway.

"Kara."

It was Sue.

I said, "Looks like quite a turnout?" My question was heavy with implication.

"Oh my, yes. Excellent turnout. A few old members returned to our group, and a few new ones joined." She lowered her voice. "Goodness, they were excited to see inside the house. I told them not to roam, but I hope you'll understand if they sneak a peek into the rooms here on the main floor."

"Of course. Do you think they'd enjoy a short tour?"

"They'd adore it. Most of these gals grew up around here but never had an opportunity to check the house out. With you here, they are extra curious."

"Me?"

"About you and your plans for the retreat. Everyone is curious. Nicole knows how to sell a house and a story. And I'm delighted." Her eyes twinkled, and she hurried to join the others in the parlor.

"Guess what, ladies and gent? Our hostess, Kara Hart, is offering to conduct a tour for anyone who's interested."

They gathered around me.

Sue did a few introductions, which I knew I'd never recall except for Reggie. As the one male, it was easy enough. Names like Jane and Claudia and Diane and Martha flowed together, but I smiled and nodded and tried to keep my polite face on. It was a sincere face. It was also my brave face. The one that made me believe I could do this. And do it better each time.

I saw Victoria carrying additional plates into the dining room. One of the ladies seemed to have attached herself to the work detail and had handfuls of silverware and napkins.

"We've got this handled, Kara," Victoria said. "Go ahead with the tour."

"Thanks." I took a breath. Facing our first guests at Wildflower House, I said, "Let's walk through, and if anyone has any questions, please speak up."

It felt natural after we got started—especially when I realized Sue was happy to contribute her own memories and opinions to my narration. It felt almost as if Mary and Rob were walking with us as we passed through the foyer and stood in the sitting room with its view of the dining room and—back across the hall—of the grand staircase. I could see, as if I were seeing it through the eyes of our guests, the great pains we'd taken in our renovations and our genuine pleasure to host them. I glowed a little, feeling the reward for our effort.

There were a few questions, mostly about the fire screen paintings, and one of the women, Elaine, noted the "Hannah Cooper vase," as she called it. Others asked about the windows and whether we were going to cover them. That last caused a discussion. The general consensus seemed to be that we shouldn't.

We exited via the front door, and I guided my troop along the side yard path and into the fringes of the woods to show them the carriage house. As we left the house behind, Judy spoke up: "All those porches! We came by a few years ago—you know, just checking on Mary and Rob—but no one was home. I took a look around outside, but the grounds were so overgrown that I couldn't see much except weeds and wildflowers."

Reggie was more interested in the carriage house and offered some details on the construction. When we emerged back into the bright day, I directed them into the backyard.

"It's still under construction," I said. "But you can see where we're headed with the flower garden. We call it the medallion. The flowering bushes are going in now, but we won't be planting wildflowers until spring. We plan to put a fountain or a statue in the center." *We.* It had always been *we* for Dad and me. After he'd died, I'd struggled trying to replace that with *I. We* felt more natural to me, and was more appropriate because it encompassed my friends and their invaluable help. "We haven't decided which way to go yet."

Jane said, "A fountain would be lovely."

"A statue would be so elegant. It would suit the house and gardens," Deborah said.

I left them for a minute, at least consciously, remembering how Victoria had once called this house monstrous. It had echoed my own feelings too closely, and I'd been angry at her. Elegant, now. I pressed my hand to my chest, feeling that squeeze again, warm and full. The word now was *elegant*. And *welcoming*.

Reggie said, "You've got quite a view out here." He pointed at the open area as it stretched from the house to the creek. "Definitely unimpeded."

I gave him a quick look. "An unimpeded view? For?"

He answered, "For stargazing. No big light sources around. I'll bet it gets dark out here."

"Yes, quite dark."

"Do you host events at night? Because I'm part of a club. We could set up our equipment out here on a clear night and . . . if that's okay?"

Stargazing. Why not?

"I'm sure we could work that out, Reggie. We can discuss it later?"

"Oh, yes, ma'am. We'll do that."

From a distance, we heard a woman's voice. We turned to look. It was Sue Deale standing on the back porch, calling out, "Food's ready. Come on in!"

As soon as the meal was finished, almost everyone adjourned to the parlor to begin their meeting. Victoria and I cleared the table, and the same silent woman pitched in to help. At one point, I asked her, "Don't you want to join the others?" She answered in a hushed voice, "I can hear them just fine." Her smile was sweet, and so I let her be. So the three of us cleaned and did our best to stay discreetly out of sight. The ladies were discussing different books, interwoven with mentions of grandbabies, crochet patterns, and stargazing. Victoria and I were washing dishes in the kitchen when Sue called my name. I stepped into their midst. The group was seated, arrayed in any chairs they could find, including the ones from the dining room. All had expectant looks on their faces.

Sue waved and cleared her throat. "I want you to know how much we are enjoying our book club meeting today. We aren't done yet, but Mitzi has to leave early, so we wanted to do this now." She glanced around the room as if seeking agreement from the membership and received smiles and nods.

The lady earlier introduced as Janet stood up and came forward holding a wrapped gift with a shiny bow. She had a shy smile and warm eyes. When she offered the package to me, I accepted it and thanked her, but I felt confused. I wasn't accustomed to hostess gifts, plus this was a business. I looked at Sue.

She said, "Janet has a special talent—skill and talent both—called paper cutting."

I nodded as if I knew what she was talking about. "How wonderful."

Janet blushed.

Mitzi said, "It's called scherenschnitte."

Sue laughed. "I always have trouble with that word." She looked at me. "Well, go ahead and open the gift. It's a very special thank-you from us for your hospitality today."

How odd receiving a wrapped gift felt—a tingling in my arms and a soft warmth in my chest. My cheeks felt hot. Dad had given me presents on the usual occasions, but he hadn't wrapped them. I hadn't expected him to.

The box was about the size of a long, narrow book, but it was thin and much lighter than that. I slid my finger under the paper fold to pop the tape.

The package held a framed white paper cutout against a dark blue background, and it was so much more than that. The pattern included birds, butterflies, and flowers, all wrapped around the *Welcome* running down the center.

"It's beautiful," I gasped. "Janet, did you create this?"

"I did. I create all sorts of scenes and even 3-D items like trees and ornaments."

"Amazing." Impulsively, I hugged her. "It's perfect."

Janet smiled broadly, her cheeks still pink and her eyes bright. "Well, some are done from patterns. But some," she added with an extra oomph, "are *my* patterns."

"It's perfect, and especially perfect and appropriate for Wildflower House." I scanned the room and the faces all staring at me. For a moment, I could only stand and feel the goodwill, the sweet energy surrounding me; then I went to a wall where the bookcase wasn't. I held the framed cutout up to the empty space. "Should it hang here? What do you all think?"

When their meeting was done, everyone lined up on the porch for a group photo.

"Smile!"

Someone yelled, "Cheese!"

They hugged each other and smiled broadly, and I snapped the picture.

"Now you," Reggie said. "Stand there with all the other ladies."

"Oh. Okay, yes." I handed my phone to him. We all posed together, and Reggie snapped pictures with a series of phones. Finally, we were done.

"Lovely. Great photo. Thanks, everyone," I said. It felt as though we'd re-created a slice of history, a vignette of this house and those women who'd posed on this porch long ago. I smiled and felt it inside and out. I may have glowed with delight.

Everyone broke apart, and the ladies and Reggie went to claim their dishes and other items. Sue stayed.

"We're your first event," Sue said.

I shook my head. "Not exactly. We aren't officially open for business yet. You are all my personal guests today."

"So we were your beta testers?"

I smiled. "That sounds right."

"Kara, listen, I have friends who might be interested in renting your place for small events over the winter. Not stay overs. For instance, the

Ladies Auxiliary was talking about holding their Christmas party here." She touched my arm. "It could be our best holiday party ever." She nodded gravely. "I'll drop by, and we can discuss it?"

Suddenly I felt shivery inside and blurted out, "Reggie wants to bring friends over for stargazing."

"Excellent. You see? Word gets around!"

Somehow one of the ladies had ended up with my phone during the picture-taking session. She was waving it at me to get my attention and apparently touched an icon inadvertently. Suddenly music issued forth—*Appalachian Spring*.

I stopped moving and stared.

Sue's eyes widened, and then she laughed loudly and clapped. "That was always Mary's favorite. Did you know that?"

"Somehow I'm not surprised."

After the photo the ladies and gentleman left by ones, twos, and threes, climbing back into the vehicles in which they'd arrived, and I waved to each departing vehicle. I felt surrounded by warm and fuzzy good feelings. This had been a confidence booster, for sure. Hosting the Ladies Auxiliary Christmas party would be a good next test. A little scary, yes, but in an exciting way.

I remembered my doubts about whether this endeavor would ever truly happen and when it had begun to feel real. Now I had evidence that it was. And that I could do this.

Nicole and I had discussed offering activities, like pottery and painting and even yoga. Now I had a book club and the Ladies Auxiliary. Even a group of stargazers. I chuckled at the idea that there seemed no limit to how high our dreams and aspirations might reach.

"What are you laughing at?" Victoria asked.

I smiled. "Nothing really. Just thinking silly thoughts."

"Good."

"Good? Why do you say that?"

"That means you're open to potential. I'm taking off now." Victoria spoke as she juggled her large tote and many bags of leftovers in containers. She held up the bags. "I left you some of the goodies."

"Not too much, I hope. Nice of the ladies to leave them behind but even nicer of you to take them."

"Mom will be thrilled."

"Thank you for your help today," I said with sincerity.

Victoria smiled. "My pleasure. It was a blast. That lady Laura was very sweet and so helpful."

"I couldn't have done this without you, Victoria."

Victoria said, "I'd say you could've, but I'll be honest. No, you couldn't have, but not because of me. It's because you aren't an octopus. I was delighted to be here and to help you, but you need to line up some guys and gals who'll be happy to pitch in and handle fixed duties for you when you host events. Even when you don't have to be out front as the hostess, it's too much to juggle. Plus, providing occasional pickup work like this creates goodwill with the local people. Nice if they can benefit. And whenever possible, please include me too."

With that, Victoria moved in a flurry of bags to her car and stowed them on the seat and the floor. I let her divest herself of the bags before saying, "Not so fast, Victoria."

She stopped and stared at me. "Did I do something wrong?"

I shook my head. "No. You did everything exactly right." I put my arms around her. I felt her body relax, the tension easing from her arms as she hugged me back. When I stepped away, I said, with a slight hitch in my voice, "Drive carefully."

"I will."

I saw her press her sleeve against her eyes as she climbed into the car. She threw me a smile, started the car, and drove off with a wave.

It seemed very silly, but that hug . . . I was getting the hang of it. I liked it.

In the sudden absence of people noise and the energy people generated, I noticed the small white car still in the parking lot. It was almost hidden by a tree and the new shrubbery. One guest remained? Or had someone accepted a ride home forgetting they'd driven? Anything was possible.

There was a small cough behind me. I turned to look back into the house. A tall, slender woman was standing half-hidden in the shadows of the hallways near the grand staircase. It was the older woman who'd been helping Victoria.

"Hello," I said. "I'm sorry; I didn't realize someone was still here." I couldn't pull her name out of my head. I kept the smile on my face as I stepped back inside.

Her face was pale. Not entirely colorless but someone who would easily fade into the background. Quiet. Perhaps timid. I lowered my voice, not wanting to overwhelm her.

"I hope you had a good time today."

She offered a shy smile. "I wanted to speak with you alone, after everyone else was gone. I apologize for not arranging it with you ahead of time, but I wasn't sure."

I clasped my hands together rather than reaching out and perhaps alarming her. "No problem." Doggone it. What was her name? "I'm glad you could join in."

"This is personal . . . I needed the chance to assess for myself before approaching you. I didn't want to assume or push in where I might not be welcome."

Laura. That was it. Her name was Laura.

"Of course you're welcome. Laura, right? Why would you think you might not be welcome?"

Abruptly extending her hand to me, she said, "Laura Harris."

I took her offered hand and gave it a gentle, reassuring squeeze before releasing her. "Thank you so much for your help in the kitchen. Victoria told me how grateful she was, Laura."

"I married Fred Harris twenty years ago, but I was Laura Stevens before that. I was adopted. Before that, I was Laura Lange."

"Laura—" My breath stopped before I could say Lange—my father's family's name.

She'd dropped the name gently, almost casually, as if it were of no importance. And she'd said something about adoption.

My entire body went numb. My face and hands tingled, but I couldn't move. This was one of the toddlers. My father's siblings. I thought I might fall flat, right here in the foyer. I put a hand against the foyer table.

Laura Lange Harris nodded. "Mr. Harris is deceased."

My weakness passed quickly. I grabbed her hand back, saying, "Why didn't you tell me sooner?"

A startled expression brightened her faded-blue eyes. She let her long, thin fingers stay clasped in mine.

"How long have you known I was here and who I was? Dad was here for a short time, but he's gone now." I was struck silent. Did she know that her older brother, Henry, had died just a few short months ago? Surely she knew.

"I found out about him, but too late. When I realized . . . sorry, it's a longish story. Please understand that I wanted to see you first, but anonymously. As soon as I met you, I knew I wanted to tell you, but it wasn't good timing with everyone here."

I snagged her other hand and held both of hers in mine. "I never expected to meet you. It would've meant so much to Dad. I wish . . ." I used one hand to gesture toward the sitting room. "Let's have a seat. I don't know about you, but I'm very thirsty."

Laura looked down at the hand I still held tightly in my grasp.

"I'm afraid you're an apparition," I explained. "If I let you go, you might . . . go. You might leave, and I'll lose this chance to speak with you. I know that sounds crazy. After all, you're here of your own volition, but . . ."

"I understand. Yes, we should talk."

Chapter Twenty-Three

Laura Harris, née Lange, turned toward the parlor.

I said, "Let's sit in here." I gestured toward the sitting room, where our chairs, Dad's and mine, were waiting. Used and long ago broken in, they were comfy. The sitting room was plain, too, I thought. Like Laura. My Aunt Laura? A blood relative? For me, that felt as rare and special as the Monet-inspired painting in front of the fireplace and the Hannah Cooper blue vase on the mantel. More so. From these chairs, we had that view but also the view of the dining room, the foyer with its own special frames hanging over the foyer table, the parlor, and also the grand stairs with their gorgeous wood and stained glass . . . they felt almost like good-luck talismans. In my humble opinion, the entirety of it was a feast for the eyes, and yet it was the comfort of the old chairs, the chairs from my dad's home on Silver Street, that I craved.

I steered her toward the larger chair, Dad's chair.

"Tea? Water?" I asked. "I have some ice water with lemon and lime in it."

"That will be fine."

"Okay. Good. I'll be right back." I paused in

the foyer. "You'll still be here when I return?"

"I will."

I tried to walk gracefully away, but my body felt awkward and jerky. I paused in the kitchen and stared blindly out the window. Everything was swirling in my head, and a feeling of not being able to catch my breath kept reminding me that I was mortal. As mortal as my parents. I had an opportunity here—one I'd never expected to have and might never have again. I told myself not to screw it up.

Glasses. I needed glasses. I took the pitcher from the fridge and poured a tall glass of fruit water for each of us. I carried the glasses back to the sitting room and set them on the coasters on the table between the chairs.

"Are you hungry?"

Laura looked surprised, then amused. "No indeed. We just finished an excellent meal."

"Oh, of course. You're right." I sat. "I'm sorry to seem so scattered. I'm just . . . I never expected to meet you, much less have you introduce yourself after a book club meeting."

"Understandable." She nodded. "I feel the same. Scattered. I missed my opportunity with Henry." She paused and added solemnly, "I'm very sorry about your father."

I was taken aback. "I'm sorry you missed the opportunity to know him. It would've meant so much to him to know that you were okay. When you and Lewis disappeared, Dad was devastated. Your father, Mr. Lange, wouldn't tell him what had happened or where you were. Later, when Dad was older, he hired a private detective but got nowhere." I asked, "What about you? Where have you been, and how did you come to be here? Will you tell me about it?"

Laura shifted in her seat, effectively turning away from me, but ever so gently. If anyone had been watching us, they could not have guessed at the extreme emotion happening between us.

Laura sighed. I had a view of her profile, the cheekbones and jawline so similar to my father's, but the light flyaway hair was her own. It was brown and threaded with gray.

"I was very young when we were taken away. I have almost no memories of those years. I have vague memories of an older boy. I'm sure that must have been my brother Henry."

"You were already back here in Louisa when Dad and I moved here. Surely other people knew of the connection between you two, even if you didn't."

"I hoped I'd come across that person—the one who'd know. But maybe a part of me wasn't too eager . . . didn't try hard enough . . . maybe not wanting to know in case the truth was too awful." She said, "You are so much bolder and braver than I ever was. When I think back, I remember being afraid and with people I didn't know. I'm sure they tried to explain and reassure, but I couldn't hear them through my fear. I was afraid, for myself and for Lewis." She stared past me. "I believe fear became a habit. An automatic response to life."

"At least in your new life you had your brother Lewis. That must've helped."

She shook her head slowly. "No. I remember him clearly. His face. His voice. But someone took me one way and him the other. I never saw him again." She pulled a folded tissue from the end of her sleeve and dabbed it at her eyes before replacing it neatly back under the hem. "I came to understand that I was adopted. My parents were kind. But Lewis wasn't there. Lewis was gone, and I was alone with strangers."

Laura sniffled. "Don't mistake me. I am grateful to my mother and father, the ones who raised me. They were loving parents. I asked about Lewis over and over early on, and that distressed them. They said they knew nothing. I thought he must be dead."

The expression in her blue eyes and in her posture was meek but tense, like the dark-eyed doe who visited my yard most nights—shy and prone to freezing or bolting. Patience, I told myself.

"When I was still very young, we moved to New Mexico." She looked me full in the face. "I didn't remember where I was from or my birth surname. When I was older, when I pressed my parents, they told me they adopted me in Virginia. They had the adoption document showing I was born in Louisa, but it only listed the new names.

"Mother said that my birth mother died and my birth father's health was failing, so he couldn't take care of us. Mother didn't remember the surname, only that it started with an *L*.

"I tried so hard to remember. The name Lane kept popping into my head, or maybe Lynn. I had some silly idea that Laura Lane or Laura Lynn was my birth name." She shook her head. "When I turned eighteen, I wanted to return to Virginia just to see . . . but my parents didn't support that wish, and then my father died of a heart issue, and I couldn't leave Mother. When I lost her, I was free to leave." She gave a quick, wry smile. "I was almost forty before I came here. Back here, I should say."

"Did you ever find Lewis?"

"No. I had no idea how to go about doing it. I checked phone books. I asked around at the library, at the sheriff's office, and so on. That's how I met my late husband. I never hired a detective. You said your father did? Henry, I mean."

"Yes, he did, but it didn't do him any good." I rubbed my temple.

"Mr. Harris wasn't from around here, either, but he did figure out that my birth name was Lange instead of Lane. One of the retired deputies knew of the Lange family but mostly of my father. He was already deceased, of course."

"And yet Dad was just an hour down the road in Richmond."

She sighed. "Even if we'd thought to look in Richmond, I would never have connected the Henry Lange of the big tire and automotive business with the older brother I hardly remembered. He was no more than a hazy memory that felt less real as time passed." She shook her head. "When I discovered the other day that I'd just missed meeting my older brother, I couldn't believe I had one more chance—the chance to meet you, my niece. As for Lewis . . ."

"We'll find him," I said.

She frowned, then smiled. "I know you mean well, but if your father couldn't find either of us, and I couldn't find anyone, then what makes you think we can locate Lewis after so long?"

"I was thinking about DNA tests the other day. Lots of people do those now. We might get lucky."

"Well, but then he would need to want to be found. To have taken one of those tests himself. Right?"

"True. I accept that we might not find him or even that he might not want to be found, but we won't dismiss the possibility entirely, right?"

"Okay."

"Excellent."

Laura smiled sweetly. "Please tell me what *you*

know—about your father? About the family I came from but don't remember?" She patted my hand. "I don't live far from here. If you want to know me better, to continue getting to know each other, I'm open to that." She clasped my hand. "We don't have to get it all done right now."

"I'm so glad you . . . oh. Wait. How did you know my father and I had moved back to the area? Who told you? How would they *know* to tell you?"

"The Ladies Auxiliary. We have speakers every so often. Nicole came to speak to us about business opportunities for women in the county and the area around. She mentioned Wildflower House and that it would be a meeting place, a retreat, available for all sorts of events, probably opening sometime early next year, and told us about the entrepreneur owner—a young woman named Kara Hart. Of course, we all knew it as the old Forster property, so it was interesting information."

"Nicole knew?"

"Knew? You mean about me? No. If she'd known, she would've said something before—in time for me to have met Henry. Nicole left after her speech, and we had our regular meeting. It just happened that Sue Deale spoke up and said it might be a great place for the book club to meet. Some of us are members of both the Auxiliary and the book club."

"I understand."

"So I happened to be on the cleanup committee with Sue, and she mentioned your father had bought the place and then died, and she'd been so worried about what was going to happen after that, but then you'd stepped up and took it all on. She mentioned his name was Henry, but of course, I assumed it was Henry Hart, being as Nicole had called you Kara Hart, and then Sue—you know how she loves to share a good story; it's because of how caring she is. Well, she said, 'Goodness, no, it was Henry Lange, who grew up in the Cub Creek area,' and how this was all like serendipity and fate and such as that."

She shook her head. "You could've knocked me right over. In fact, Sue grabbed me and put me in a chair. She assumed I'd overdone. I didn't tell her otherwise because Sue is all heart. If you tell her something, she'll open that heart to anyone who cares to listen." She took a deep breath. "I knew this was an opportunity. I'm sorry I missed Henry, and I wasn't about to miss you too. Yet I needed to see who you were . . . the kind of person you were first. Does that make sense?"

I nodded. I was almost afraid to speak. As if this moment might somehow evaporate, just like a dream.

She squeezed her fingers together. "I confess that I hadn't been participating in the book club for nearly a year. But this month I made sure to attend."

Her eyes were suddenly bright. I knew that feeling—the sting of tears. She plucked out her tissue again and mopped at her lashes.

"I thought I was fresh out of family, Kara. I had dear friends, but God didn't bless Mr. Harris and me with children. I can't begin to tell you what it means to know I have a niece. I can dare to believe that one day Lewis will show up too."

We talked awhile longer, and during a lull, Laura said, "I should be going. I didn't intend to take up your whole day."

"Must you?"

"No, but I'm sure you have things to do."

"Why don't you stay, and let's chat awhile longer."

Laura did. She told me about her life, mostly the highlights, I suspected. Releasing those words— such personal words—seemed as awkward for Laura as the same act had been for my father. For my own part, I tried to be open with her. I wanted to give her my memories of my dad because it was the only way I could share him with her. But as I sensed she was doing, I also kept it to the lighter moments and skimmed somewhat over the darker parts. We didn't have to get everything said today. And that was a comfort.

Later that evening, we raided the fridge and picked through the leftovers Victoria hadn't taken.

Was this the first time I'd eaten a meal with laughter and light at the table with me? Surely not, but I had trouble remembering when a shared meal had come close to the pleasure of this one. With the exception of Will . . . but even that was different. I'd felt a certain pressure on the date with Will, hoping, and wanting to hope, for more. It was different with Laura. She just felt like family. As if DNA recognized DNA. We speculated about ways we might try to find Lewis and made a pact to do that DNA test. Maybe Lewis had already done one, and it would help us find him. Before we were done, I had Laura's phone number, her address, and her promise not to disappear on me.

"Disappear? I assure you that won't happen."

"I know." I touched my forehead and then placed my hand over my heart. "I understand that logically, but I've lost a lot of people. Chance? Fate? I always blamed fate. Maybe fate is making amends."

I walked her not only to the door but all the way to her car.

We stood there with the moon rising above the treetops and the stars winking on.

"This is an amazing place, for sure, Kara, dear. I doubt the house ever looked this good, not in its entire history."

"I don't know. One thing I do know—it's not the size or the fanciness of a place. The places in which we live are made livable, or not, by those with whom we share them."

Laura sniffled. "I'm sorry." She grabbed that tissue. "I know what you say is true. I had a good life, but never what I'd call happy. Seemed like the losses—even though they were bits of old memories and so very vague—haunted my life. Now I feel like someone opened a door." She smiled. "And I found you waiting to greet me on the other side of it."

Chapter Twenty-Four

Between the book club and meeting my aunt, my brain and heart were overfull. How was I supposed to shut the emotions off and get to sleep? I called Will, wanting—needing—to talk about the book club event and Laura. He said the right things, showed all the right interest, laughed at the appropriate moments, and gave no advice or lectures. I felt so grateful.

"Thank you for listening, Will."

"Anytime, Kara. Thanks for calling to tell me about it. You had an amazing day."

"I did." I paused before adding, "It feels like the right time to inter Dad's urn."

"I'll need a couple of days to get the vault ready. I'll come over tomorrow and get it started."

"Thank you so much." I would have Will's help and the added pleasure of seeing him. "Come at lunchtime, and we can have a picnic."

"I'll be there. And Kara?"

"Yes?"

"Congratulations again on a successful event with a major bonus. An aunt. Astounding. Suppose you hadn't done this—creating Wildflower House and all? You might never have met her."

Astounding, indeed. And a near miss when I considered it.

After we said our goodbyes, I called Nicole to give her a heads-up.

"I'll be there," she said with a sigh. "Thank you, Kara."

I considered whether to include Laura but decided not to. A burial would be too sad an introduction to a brother she hardly remembered.

Will joined me on the porch. "You look beautiful," he said.

I'd opted for a simple dress and sandals. Will was dressed in jeans and a suit jacket. His tone was quiet, almost formal, as he asked, "Are you ready?"

I nodded and took his hand.

No time like the present, as Dad might've said.

We walked around the side path and into the backyard to the new garden. It was much smaller than the original wildflower field and certainly tamer. There were no flowers yet, but they'd be here come spring. I missed the vibrant joy of the wildflower field as I'd first seen it, but when it came to living and incorporating the flowers into our lives, this was more fitting.

Will released my hand and stood back. I walked into the garden alone. The symmetry appealed to me. It would've pleased Dad too.

"It's perfect, Will." I took a deep breath. "I'll get the urn. Nicole should arrive anytime now."

"I'll be here."

I went upstairs alone and stood in Dad's room, staring at his urn for a long moment before picking it up. I cradled it in my arms carefully. "Already dusty, Dad. I fell down on the job." Dusting had always been my chore, so this was a small joke—a private one between me and my father.

Carrying the urn carefully down the stairs, I went back outside. Nicole was walking across the yard toward Will. She'd followed our new path around the house just as Will and I had done. The path was a far cry from the green, tangled jungle Dad and I had found when we'd moved to Wildflower House six months before.

"Hi, Nicole."

She gave me a sad smile. "Thanks for inviting me." She reached toward me and ran her hand over the satiny finish of the urn, then slowly traced the etched name with her fingers.

Nicole was wearing a blue dress—a very bright blue. Not her usual. She noticed me giving her dress a second look and said, "It was Henry's favorite."

I patted her arm and said, "You look lovely."

Will joined us.

Suddenly unsure, I said, "I didn't plan anything, really. Not a proper ceremony."

He saw my panic. "Calm down. It's okay."

"I don't know what to say, Will. I thought the right words would come to me."

"You and your dad said what needed saying while he was with you. Anything else, anything omitted, probably didn't need to be said anyway."

It was true that my father had shared memories about my mom and his own history with me here at Wildflower House. He'd told me much about his childhood and explained his reasons for wanting to retire here. He should've told me these things sooner, and there was more that he should've told, but he'd tried, and in some part he'd succeeded. I was grateful for that. Not every success could be total, but my dad had done his best, and that was all anyone could ask.

I turned to Nicole. "Would you like to say anything?"

She shook her head. "No, this is hard enough as it is."

I held the urn closely and touched my cheek to it. "Goodbye, Dad."

With Will's help, I set the urn containing Dad's remains in the small recessed burial vault.

"When you and Nicole are ready, let me know. Take your time."

As he rose to his feet, I touched his arm. "Now is good," I said. Nicole had moved up next to us. I asked her, "Are you ready?"

She repeated her sad smile in lieu of words.

Will gave me a long, questioning look; then he lifted the vault lid and set it gently over the box, working to ensure the joints between the lid and box met securely. He removed his suit jacket, and I took it from him. He rolled up his sleeves, then put his bare hands into the nearby pile of dark earth, drew it over the edge of the hole, and let it cascade in.

My heart was hurting. My eyes were stinging. On impulse I tucked my arm through Nicole's. She glanced at me and responded with a tightening of her own arm. Together, we watched Will pull the dirt forward with great care—as if the very earth itself were precious—into the depression until it covered the lid and filled in the hole.

He patted the dirt until it was smooth. "The statue will go here."

"With the engraved memorial stone at its base," I said. "I gave the memorial company the text. *You can't choose where you're born, but you can choose where to grow.*"

Will stood, brushing the grains of dirt from his hands. The dirt from my father's grave. Wildflower House earth. He reached over, took my hand in his, and held it tightly.

In my head, I heard words whispered: *You can choose where to grow . . . and with whom.*

Nicole gave each of us a silent hug and solemnly walked away. She headed around to the front, to the parking area.

Will asked, "Is she okay?"

"Nicole is fine. She needs a little privacy to

remember and mourn." I squeezed his hand. "Thank you for today."

Instead of answering, he offered the comfort of his arms. I accepted the gift, the simple gift of being with someone who cared and for whom I cared. I sensed a future that was wide open for each of us and filled with potential.

It was important to know when to let go. When to move on. But I tightened my arms around Will because one thing was certain—if fate even looked like it was about to take another spin and re-sort my life again, this time I was going to grab hold of that spinner and fight for it. Because, as Dad might've said, anything worth doing was worth working for, and now I understood it was also worth fighting for.

Chapter Twenty-Five

On a beautiful autumn day a couple of weeks later—barely autumn, but the leaves were already yellow atop the tall tulip poplars—a day when I would certainly leave the front door open to welcome a breeze, I stepped out to the front porch and saw a small dusty car parked in the driveway. A girl was sitting on the bench. More of a young woman, really, but she seemed so slight, so young. Hardly out of her teens, I thought.

"Hello?" I asked.

She jumped, startled, but stayed seated on the bench. "Sorry. I wasn't paying attention."

The young woman brushed her short brown hair away from her face, and when she looked at me, I saw more pain in her blue eyes than youth should know. Not a teenager. Early twenties, maybe. I waited.

"Will said you wouldn't mind."

"Mind?"

"Letting me see the paintings? The fire screen paintings? How they look in your house?"

"You're Brittany?"

"That's me. But call me Britt."

In my heart, I knew how much it had cost Will's sister to come to a stranger's home, to sit on the porch getting up her courage to knock and risk . . . what? Rejection? Disappointment? I'd never been one to trust strangers either. Everyone was different, including how they dealt with injury and recovery. But a welcome was a welcome, and I knew how to offer that.

"Absolutely." I stepped forward and extended my hand. "Come inside?"

She accepted my hand and held on to it as she stood. I noticed then the heavy brace on her lower leg. She saw me glance at it and tugged at her hand as if to pull it away. I tightened my grip firmly but gently, and she met my eyes in a challenge.

Softly, I said, "I had an accident a couple of years ago."

"Will told me." Britt looked almost contemptuous, but that wasn't the tone I heard in her voice. She looked past me. "Who's that?"

Maddie Lyn was peering at us through the screening of the door.

"My friend Maddie. We were just about to have a tea party—with crazy-good fudge. Would you join us? I hope you will."

Britt nodded. I released her hand and held the door wide as we entered Wildflower House together.

Epilogue

In late October, Sue had said, "The Ladies Auxiliary needs a place to hold their annual holiday party. We put it on every year for the community. I'm sure you remember me mentioning it?"

We'd been in the sitting room that day. Sue had brought me a set of china teacups and saucers. She'd handed them to me when she arrived, saying, "Mary treasured this set. I have my own, so I was hoping you could find space for them?" I accepted the teacups and saucers from her. As a thank-you gesture, I'd fixed tea, but I knew what was on her mind: the Ladies Auxiliary annual party.

Sue had continued, "We've been meeting in the fire station, but there's always the possibility of emergency interruptions and, of course, hard concrete floors. There are a couple of other places we've met, depending upon the members' connections, but each has its negatives. The fellowship hall of the Baptist church has been the best place, but the roof there is undergoing repairs. Our annual party is very popular," she said. "And important to the people around here."

"We aren't open for business yet. Not officially.

We're approved for day events, but I don't have staff yet."

"That's the beauty of this. We—the Ladies of the Auxiliary—will do all the work." She touched my arm as if to make sure my attention was properly focused. "We can accomplish two things with this one event, Kara—our party and your open house. There is no better time than early December for an open house. People are out and about getting ready for Christmas. It's perfect."

As much as I liked the idea, I suspected it wouldn't be quite as simple as staying out of their way. Regardless, I wouldn't let these women down.

"How many attendees are we talking about?"

Sue laughed softly and waved off my concern. "Just the usual open house kind of thing. People will be coming and going. We aren't talking a sit-down dinner or anything like that. The Ladies of the Auxiliary will decorate. They'll be happy for the chance to show off their hobbies and talents. You're a member now, after all. We're all in this together, so to speak."

"A member? Me?"

"Honorary. We held a special meeting and voted you in."

"Is that so?"

Sue added, "No obligation, of course. We don't want to take advantage."

I'd first seen Wildflower House in the spring when the locals had still called it the old Forster place. The grounds had been overgrown, but the flowers had been wild and stunning. Spring had been a time of healing until my father died. Summer had become a season of grief and also of fear—the nearly paralyzing fear of making choices alone and failing. But the end of summer, as it began to transition into autumn, had been a turning point for me too. My heart had finally allowed a lifetime of memories with my dad, and even the memories with my mom, to displace my stubborn grief, giving me emotional permission to follow this course I'd chosen.

The renovation of Wildflower House wasn't complete yet. There was work still to be done upstairs, and that would begin in January, but the main floor was finished. Ready for prime time, one might say. And that was good, because between Nicole's and Sue's efforts, local curiosity about this place was buzzing.

Thus, when Sue had brought the teacups and asked about the Ladies Auxiliary holding their annual event at Wildflower House, I'd agreed. I did need to open the doors to the outside world. What better way to do it than with the help of friends?

Now we were in this miraculous time between Thanksgiving and Christmas. As we slipped across the calendar boundary between November and December, Wildflower House bloomed.

I wished Dad could've been here to see the delicate paper snowflakes snipped and trimmed by Janet's petite gold scissors. The snowflakes were hanging by nearly invisible threads from the foyer ceiling. Green garlands and crystal candlesticks adorned the mantels, along with so many other decorations—including a decorated Christmas tree in each of the three main public rooms. Many of the items on the trees represented the hobbies and skills of the women who'd organized this open house and, as Sue had said, had done the work. Despite the inconveniences, the joy and laughter of numerous people was woven throughout, and I felt like the primary beneficiary.

I'd kept at it—had stayed the course—and had received this amazing gift.

My Aunt Laura and Will's sister, Britt, were my right-hand helpers, organizing the decorating groups and coordinating refreshments. Victoria was there, of course, keeping everyone in motion and not working at cross-purposes. Maddie Lyn was dressed in velvet and lace with shiny white shoes that when worn on Maddie's feet were obviously made for dancing. I twirled with her once or twice, but then I left her with Mel and went back to work. Truly, I had no idea how many guests to expect.

I stood on the porch considering how to

manage overflow parking. If Sue and the others were right about the likely turnout, my new parking lot was going to fill up quickly. Luckily, the pines outside of the official parking lot were widely spaced, and the ground was level and hard packed, so there was room for spillover. The workers, including family and friends, had spread their cars out along the wider areas of the drive and into that spillover area.

Britt joined me. "Kara?"

"What? How's it going in there?"

"Fine. Will needs you in the carriage house."

The carriage house? We'd done a little decorating out there, but not much. Frankly, it was cold outside. I didn't expect many people to wander that way, especially as it would grow still colder with evening.

"Okay. Thanks," I said as I twisted the wire tie to secure a loose sprig of holly berries on the porch railing.

Something about the look on her face . . . was it anxiety? Eagerness?

"Is something wrong? An emergency?" I asked.

"No, not an emergency, I don't think. He seemed . . . concerned." She added, "No one should arrive for another hour yet, so there's time for you to check."

"I'll go see." Will wasn't a worrier, so if something was causing him concern, then I wanted to know exactly what it was. I headed to the kitchen and the back door. I didn't stop to find my coat. I wouldn't be out long.

But when I stepped onto the back porch, I paused, mesmerized. The medallion garden was lit by colored floodlights, blue and green, directed toward its interior. Electric lanterns were arranged around the perimeter. The sculpture at the center had been put into place a week ago. I'd chosen one that reminded me of a statue I'd seen in Central Park in New York City. Years before, I'd gone there on a college group trip to see the sights. This sculpture was only vaguely similar, but as soon as I'd seen it advertised, I'd contacted the sculptor and ordered it. A young woman, slender and dressed in a thin garment, was holding a shallow bowl. Around the bowl, birds were perched. Several large butterflies had alighted on her hair and shoulders. As if . . . as if one with her. As if they belonged there and they all belonged together. As I stared from the back porch, caught by the soft lighting, a snowflake landed on my nose. Another followed swiftly.

Flurries. They were calling for only flurries, and that was important. If we had a real snow, many of our guests would take it in stride, but many would not. This was important to me and to everyone who'd worked and planned for the event this evening.

Lanterns were hung along the path to the carriage house. More than I thought necessary, but Will had argued that it was a safety factor as well as decoration. The wires were cleverly concealed. He'd strung old-fashioned white lights across the front of the carriage house, and as I approached, I saw that only the exterior of the building was lit. The inside of the carriage house looked dark. A power problem?

As I entered, I called out, "Will?"

Gray stone exterior and teal-painted woodwork defined the outside, but inside the old wood beams were solid, and clean straw had been spread across the dirt floor. In the near dark, it smelled fresh yet well aged at the same time. As I stood there, soft, warm lights came on overhead, brightening the old wood and the stone and revealing heavy fir boughs secured to the beams with twine. A huge ball of mistletoe was suspended from the ceiling high above by a long red ribbon.

I whispered, "Will?"

"Here," he said. He was standing on the stairs, wearing spotless blue jeans and a crisp white dress shirt.

I said, "It's beautiful in here. So beautiful, Will. I have no words."

"I'm glad you approve. I kept it simple."

Simple. Yes, all the best, truest, most important things in our lives should be simple.

From somewhere around us, music began to play. I followed the sound with my eyes and saw small speakers mounted in the junctions of the crossbeams.

"Music too." I smiled at him. "You told me you liked to stay busy, but you've outdone yourself." I listened to the melody and the singer's voice filling the air around us. "What is that song?"

" 'Christmas Waltz.' Nancy Wilson's version. My grandparents loved this one. They danced to it every Christmas." He stepped down to the floor. "When I was deciding what music to play, I thought of you, and then I thought of this." He looked a little awkward. "Don't really know why."

It wasn't *Appalachian Spring*, but then again, this was winter. And this was with Will. It wasn't merely simple. It was also undeniable.

I held my hand out toward him. "I know why."

He said, "I'm not much of a dancer, but if you're willing to take the risk?" He walked to where I stood and took my hand. "We have only a little while before the guests arrive."

The music came from the speakers, but it filled the eaves and echoed in my heart.

I said, "I've been waiting for this dance for a long time, Will. We have all the time we want. It's up to us to claim it. The rest of the world can wait."

Acknowledgments

My sincere thanks to everyone who contributed their talents and skills to *Wildflower Hope*, especially my editor, Alicia Clancy, who gave this series the opportunity to be published by Lake Union Publishing, and Tiffany Yates Martin, the developmental editor who brought her skills to bear on *Wildflower Hope* to make it shine. There are many hands and hearts that contribute to the production of a book. I know I can't thank everyone, but I'd like to call out special thanks to Caroline Teagle Johnson for her cover creation; Nicole Pomeroy as production manager; the author relations team under Gabe Dumpit, especially Kristin King; and the copyediting magic of Riam Griswold and proofreading dedication of Stephanie Chou.

I extend extra heartfelt and hope-filled thanks— and virtual hugs—to my readers. You make this endeavor worthwhile and joyful for all of us.

Author's Note

Wildflower Hope is a novel of fiction and is not intended to be a resource about addiction or to offer advice about managing addiction, but I believe everyone should be aware of the potential for misuse of prescription drugs and understand what opioid and prescription drug addiction is and how easily any addiction can reach into our lives and destroy them. Whether through appropriate use or misuse, if opioids or other drugs or substances interfere in your life, I urge you to seek help with local medical professionals. For information on this subject, here are some resources I found online:

Substance Abuse and Mental Health Services Administration:https://www.samhsa.gov/find-treatment

Hazelden Betty Ford Foundation: https://www.hazeldenbettyford.org/addiction/types-of-addiction/opioids

Al-Anon and Alateen (for people impacted by the drinking of others): https://al-anon.org/

Alcoholics Anonymous: https://www.aa.org/

Narcotics Anonymous: https://www.na.org/

Questions for Discussion

1. Kara was impulsive but sincere when she declared her intention to turn Wildflower House into a creative retreat and day event facility, but the doubts soon rolled in. Doubt is normal, but Kara's biggest problem was that she wanted to have a surface "change of heart" and leave the fear, anger, and resentment locked away inside. Is it better to leave unhappy memories undisturbed? Can we be our true selves if we live only on the surface? How much of who we are gets buried with the bad memories?

2. Kara had trouble accepting her father's death. This isn't unusual, but as with the death of our own loved ones, one's experience is colored by the relationship one had with the deceased. Kara and her father had a truce of sorts—they showed their love and respect by not rocking the boat. Might Kara's reluctance to move on with her life have been due in part to the unresolved questions? Or the loss of her father as her support system and rescuer? What other factors may have played a part?

3. Letting go can be a challenge for more than parent-child relationships. Sometimes people cling to love relationships beyond the time when they should gracefully let them go. Did Kara do that? Why? Do you think Seth or Will was the better match as a love interest for Kara? Why?

4. What about Victoria? Why do you think she was so determined to confront Kara, especially in the face of Kara's extreme hostility? Kara didn't open Victoria's note. Do you think she should have? What do you think Victoria wrote?

About the Author

Grace Greene is an award-winning and *USA Today* bestselling author of women's fiction and contemporary romance set in the bucolic reaches of her native Virginia (*Kincaid's Hope*, *Cub Creek*, *The Happiness In Between*, *The Memory of Butterflies*, and *Wildflower Heart*) and on the breezy beaches of Emerald Isle, North Carolina (*Beach Rental*, *Beach Winds*). Her debut novel, *Beach Rental*, and the sequel, *Beach Winds*, were both Top Picks by *RT Book Reviews* magazine. For more about the author and her books, visit www.gracegreene.com or connect with her on Twitter @Grace_Greene and on Facebook at www.facebook.com/GraceGreeneBooks.

Center Point Large Print
600 Brooks Road / PO Box 1
Thorndike, ME 04986-0001 USA

(207) 568-3717

US & Canada:
1 800 929-9108
www.centerpointlargeprint.com